Nowhere Else to Run

Eddie Martin

First published in 2016

Beecroft Publishing
Beecroft
Crittenden Road
Matfield, Kent
TN12 7EQ
United Kingdom

www.beecroftpublishing.co.uk
email: sales@beecroftpublishing.co.uk

ISBN 978-0954618-66-7

Table of Contents

Chapter 1 – Heathrow Airport 1

Chapter 2 – Journey to Rio 13

Chapter 3 – Making Contact 28

Chapter 4 – The Abduction 39

Chapter 5 – Rescued at the Sambadrome 56

Chapter 6 – Iguassu Hotel 78

Chapter 7 – To the River 96

Chapter 8 – At Iguassu Falls 120

Chapter 9 – Terror in the Favela 136

Chapter 10 – Finding Antonio 160

Chapter 11 – The Man in Black 183

Chapter 12 – Downtown Rio 193

Chapter 13 - The Double Cross 216

Chapter 14 – Final Day Sting 229

Chapter 1 – Heathrow Airport

George glanced up at the overhead departure monitor, then across the table to his wife Maggie.

"What do you want for breakfast?" he asked, scanning through the breakfast menu.

The smell of coffee and toast wafted through the air while they waited to be served. They were at a café in the departure lounge at London Heathrow airport. The time was 6:15 a.m. on a cold February morning, but warmer inside the building. The airport was awakening for the day.

"I don't know yet," Maggie said, "I can't decide what to have. Have you chosen?"

George looked at the menu again in a habitual way and scratched his head, but had already made up his mind.

"I will have the full English breakfast," he said, "It has to be done. We're going abroad, and I'm not sure when we will have a proper English breakfast again."

George and Maggie were waiting to catch a flight to Brazil, their first trip to that amazing country. It was carnival time in Rio de Janeiro, and for many years, they both wanted to experience the festival, which was one of the world's most spectacular events. The couple were going to spend six days in Rio to enjoy the carnival, the beaches, and the Brazilian culture. It was to be the holiday of a lifetime, and the trip was booked months in advance. George and Maggie were eager to board the plane, but breakfast was foremost on their minds at 6:15 am.

Maggie deliberated over the menu a minute longer.

"I know," she said, "I'm going to have scrambled eggs on toast, with tomatoes, and a pot of tea."

"I think I'll have coffee," George said, "I need my coffee first thing in the morning."

"Shall we have orange juice as well?" Maggie asked.

"Good Idea," George replied.

George looked for a waiter, but couldn't see any nearby; they were all busy behind the serving counter. He tried to get their attention by waving his arms in the air, but no one was looking in his direction. He gave out a deafening wolf whistle, which was unbecoming for that time of the morning, but it caught the attention of the catering staff. One young lady acknowledged George and immediately proceeded to the table with a notepad in hand.

"Sorry about that," she said, "It's early, and we were just getting things ready. How can I help you?"

"It's alright," George said, "we're all asleep at this time of the morning."

It was a sarcastic remark, and Maggie looked at George with disgust. She raised her eyebrows, as if to say, '*That wasn't necessary.*' The waitress was not bothered; she had heard remarks like that many times before and just ignored the comment.

"What would you like?" she asked.

George opened his hand towards Maggie and offered her to speak first. Maggie took the opportunity and said to the waitress.

"I would like the scrambled eggs, please, with fried tomatoes, and two slices of toast."

"Anything to drink?" the waitress asked.

"Ah! Yes. A pot of tea, please."

The waitress then looked at George nonchalantly.

"And for you, Sir?"

"I will have the full English breakfast, thanks, with coffee, black coffee."

"Will that be all?" the waitress asked.

"I think so," George said, while looking at Maggie in case there was something they forgot.

The waitress was about to walk away from the table when George remembered he had forgotten to order something.

"Hold on," he said.

The waitress turned around and returned.

"Can we both have orange juice as well, please?"

"Yes, certainly, Sir," the waitress replied.

She completed the order and made her way back to the service counter. It was not long before she disappeared through the swing doors to the kitchen.

George and Maggie both looked up at the departure monitor again. The flight to Rio de Janeiro was non-stop from London Heathrow by British Airways and was on time. Earlier that morning, they had checked in and disposed of their luggage, just retaining their hand baggage. George and Maggie were seasoned travellers and always arrived at airports early to avoid queues and delays. The flight departed at 9:30 am, and there was ample time for breakfast and for some duty-free shopping.

George was a gregarious man, five feet ten inches tall, medium built, aged 52. His eyes were light blue, with a brown speck in one iris, which was most noticeable when you looked directly into his eyes. His hair was curly and light brown in colour, with a touch of grey at the sides. Compared to many men, he still had a full head of hair for his age.

Maggie was the more cautious of the two. Five feet two inches tall, and attended the gym twice a week to keep fit. Her eyes were brown, which matched the colour of her shoulder-length hair. Maggie was approaching the age of 50 in a month.

The holiday to Brazil was a special trip to mark the occasion. Two years ago, they went on a similar trip to Thailand to celebrate George's 50th birthday. The couple always celebrated landmark birthdays with special occasions, and sometimes threw a party for friends and relatives. At other times, as on this occasion, they organised a trip to some faraway exotic destination.

The clink of a coffee cup behind George prompted him to turn around, and he noticed two well-dressed men seated a few tables away from them. The men were swarthy in complexion with black hair, and he assumed they might be from South America. Dressed in black suits, suggested they might be businessmen. George noticed two unusual things about the men. One had a three-inch scar on the right cheek, and each man wore a diamond-encrusted earring. The men spoke in a foreign language, which wasn't easy to decipher as they were

3

some distance away from George and Maggie. They were eating breakfast, and the sight of their breakfasts made George hungrier.

"Lucky fellows," George said, "they've got their breakfast already."

The men overheard George and stared intensely towards the couple. This sent a shiver down George's spine, for no reason other than being stared at by a man with a three-inch scar on his face. This made George feel uncomfortable, and he looked at Maggie with raised eyebrows. He gave a wry smile, as if to say, '*I should have kept my mouth shut.*'

Maggie was sympathetic to George's reaction and changed the subject.

"What do you need in duty-free?" she asked.

"The usual, I guess. A bottle of rum for me to have in the hotel room, and whatever you wish to drink."

"I don't know what I want," Maggie said.

"You normally have sherry, or sometimes wine."

Maggie looked puzzled at George for making such a crass remark, but knew he was probably correct in his assumption.

"I'll think about it," she said.

"I need to buy some after-shave lotion as well," George said, "but I think I'll get that on our return journey. It's too heavy to take there and back."

At that moment, two young men approached the table adjacent to George and Maggie.

"Good morning," one of the men said.

The man spoke with a foreign accent, possibly German.

"Good morning," George and Maggie said together.

The men took off their jackets and sat down. Both men wore T-shirts, jeans and trainers. On the front of one T-shirt was written 'AC/DC' across a picture of an electric guitar. The other man wore a red T-shirt with no markings. The men looked to be around 25 years old and over six feet tall. Their arms bulged with muscles, indicating they kept themselves fit. Both men sported prominent tattoos on their arms. The man with the 'AC/DC' T-shirt was tattooed on the right arm with 'AC/DC.' The other man was tattooed with a sword on one arm, which stretched from his elbow down to his wrist. The appearance of both men looked menacing, but they seemed like good friends and were well-mannered. The men spoke German, which confirmed the thoughts of George and Maggie.

George scanned around the café to see who else was seated. On another table sat four young men, and glasses of beer in front of them. It was early for alcohol, but they seemed to be starting a holiday in a manner they wished to continue. Another man sat in the corner of the café wearing a brown leather jacket. He was sipping coffee and reading a newspaper, and looked familiar to George. A group of schoolgirls, aged 12-14, approached the café, and the noise emanating from the group of teenage girls at 6:30 in the morning was horrendous.

Seconds later, the waitress arrived with the breakfasts and set the plates on the table in front of George and Maggie.
"Here you are," she said, "I brought you some toast as well, Sir, I thought you might like some."
"Ah! Thanks very much," George said, "I forgot about the toast. Thank you very much."
The waitress unloaded the tray of beverages, orange juice and toast onto the table.
"Enjoy your breakfast," she said, and turned around to serve the Germans.

George and Maggie had left home about two hours before, allowing for traffic delays, and checking in early. The journey to the airport took an hour, and the check-in was swift. They were hungry and looked forward to breakfast, only managing to have a cup of tea before leaving home. The couple spent the next half hour eating until about 7:15, when George looked up at the departure monitor again. He noted the flight to Rio was still on schedule.

"Are you ready to do some shopping?" George asked Maggie.
"Yes, let's go. Time is ticking on."

The couple stood up, collected their hand luggage, and were about to walk away when one of the Germans at the next table bid them farewell.

"Hope you enjoy your holiday, wherever you are going."

The German spoke with an accent, but his words were understandable.

"Thanks, and you enjoy yours as well," Maggie said.

As they walked away from the table, George glanced over his shoulder at the two men in black suits seated further back. Once again, both men were staring intensely at them, and it was very unnerving. George decided to ignore it and walked on.

The couple made their way to the Duty-Free shops and meandered around searching for booze and perfumes. Maggie paused at a counter to try out a perfume, spraying one on a tester and dangling it in front of her nose.

"Hmm! That smells good. What do you think?"

She handed the tester to George, who held it close to his nose.

"Too sweet, and too overpowering. I prefer something earthy."

"What do you mean, earthy?"

"Like musk. You know! Musk from animals."

"Well, I like this one," Maggie said.

"Ok, get that one then," George replied.

At that moment, there was a shriek from one of the female staff members on the other side of the duty-free shop.

"Stop, thief, stop," she shouted.

The disturbance caused everyone in the shop to look in the direction of the noise. A man was seen running away from the shop, with two bottles of booze in his hands. He was closely pursued by a security guard on duty. The chase was short, and the thief was soon apprehended by another guard from a nearby shop. One of the security guards held the man firmly by the arm, while the other called the airport police on his Walkie-Talkie. It was not long before a small crowd gathered around the man and the security guards. Interested, the crowd ogled, while the guards sternly spoke to the thief. The police soon arrived on the scene, and after a brief discussion with the guards, led the captured man away for interrogation. The episode reminded

George and Maggie to be vigilant at airports and to ensure their belongings were safe, wherever they travelled.

The commotion soon died down, and George glanced around the duty-free shop to observe the reaction of the other people. Most of them looked shocked, and people were murmuring to each other around the shop. While George scanned, he noticed the two men in black he had seen earlier were also in the shop, staring at them. The men quickly turned away and pretended to shop, but George thought otherwise.

"Look, Maggie, those guys are staring at us again."

"What guys?" Maggie asked.

"The men we saw in the café, the ones who stared at us before. If I'm not mistaken, I think they are following us."

"Don't be silly," Maggie said, "It's just your imagination. No one is following us. Why would they follow us?"

"I don't know, it just seems odd that since we were in the café, they always seem to be near us."

"It is an airport after all," Maggie said, "People are allowed to move around."

"Yes, I know, but I am getting an unusual feeling about this."

The two men left the shop, and George, who still felt unnerved, eyed them all the way. George and Maggie continued shopping and purchased a bottle of Eldorado Demerara rum from Guyana. It was matured for 12 years, and a favourite of George. The purchases included a bottle of French Merlot and a 50ml bottle of Chanel No. 5 for Maggie.

It was 8 o'clock when they left the duty-free shop, and they located the nearest monitor to check on the departure flight times. On this occasion, the display indicated the departure gate number. Boarding was at 8:30, so they needed to make their way to the departure gate as soon as possible, and proceeded to it. On the walk, the two German men who sat at the table next to them in the café were about to overtake the couple. The Germans seemed to be in a hurry, but George decided to speak to them anyway.

"Hi there again," George said.

The German men were startled by the remark and slowed down to match the couple's pace.

"Hi," one of the men said, "We meet again."

George then thought to make a flippant comment.

"You're not following us, are you?" he asked.

All four thought the comment was funny and laughed, and one of the Germans, in not-so-perfect English, said.

"No, we are going to Brazil."

"Really!" Maggie exclaimed, "What a coincidence? We are also going to Brazil, and will be staying in Rio."

"On the 9:30 flight to Rio?" the other German asked.

"Yes, what a coincidence," George said, "It's the same flight as ours. I think it's going to be a long flight."

"Ah, yes!" the same man replied.

He held out his hand towards George, and all four introduced themselves. The Germans were called Karl and Helmut from Frankfurt.

"We will probably see you on the plane," Karl said.

"Yes, have a good trip," George replied.

The Germans then walked on ahead, leaving George and Maggie to walk at their own pace.

"They seem like nice guys," Maggie said to George.

"Yes, they do. I wonder where they are staying in Rio."

The Germans were fit men who walked at a quick pace, and soon disappeared among the passengers ahead.

George and Maggie arrived at the departure gate and searched for a place to sit in the waiting area. The departure lounge was packed with people of varying nationalities, all waiting for the flight to Rio. There must have been hundreds of people waiting, and to accommodate the volume, British Airways laid on a Boeing 777 airliner, which can seat 400 plus passengers. George went to find bottled water, while Maggie searched for two vacant seats and waited for him to return. They sat down to relax until the flight was called. George and Maggie looked up at the departure monitor again to check that the flight was on time. It seemed excessive to scan the monitors so often, but they are informative and relieve the boredom of waiting.

Boarding was not for another few minutes, and to pass the time, a bit of people watching was necessary. It was a normal pastime for people waiting in a crowded area, and George and Maggie were no exception to the pastime. George noticed three men standing not far from the departure gate, whose appearance seemed Brazilian, and they seemed to be somewhat agitated. One wore a black zip-up cardigan and was listening to music through his headphones. The second sported a green casual jacket, while the third wore a black lounge jacket. All three wore blue denim jeans, and each held onto a small black trolley bag. George thought they were an odd-looking bunch.

A few jets were glistening in the sunlight through the windows. Some waited on the tarmac for permission to take off, while others were being refuelled at the docking areas. Many people were seated in the departure lounge. Some were families with children. Most of the children seemed bored and played quietly. Others were boisterous and ran around, causing havoc among the other passengers. The lounge area was normal for an international flight, with the murmur of various conversations in a multitude of languages. Many people, however, remained seated and watched the BBC news on the large TV screens.

George leaned across to Maggie and spoke quietly to her.
"I don't believe it."
Maggie looked at George strangely.
"Don't believe what?" she asked.
"Those two men in black are standing over there."
George tried not to look up, but indicated surreptitiously with his right hand to Maggie.
"Over where?" she asked.
Maggie was about to look in the direction in which George pointed, but George interjected quickly.
"No, don't turn your head, they're looking at us."
Maggie decided to look up at the ceiling, pretending to glance around, and did not make it obvious that she was going to look at the men. She eventually looked in the direction George indicated.
"I can't see any men," Maggie said, "where are they?"

George looked over and couldn't see the men either, and assumed they must have moved on from where he last saw them. His hands began to sweat, and he felt a shiver come over him.

"They were there. I tell you. They were," he said.

"You're just being paranoid," Maggie said.

"No, I'm not," George snapped back, "they were there, where I told you."

"If you feel so strongly about it, why don't you report them to the authorities?"

"Report them!" George said, "That seems over the top, don't you think?"

"Well, you are the one who seemed concerned. Do something about it or shut up, because you're making me nervous now."

George did not want to ruin the special holiday in Brazil, so he thought it best not to mention the men for the time being.

'Bing-bong' rang out on the intercom in the departure lounge, and the flight was called for boarding. Most people stood up immediately and collected their hand luggage. Some hurried and pushed their way to the front of the queue, which formed quickly. George and Maggie were travelling in Economy Class, as their funds allowed, and eventually joined the lengthy queue that had already formed. Business and First-Class passengers were allowed to pass through the fast-track channel, which made George and Maggie envious. *'If only,'* they thought, as they shuffled along.

George took the boarding passes and passports from his hand luggage and presented them to the lady in charge of boarding.

"Good morning, Sir, good morning, Madam. How are we today?" the lady asked.

"We are fine," George replied.

George glanced down at the name badge pinned to her blouse.

"And how are you, Elizabeth?" he asked.

"I am also well," she replied.

"Are you looking forward to the flight?" Elizabeth asked.

"Very much so," Maggie replied.

Elizabeth paused for a moment and tapped a few letters on the keyboard in front of her. The short delay caused George to make a flippant remark to Elizabeth.

"Is something wrong with the plane?"

Elizabeth looked up at George strangely.

"No, I've got some good news for you," she replied.

"Oh!" George said.

Maggie looked on with interest while Elizabeth typed a few more letters onto the keyboard.

"It's your lucky day," she said.

She looked up at George and Maggie and smiled.

"I'm going to upgrade you to Business Class."

The couple were elated, resulting in a great big grin on their faces, and raised arms ecstatically in the air.

"Wow!" George and Maggie said together.

"I don't believe it," George added.

Elizabeth reprinted the boarding passes with the new seat allocation and handed them to George.

"Have a good flight," she said.

"Thank you," the lucky couple said.

George and Maggie made their way to the door to board as Business Class passengers. They were filled with excitement now that they were on their way, and the unexpected seat upgrade.

The couple boarded the plane and were escorted to their seats by Philip, one of the cabin crew.

"Would you like a hot towel now, and a glass of champagne?" he asked.

"Yes, that would be great," George replied, "sounds good to me."

"Yes, please," Maggie added.

Philip then left the couple to settle in and went away to prepare the champagne and towels.

"This is the life," George said to Maggie, "the way to travel."

"Certainly is," she said, "we should travel business class more often."

"Yes, I would like to, if only we could afford it."

George and Maggie sat back in the seats and closed their eyes to relax. They were not used to Business Class and wanted to take in the atmosphere. The cabin was fairly quiet, with only the air-conditioning noise, which broke the silence. Philip soon returned with a basket of hot towels and two glasses of champagne.

"Enjoy your drink," he said, "Is there anything else I could help you with?"

"No thanks, Philip," George said, "I think we're fine now."

Philip walked away from the couple to attend to other passengers. George pulled out the food table from the side console and rested the champagne glass on it. Maggie did the same, and they both refreshed their faces with the hot towels. George and Maggie picked up their glasses and clinked them together to toast their holiday.

"Enjoy the holiday," George said, "I hope we have a great time."

"Yes, same here."

The couple sat back in the seats and slowly sipped the champagne. The cabin was warm and comfortable with subdued lighting. The seats were spacious and could be converted into flat beds for sleeping. The couple were relaxed and now felt it was the real start of their exotic holiday.

Chapter 2 – Journey to Rio

The other passengers boarded the plane promptly, and it was ready to leave the docking area at 9:30. The 'fasten seatbelt' light turned on, and the cabin crew completed the safety checks while the plane taxied onto the runway. George paid attention to the safety procedures, while Maggie read the flight magazine located in the side pocket. The safety procedures were completed once the plane reached the start of the runway. It remained still for a few minutes until the pilots were given the go-ahead from the control tower to take off. The captain said a few words to the cabin crew over the intercom, and the cabin crew duly sat and fastened their seat belts.

The plane moved slowly at first, and then gained momentum as it sped along the runway. Because the flight was full, it seemed ages before the aeroplane rose from the ground, probably because the flight was full. It soared into the sky for an uneventful lift off. The passengers remained silent, which was normal for take-off and landing. Perhaps passengers always anticipated something might go wrong at these critical times of a flight. After a few minutes, the plane cleared the London airspace, and it was not long before it reached a height of 6,000 metres, still climbing. It soon flew over the southern coastline of the UK and eventually reached a height of 12,000 metres, an optimum height for flying. Viewing the ground from that high was a humbling experience. The patchwork design of the land, bordering the blue sea, was always a sight to behold.
The general din of people's voices merged with the background noise from the plane's air-conditioning when the plane's intercom sounded. 'Bing-bong.' The captain spoke, first in English and later in Portuguese.
"This is your captain speaking. My crew and I would like to welcome you on board this British Aircraft flight to Rio…."
He continued the oration, and most people listened to his words, which had been repeated on so many occasions in the past. It was the norm for him, and for some of the passengers, who had heard it all before. Those passengers settled down to get some rest before breakfast was served. They were not interested in

the speed of the aircraft or even the height at which it was flying. The intercom went silent for about five minutes, and then sounded again.

'Bing-bong' rang out over the intercom, and the 'fasten seat belt' sign was extinguished. This was followed by the loud noise of seat belts unclicking. Some people stood up straight away and made their way towards the washrooms, where queues began to form. Most passengers now felt at ease, and a general din of voices and laughing was heard throughout the aircraft.
"Finally!" Maggie said.
Feeling stressed during liftoff, she immediately unbuckled her seat belt. Maggie always felt nervous during take-off and landing, but now sat back in the seat to relax.
"I could do with another drink," George said.
He looked for Philip and saw him preparing the Business Class cabin with the rest of the crew. Curtains were drawn across the aisles to separate Business from Economy Class. Then the clinking of glasses could be heard as the cabin crew prepared more champagne for the passengers.
"Music to my ears," George said.
He sat back and waited for the champagne. After a few minutes, drinks were served with nibbles, and everyone seemed completely at ease. The cabin crew began to prepare the breakfast trays, and the familiar scent of bacon and eggs wafted through the air.

George and Maggie had already eaten breakfast in the departure café at Heathrow airport, but that was over three hours ago, and the smell of bacon and eggs enticed them into having a second breakfast.
"I'm going for a walk before breakfast," George said, "I'd better stretch my legs before eating again."
"Good idea," Maggie said, "I will go when you come back."
George took his shoes off and stood in the aisle. He stretched his arms high in the air and was soon noticed by other passengers, who seemed envious of the exercise. He proceeded slowly to make his way to the back of the plane and paused now and then to stretch his arms. As he passed through

14

the curtains separating Business Class from Economy, George was met by a sea of passengers, some looking up at him.

"Good morning," he said to the first two rows of passengers, and continued to walk.

As he walked along the aisle, George looked at the people seated and often smiled when they glanced up at him. Some were family groups, while others seemed to be travelling alone. George passed a man in a brown leather jacket, and thought he had recognised him; he was sure he had seen him somewhere else before. It was the same man who was seated in the corner of the café, where George and Maggie had eaten breakfast earlier.

After he passed about ten rows, he came upon Helmut and Karl, the two Germans. Helmut was asleep, and Karl was reading a book.

"Good morning again," George said to Karl.

Karl looked up, surprised.

"Ah! Good morning. How are you?" Karl asked.

"Feeling a bit lazy," George replied.

George glanced over to Helmut and nodded his head towards him.

"Helmut seems to be away with the fairies."

"Huh!" Karl exclaimed, "Away with the fairies?"

George realised he just blurted out a typical English phrase, which Karl did not understand.

"In a dream world," George said, "asleep."

Karl smiled, for he now knew what George meant.

"Ah! I understand, away with the fairies. We've had a long journey, and I think Helmut is very tired."

"I will leave you guys to rest then," George said.

He put his hand on Karl's shoulder and walked on.

George continued the slow walk to the back of the aircraft, where the aisle crossed over to the other side of the plane. The aisle was hidden from the view of the other passengers, and George was about to traverse it when he met one of the men in black coming the other way. It was one of the men he saw at Heathrow airport, the same man he saw in the café earlier that morning, the one with a scar on his face. No one else was around, and the man grabbed George by the throat. He pushed George up against the wall and spoke to him in a quiet, threatening tone.

"We know who you are, and we know you have the package."

George was taken aback, and his adrenaline level rose immediately, causing the blood to pump through his veins quickly. The grip on his throat was painful, and he could hardly breathe. George was bewildered and in complete shock.

"Get off of me," he tried to shout.

The man's grip on George's throat was so tight that it caused the words to come out in a gruff manner. George tried to kick out at the man, but the man pressed his body firmly against the wall. George tried to use his arms to fend off the assailant, but the man leaned harder against his body, and George could make no headway. The man then punched George in the stomach, causing him to slump in pain, and he could not do anything.

"You understand what I am saying?" the man whispered in George's ear, "I want the package."

"What package?" George tried to say, but the words came out gruffly again.

"The one you have with you."

"I don't have any package, get off of me. I think you have the wrong person. I don't get involved in anything like this."

George recognised the man's accent and guessed he was Brazilian. The South American tightened the grip around George's throat.

"You deliver, or else!" he said.

The South American released the grip on George and disappeared up the aisle back to his seat. George slumped to the ground in pain, holding his throat and stomach.

'*What is going on?*' he thought, '*What am I going to do? Shall I report him?*'

George was somewhat scared and did not want to make any rash decisions.

Another passenger, also stretching his legs, came upon George. He found him slumped on the ground and became concerned.

"Are you ok?" he asked, "Do you need help?"

George looked up at the man, smiled with a grimace, and took a deep breath.

"Yes, I'm fine. I just tripped and fell," he said in a croaky voice.

George did not want to raise any suspicion and acted nonchalantly when the man bent down to help him up from the ground. George stood up and rubbed his stomach to relieve the pain, but he was aching; a frown showed on his face.

"You should be careful," the man said.

"Yes, I know, it was silly of me. Thank you very much for your help."

"Are you going to be alright?"

"Yes, fine, and thanks again for your kindness."

The man left George and continued to walk up the aisle. George stretched and arched his body to try to relieve the pain and slowly returned to his seat.

"Where have you been?" Maggie asked.

George held his stomach and groaned while he sat down. His face was ashen, and he broke out in a sweat.

"What's wrong? Maggie asked, "You look as if you've seen a ghost."

"It's alright, I tripped and fell over at the back of the plane."

Maggie looked surprised at George and was not impressed with him.

"You what! You silly man."

Not wanting to alarm Maggie, George was unsure whether to tell her about the incident that occurred. Instead, he made out that the ache in his stomach was from the fall.

"I must have twisted my body when I fell and pulled a muscle in my abdomen," he said.

The other South American stood in the next aisle and caught George's attention. Maggie's back was to the man, and she was not aware he was looking at them. The South American raised his hand to his face and pointed to his eyes with his middle and index fingers. He then immediately pointed both fingers towards George to indicate they were watching the couple closely. George looked away from the man, sat back in his seat, and closed his eyes.

It might have been the trauma that just occurred, but George somehow drifted off to sleep. Maybe it was the body's natural reaction to the turmoil. Maggie was concerned about George and wiped the sweat from his brow while he slept. Breakfast was soon served, which, for a while, distracted Maggie from George's plight. Not wanting to wake him, she sipped her coffee while he slept. An hour passed, and George was sound asleep when he was awoken by the plane shaking. The aircraft had entered an area of turbulence, and the plane shook erratically. The intercom rang out, 'Bing-bong' followed by the captain's voice.

"Ladies and gentlemen, please fasten your seat belts. We are passing through an area of turbulence, and the aircraft will be unsteady. It shouldn't last for long, and we hope to be out of it soon. You can then relax and enjoy the rest of your journey."

There was the sound of seatbelts clicking as passengers fastened them. George looked bleary-eyed at Maggie, and then at other passengers, some with anxious looks on their faces. The couple had experienced turbulence before on many of their trips and waited for it to pass. After a few minutes, the turbulence abated.

"I think I need the washroom," Maggie said.

"Yes, me too, and I need to stretch my legs."

George and Maggie unfastened their seatbelts and stood up. There were not many people waiting for the washrooms, so wanting some exercise, they slowly walked towards those at the rear of the plane.

On the way, the couple had to pass by Karl and Helmut, who smiled at them when they saw them coming.

"Well, hello," Karl said.

"Hello," George and Maggie said together.

"I missed you last time," Helmut said, "I was asleep when you came by before."

"Yes, you were," George said, "Are you feeling rested?"

"Yes, much better."

"Are you staying in Rio for long?" Karl asked.

"For a week," Maggie replied, "we are hoping to see much of the city, including the Sugarloaf and Corcovada Mountains."

"Where are you staying in Rio?" Helmut asked.

"At the Rio Othon Palace," George replied.

"Where is that?" Karl asked.

"Copacabana Beach," George said, "right on the sea front."

Unbeknownst to George and Maggie, the two South Americans seated three rows away on the other side of the plane overheard the conversation. They now knew the address the couple would be staying at in Rio, and it was unfortunate for George and Maggie, but a lucky break for the South Americans.

"What about you two?" Maggie asked the Germans, "Where are you staying?"

"Oh, we are staying in a hostel, in downtown Rio," Helmut replied.

"We book cheap accommodation sometimes," Karl added, "We prefer to spend our money on fares rather than accommodation."

"Well, if needs must," George said.

George felt embarrassed for the crass remark he had just made and tried to change the conversation.

"We were just stretching our legs, and...."

Before George could finish the sentence, a fracas started between two men in the other aisle, two rows up. Everyone within hearing distance looked up at the disturbance, and no one was sure what the altercation was about. The two men were pointing fingers at each other and swearing loudly. One man sat on one side of the aisle, while the other sat on the opposite side. Both men were sturdily built, which seemed an awkward fit for the restricted economy class seats. Passengers next to them didn't want to get involved and leaned away from the brawl.

"Why the hell don't you pay attention?" one of the men said.

"Excuse me!" the other man replied, "I did say sorry."

It seemed the two men may have bumped into each other by accident.

"You think you own this plane!" one of the men said.

"You certainly don't," the other shouted.

"Fuck off," the first shouted.

"Don't you swear at me," the second shouted back.

The first man stood and pushed his hand against the other man's body.

"I'll do what I want," he said.

The second man also stood up, and together, the size of the two men did not leave much room in the aisle. He then pushed his opponent hard, causing the man to stumble back into his seat.

"Stop it," a woman sitting in the next seat shouted, "stop it."

One of the men turned around and looked at the woman.

"Shut up, woman," he shouted, "stay out of this."

Another male passenger nearby also stood up to give her moral support.

"Leave her alone," he shouted, "I agree with the woman. Now just shut up, sit down and be calm."

The two brawlers looked at the male passenger.

"Piss off," they both shouted.

By now, many passengers were standing and shouting at the two men to stop the fighting. But it was in vain, and the two men began to punch and say expletives at each other. The confrontation became serious, and other passengers nearby cowered down to avoid being hit. The two men punched and kicked each other while they stood in the aisle, and the altercation was getting out of hand.

The three Brazilian men whom George noticed at the departure gate before take-off were seated two rows in front of the men in black. One of them stood up and went over to calm the brawl.

"Gentlemen, stop fighting, or else I will have to arrest you," he said.

Both men paused the fighting.

"Who the hell are you?" one of the men shouted.

"You'll have to stop fighting," the Brazilian said.

"Yes? Who do you think you are?" the other man said.

"Stop fighting," the Brazilian said, "or else I will arrest you."

"Piss off," one of the men replied, "You can't arrest us."

The Brazilian pulled out a Warrant badge from an inside pocket and showed it to the two men.

"I can," he said, "I am an Air Marshal, and I will arrest you if you don't sit down and be quiet."

One of the men pushed the Air Marshal away and delivered a punch to the other man's face. The Air Marshal stumbled to the ground, but was soon on his feet again. His two colleagues, also

Air Marshals, rushed over to help him immediately, and together they apprehended and arrested the two men. The brawling men were handcuffed to the armrests of their respective seats and told to be silent. This was followed by an uproar of applause and whistles from the other passengers, who were happy to see the men restrained.

Most passengers sat down again, and there was a din of murmurs around the aeroplane, as they spoke to each other. The captain was informed of the brawl and made his way to the location of the fracas, where he was able to talk to the three Air Marshals. The passengers were somewhat anxious because of the scuffle, and the cabin crew were busy trying to calm them.

George and Maggie were still standing next to the Germans and were about to head for the washrooms when George realised the presence of the Air Marshals could be beneficial to him. He wondered whether to inform them of the two men in black, especially the one who assaulted him. George looked over at the men, only to find they were staring back. He was keen to talk to an Air Marshal, but sensed that the looks from the men in black were warning him not to do so. George looked at Maggie and then back again at the men. He didn't want to get Maggie involved and thought it better to play it safe, so he decided not to approach the Air Marshals. At least, not for the time being. George and Maggie bid temporary farewells to Karl and Helmut and continued to the washrooms.

The remainder of the flight to Rio was quiet and uneventful. The passengers were shocked at what had just happened, so they remained in their seats, only getting up to go to the washrooms. George made two attempts to contact the Air Marshals, with no success. On one occasion, he walked down the opposite aisle to the Air Marshals and tried to get their attention by waving his arm, but none of them were looking up at the time. The men in black were astute, though, and saw George, who immediately retracted his arm. He raised his arms up and down to make them think he was exercising. The second time, George approached the Air Marshals in the aisle where they were seated and paused at their row. They looked up at him and waited for George to speak. But before George said anything, he glanced over to the men in black, only to see them staring intensely at him. He bottled out and continued to walk along the aisle, returning to his seat.

After a twelve-hour flight, the plane landed safely in Rio, and the passengers disembarked, First Class, then Business, and lastly, Economy Class. Once landed, the travellers were grateful to forget the events of the flight. George remarked to Maggie while queuing at the immigration desk.

"Phew! I'm glad that's over. I wouldn't like to experience a flight like that again."

"No," Maggie replied, "me neither. It was very enlightening, though."

George felt edgy and kept looking over his shoulder every few seconds. He was still anxious that the two men in black would catch up with them.

"I wish the queue would move faster," George said.

On the whole, the queue was moving quickly, but George was nervous, and he felt it was taking a long time to be processed through immigration. Maggie sensed his nervousness.

"Relax," she said, "we are on holiday, and you should be enjoying it."

"Yes, you're right," George said.

He glanced over his shoulder once more to check. The queue moved quickly, and they were soon through immigration. They still needed to collect the luggage, so they made their way to the baggage retrieval area.

As they approached the carousels, George looked up at one of the monitors to check which carousel their luggage would arrive.

"Number 3," he said to Maggie, "let's go quickly."

George was keen to retrieve the luggage swiftly before the two men in black came through immigration.

"Slow down," Maggie said, "What's the hurry? We need to get a trolley."

Maggie found one at the trolley ranks, and they shuffled along to the carousel. A few suitcases had already appeared, and the quality of luggage indicated they belonged to First Class passengers.

"Where's our luggage?" George asked, "They should be here by now."

"Patience," Maggie replied, "Do have some patience, I'm sure they will come soon."

George glanced around to see if passengers from Economy Class were joining them, but none could be seen as yet. However, it was not easy to spot the difference between the travel classes these days, as many people dressed the same.

Some passengers collected their luggage and disappeared through Customs. There were about fifty other passengers still waiting for luggage when another batch came through on the conveyor belt. George moved closer to the spot where the luggage entered the hall, but could not see theirs as yet.

"What kind of service is this?" George mumbled to himself. He was anxious, and it was a rhetorical question to no one in particular.

"We travelled Business Class, and I expected to see our luggage by now," he said.

Other passengers looked at George and sensed his impatience. He noticed this and humbly looked down at the carousel. Maggie followed closely behind George with the trolley and overheard the comments.

"I think you need to be patient," she said, "If you remember, we didn't book into Business Class initially, so our luggage is in with Economy Class."

George thought for a moment and realised he was being foolish.

"I guess you're right," he said, "We'll just have to wait. I am getting tired, and I want to get to the hotel."

About ten minutes had passed since they arrived at the carousel, and passengers from Economy class began to enter the area. George glanced up to check if the two men in black were coming, and to his shock, saw them approaching. This made him even more nervous. He quickly lowered his head, took out a cap from his hand luggage, and put it on his head. He hoped the disguise would give him some anonymity.

Luckily for George and Maggie, their suitcases came through together, just as the two men arrived at the carousel. The men stood further along on the opposite side to them and did not notice the couple among the throng of waiting people.

"Thank god for that!" George said.

He barged through the people to get closer to the carousel and quickly grabbed the luggage. Other luggage items were now coming through, and most people gathered nearer to the carousel, so George forced his way back through the crowd with the luggage. He hurriedly put the bags on the trolley and was keen to exit the baggage collection area. George took control of the trolley and hastily began to walk towards the Customs declaration area. He wanted to leave the airport as quickly as possible, to get away from the two men.

"What's the hurry?" Maggie asked.

She tried to keep pace with George and was almost running.

"Slow down," she said, "you're going too fast for me."

George slowed the pace, but made sure he faced away from the carousel. They were on the way to Customs and were crossing an area sparse of passengers, when a voice echoed across the concourse.

"George, Maggie, hi guys, Auf Wiedersehen, and have a good holiday."

The couple turned to see who was calling and saw Karl, one of the Germans, waving his hand frantically. This was the last thing George needed; it drew attention to the other passengers waiting to collect their luggage, including the two men in black. George was not keen to look up; he was anxious not to be recognised, but Maggie was friendly towards the Germans and waved vibrantly at them.

"Hi Karl, hi Helmut," she shouted, "We are on our way now. You have a good holiday as well."

George did not wish to be unfriendly or impolite to the Germans, and half glanced up at them. He waved his hand chest high at them and walked through the green channel in the Customs area. The two men noticed them leaving and hoped their own luggage would come through quickly.

George and Maggie made their way out of the airport building and were enveloped by the evening's humid air on the outside. The BA plane and the terminal buildings were air-conditioned, and this was the first time they felt the hot Brazilian atmosphere. As a result of their haste and eagerness to leave the building, the couple began to sweat profusely, and their clothes soon became damp. Because of their fair skin, they were immediately recognised as tourists, and soon accosted by a local man who ushered them towards the taxi rank.

"Taxi?" the man asked.

The man looked at them, hoping they would speak, so that he could determine their nationality, but George and Maggie remained silent.

"German? American? British?" he asked.

"British," George replied, "And yes, we do need a taxi."

The man ushered them closer to the nearby taxi rank.

"How much does the taxi cost to Copacabana Beach?" George asked.

"For you, a special price, one hundred and ten Real," the man replied.

George knew the approximate fare to Copacabana Beach as he had done some research in the UK before leaving for Brazil.

"No, too much," George said.

"Ok, I'll do it for one hundred Real."

"No, still too much."

George knew the fare should be about eighty Real.

"Eighty," George said to the man.

The man waved his index finger.

"No, can't do," he said, "but you will get a good taxi for one hundred Real."

George was uninterested and ignored the man's bartering. He looked around and noticed the two men in black emerging from the airport building. He needed to think of a solution quickly and saw a taxi approaching on the road, away from the taxi rank.

"We'll get our own taxi," he said, "Come on, Maggie, let's flag this taxi down."

George grabbed his suitcase and ran towards the road, where he flagged down the passing taxi. Maggie was bewildered at George's reaction, but followed him closely. The cab slowed and stopped suddenly when George jumped out in front of it. George approached the driver's door.

"How much is the fare to Copacabana Beach?"

The taxi driver understood English and nodded his head

"Eighty-five Real," he said.

"Ok, that's fine," George replied.

George took the suitcase to the rear of the car, and Maggie soon caught up with him. The driver got out of the car, opened the boot, and placed the suitcases inside. George quickly ushered Maggie into the backseat of the taxi before getting in. He glanced out the back window at the two men and saw them staring at him. One of the men put his index and middle fingers to his temple in the form of a handgun, indicating they were going to get them. George was now anxious to get going to the hotel.

"Let's go, driver," he said, looking out of the back window, "hurry, let's go."

"What's the rush?" Maggie asked, "We seem to be rushing all the time."

George ignored Maggie's comment, and the taxi hastily sped off. He sat back to relax and was sure the men in black had been given the slip.

The time was now 19:30, and as the taxi sped off, it narrowly missed another car emerging from the taxi rank. The incident caused George and Maggie to inhale deeply, but the unconcerned taxi driver smiled at the couple in the rear-view mirror. Speeding was common in Rio. It was just after rush hour, so the roads were still busy, and the journey to the hotel would take thirty minutes. The taxi was air-conditioned, which gave some comfort to the couple on the journey. As soon as the cab joined the highway leading to town, the driver was eager to get to the hotel quickly. He constantly swapped lanes, passing cars at high speeds on both sides, and often sounding the horn. Maggie did not care for fast driving and felt she was experiencing a white-knuckle ride. A bit worried, she held on to the armrests in the car for dear life. George sensed Maggie's fear and was also not happy with the erratic driving.

"Hey! Take it easy, driver," George shouted, "we want to arrive safely, and in one piece."

The taxi driver seemed to ignore George's remark and continued to drive at speed. George thought that maybe the driver did not understand him properly.

"Driver, slow down," he shouted.

The driver looked at George in the rear-view mirror and smiled. George immediately waved both hands at the driver to indicate that he should slow down.

"You seemed to be in a hurry and wanted me to go quickly," the driver said.

"No, not now, driver," George replied, "We want to enjoy the night scenery of Rio."

The driver looked confused at the couple.

"Ok, boss," he said.

He immediately took his foot off the accelerator and slowed the car down to match the speed of the other traffic. George and Maggie felt very relieved.

The taxi soon arrived in the built-up area, and came to a slow crawl anyway. It was Carnival time in Rio, and the streets were bustling with people. The next day was the main day to celebrate carnival, when the carnival processions stomped their way through different parts of Rio. Tomorrow night was when the large Samba schools congregated at the Sambadrome in the centre of Rio. There, they would parade in front of thousands of people, all having a good time. Revellers began to party early that evening, and samba bands were already moving through the streets. The bands were followed by crowds of people, disrupting the traffic. The carnival weekend had begun, and Rio was coming alive with sound and colour. The driver diverted through some of the side streets to avoid the samba bands, which at times seemed to the couple that he was taking the longest route to the destination. However, the driver knew the shortcuts, and they soon arrived safely at the Rio Othon Palace hotel on Copacabana Beach.

Chapter 3 – Making Contact

The Rio Othon Palace was one of the largest hotels in Rio, located directly across the road from the superb and world-renowned Copacabana Beach. It towered some thirty floors high and completely dwarfed nearby buildings. The hotel had 570 rooms and suites, some of which featured balconies. Most rooms had sea views and overlooked Copacabana Beach; some also had spectacular views of the famous Sugar Loaf Mountain. A rooftop swimming pool was available for guests who preferred to avoid the beach. It was a warm evening, and the hotel's air conditioning made the environment comfortable. The hotel seemed busy and was fully occupied for the carnival by people from all over the world. On entering the hotel, the couple passed the bar in the foyer and noted the lively atmosphere with groups of partygoers. It seemed the choice of hotel was ideal for the couple.

George and Maggie checked into the hotel and were escorted to the room by a steward. They waited for a lift to take them to the 27th floor.
"Hold on a moment," George said, "I need to do something else. Wait here for me."
George rushed back to the reception desk and disappeared from Maggie's view. She stood beside the lift, looking perplexed at the steward. George approached the clerk behind the desk.
"Can I use the safety deposit box here, please?" George asked.
The clerk was the same male receptionist who checked them into the hotel.
"You have one in your room, Sir," he replied, "You will probably find it more convenient."
"I know," George said, "but I need to use this one as well. I have something special to store, and I think it will be safer here."
"Ok, Sir, what would you like to leave with us?"
George unzipped the back compartment of his hand luggage, took out a small flat package, and handed it to the clerk.
"Here it is. Can I have a receipt for it?"
"One moment," the clerk replied.

He reached under the reception desk and took out a large envelope with a label attached. He wrote some details on the label, tore off half the label, and handed it to George. The clerk put the package into the envelope and sealed it tightly. He then opened the safety deposit box located under the reception desk, placed the package inside, and then locked the door.

"That's it," he said, "all done."

"Thanks," George said, "one other thing. Do you have a street map of Rio?"

The clerk leaned over to a rack of brochures, which included a selection of maps. He extracted one and handed it to George.

"Thanks again," George said.

He strolled back to meet Maggie at the lift, who was somewhat annoyed at being left alone with the luggage.

"Where have you been?" Maggie asked, "You left me here all alone with the luggage, what's wrong?"

"Nothing," George replied, "I just wanted to get a street map of Rio."

"And it took that long?" Maggie asked.

George detected Maggie's sarcasm and needed to think of an answer quickly; she was still unaware of the package he had brought from London.

"There was a queue at the desk, and I had to wait," he said.

Maggie was not convinced by George's answer, but decided to accept the excuse. The lift arrived and took them to the 27th floor, where the couple were escorted to the room by the steward. He showed them around the room and was tipped generously. The room was a good size, with an en-suite bathroom and shower. Air conditioning was provided, and it was necessary for that time of year. The room had ample storage space, a dressing table/desk, and a separate dining table and chairs. A sliding door opened onto the balcony, which overlooked Copacabana beach. The panorama from the 27th floor was superb. The views of the bay around Copacabana beach and Sugarloaf Mountain were exquisite, especially at that time of night with the lights dotted around the bay.

George and Maggie were on their own for the first time since leaving home that morning. Maggie checked the en-suite

29

bathroom, while George threw himself onto the king-sized bed in the middle of the room.

"What a day!" he said.

He rested his head on the pillow and, looking up at the ceiling, put his hands behind his head.

"What a day!"

Maggie heard George's comment from the bathroom.

"Yes, I wouldn't want to experience that again," she said.

George stared vacantly at the ceiling until Maggie returned from the bathroom a couple of minutes later. She noticed George was lying on the right-hand side of the bed.

"I see you've decided which side of the bed you're going to sleep on," she said.

George, being used to Maggie's sarcastic remarks, ignored the comment. He always chose to sleep on the right-hand side of the bed. Maggie soon lay down beside him on the other side. They were both tired from the journey and wanted to rest, but it was early evening, and they felt the need to make the most of their stay in Rio.

"Shall we go for dinner?" George asked, "And we can determine how we feel about doing something else afterwards."

"Yes, good idea," Maggie replied, "but first, I would like to have a shower."

"Likewise," George said, "I think I smell from the journey."

They rested there for a while contemplating the trials of the day, and soon fell asleep. About fifteen minutes later, they were abruptly awoken by a knock at the bedroom door.

"Who is it?" George asked.

"Room service," a voice from outside the door replied.

George and Maggie jumped out of bed quickly, and George went to open the door. A waiter stood in the doorway with a big smile on his face. He was holding a tray aloft, balancing a bottle of champagne and two glasses.

"Good evening, Mr and Mrs Peacock, or should I say, boa noite," the waiter said, "compliments of the hotel."

Maggie looked at the well-dressed waiter standing at the door.

"This is a surprise!" she said.

"We try our best," the waiter replied.

George pointed to the table by the window.

"Put it over there," he said.

The waiter followed as ordered and placed the tray on the table.

"Would you like me to open it, Sir?" the waiter asked.

"Yes, please," George replied.

George noticed the man's English was almost perfect.

"Your English is excellent," he said.

The waiter smiled and began to open the bottle of champagne.

"I lived in London for nearly ten years," he said, "so I hope I picked up the language."

'POP' went the champagne cork, and the waiter poured the champagne into the two glasses.

"Thank you very much," George said.

"Yes, thank you," Maggie added.

"You're welcome," the waiter replied.

George handed a small tip to the waiter before he left the room. And returned. Picking up the two glasses, he gave one to Maggie. They raised glasses, clinked them together, and toasted the holiday.

"Ah! What a life!" George said.

Maggie sipped the champagne and immediately put the glass down.

"I must go to have a shower, if we want to have an early dinner," she said.

Maggie made her way to the bathroom and left the door ajar. In the meantime, George opened the sliding doors to the balcony and went outside to take in the view of Copacabana at night. It was not long before he heard the noise of the bathroom shower, but it was overwhelmed by the evening chorus of the cicadas outside.

George had other things on his mind, though. He needed to make a phone call to a contact whose details were given to him in the UK when he was asked to take the package to Brazil, the same package he had left at reception earlier. He went into the room to collect his phone and returned to the balcony. George took the piece of paper with the contact number from his pocket and dialled the number on it.

31

"Hello," someone answered in Portuguese.

"Hello, can I speak to António?" George asked.

"What?" the person asked.

"António," George repeated.

"One moment," the person said.

The person rested the telephone on the table, and George overheard a voice at the other end of the line speaking in Portuguese. There was silence for a few moments, and then George heard footsteps walking towards the phone. Someone picked up the phone and spoke.

"António here. Who's calling?"

"It's George, George Peacock from England."

"Ah, George!" Antonio said, "I was expecting your call. How was your flight?"

George detected a Brazilian accent in the voice.

"It was ok, a couple of minor things happened, but on the whole, it was alright."

He was trying to give the impression that there were no problems during the journey.

"When are we going to meet?" Antonio asked.

"I'm not sure. I have my wife with me, and it may be awkward to get away."

"We have to meet," António insisted.

"Yes, I know. I'll contact you again soon. I just wanted to let you know we arrived in Rio."

"Do you have the package?" António asked.

"Yes, it's safe."

"Don't lose it now," António added.

At that moment, Maggie emerged from the bathroom, her body wrapped in a towel. George hastily ended the call, but still held the phone in his hand, which Maggie noticed.

"I thought I heard voices," Maggie said, "who was on the phone? Who were you speaking to?"

George entered the room from the balcony and put the phone on the table. He needed to give a reason and wanted to say something seemingly innocent.

"It was only my sister, I told her I was going to call and let her know we arrived safely," George replied.

"How is she?"

"She's fine, she was pleased to hear we had a good journey and arrived safely."

George did not like to fib to his wife, but on this occasion, he felt it was ok to tell a white lie.

"Are you going to have a shower?" Maggie asked.

"Yes, I'd better."

George stripped off naked, threw the clothes on the bed, and hurried into the bathroom to take a shower. While they were getting dressed, the couple unpacked their suitcases.

George and Maggie decided to eat at the hotel that evening, and arrived at the restaurant on the first floor by 9 pm. The restaurant was laid out for buffet and à la carte dining, and was decorated in an Art décor style. The tables were covered with white tablecloths, stainless steel cutlery, crystal wine glasses, a candle in a crystal glass holder, and a small bunch of flowers at the centre. The couple introduced themselves to the maître d and were shown to a table at the front of the building, overlooking Copacabana Beach. The beachfront was illuminated by subdued lighting from lamp posts dotted along the street. As the lights were not too bright, they added to the ambience of the famous beach at night. Many people out for a walk were pestered by street vendors, which was a normal occurrence. It seemed that in most parts of the world, street vendors are always around to make a quick buck; their livelihood depended on it. Nevertheless, George and Maggie enjoyed the view from the panoramic glass window which overlooked the seafront.

Unbeknownst to the couple, a waiter approached and stood next to the table.

"Good evening, Sir, Madam. Anything to drink?" he asked.

George and Maggie were startled by the voice and turned around instantly.

"Good evening," Maggie said.

She looked at the well-dressed waiter and thought about the question for a moment.

"I'll have a cocktail before dinner."

"What cocktail would you like, madam?" the waiter asked.

"I don't know," she replied.

Maggie paused for a moment, looked at George and shrugged her shoulders. She looked back at the waiter.

"Is there a local cocktail, specific to Brazil?"

"Certainly, Madam. I will get the barman to surprise you."

The waiter then looked across at George.

"And what will you have, Sir?" he asked.

George looked up at the waiter, who reminded him of one of the South Americans on the aeroplane. He stared at the waiter for a few moments.

"Sir," the waiter said, prompting George.

"Um! I'll have a beer. I always like to have a beer before dinner."

"Any wine with dinner?" the waiter asked.

"I guess so," George replied.

The waiter handed George the wine list, but before he could say anything else, Maggie interrupted.

"We still have some champagne back in the room. Don't you think we should finish it first when we get back?"

George looked at the wine list and thought for a moment.

"I suppose we should finish the champagne. We'll leave the wine for now," George said.

He handed the wine list back to the waiter and began to feel anxious again, because the waiter reminded him of the South Americans. He looked over to the entrance of the restaurant in anticipation that they might be standing there, but the only people he saw were the maître d and two guests. A few minutes later, the waiter returned with the beer and cocktail, placing the cocktail in front of Maggie.

"Here you are, Madam," he said, "I'm sure you will enjoy this, the barman is very creative."

The waiter then placed the beer in front of George.

"And for you, Sir," the waiter said, "a Brazilian beer for you."

The silver service waitress stood behind the waiter and approached the couple's table once the waiter departed.

"À la carte or Buffet?" she asked.

George looked at Maggie.

"What do you think?" he asked.

"I think a Buffet, at this time of night. We don't want to be too long, we've had a long day, and I need to get some rest."

George looked up at the waitress.

"We'll have the Buffet."

"Ok," the waitress replied.

She pointed over towards the buffet bar.

"Please help yourself over there. Just ask if you need anything else, and enjoy your dinner."

As the waitress walked away, the maître d approached George and Maggie's table.

"Mr Peacock?" she asked.

"Yes," George replied.

"There is a phone call for you."

George looked surprised at her and wondered who could be calling him.

"Me!" he said, "who can be calling me? Are you sure?"

"Yes," the maître d replied, "You can take the call on the phone just outside the restaurant."

"Ok," George said, "I'll take the call."

He stood up, shrugged his shoulders at Maggie, and looked at her in amazement.

"I don't know who could be calling me," he said.

Maggie sat puzzled and watched George as he walked away from the table. He followed the maître d to the entrance of the restaurant, where she pointed to a telephone on a table just outside the door. George picked up the phone.

"Hello, George Peacock here. I believe there is a telephone call for me."

"Oh yes, Mr Peacock. I'll put you right through," the receptionist said.

The telephone went silent, and George waited for a few seconds. Then a deep, gruff voice spoke on the other end of the line.

"Mr Peacock?"

"Yes," George replied, "who is this?"

"Hello, Mr Peacock," the person said, "You don't know me. I am one of the men who followed you from England."

George became anxious, his mouth dried up, and his hands began to shake.

"Followed me?" George asked.

"Yes, I am one of the men you first saw at Heathrow airport; my colleague was the one with the scar on his face."

George took a deep gulp and looked around to see if there was a familiar face nearby. His hands began to sweat, and he could feel the blood rushing through his veins. He became very nervous and spoke in a mumbled voice.

"Who are you?" he asked, "Where are you? How did you find me here?"

George thought he had given the South Americans the slip, but it was obviously not the case.

"It was easy," the person said, "we overheard you on the plane talking to the other passengers, and you gave them the name of the hotel you were staying at in Rio."

George detected a Brazilian accent in the man and thought for a moment. *'The only passengers they talked to near the South Americans were the Germans. Were they in on this as well?'*

"Who are you?" George repeated, "What do you want?"

"My name is Marco, and my colleague is Fabio, the one who spoke to you on the plane."

George recalled being accosted by one of the South Americans on the plane, and now knew it was Fabio. He remained silent and looked around again to see if anyone was nearby. These men were definitely the Brazilian thugs.

"You still there?" Marco asked.

"Yes, I'm still here. What do you want?"

"We want the package. Give it to us, and we will not bother you anymore."

"I don't have any package," George said, while trying to sound innocent.

"We know you do, Mr Peacock. We have been well informed, and that's why we followed you."

"Informed? Who told you about me? I think you have the wrong person."

"We know we don't, and that's why I'm calling. We want to arrange the collection of the package."

"I told you I don't have any package, so why don't you leave us alone?"

George slammed the telephone down very hard and looked at his hands, which were still shaking. *'Who are these people?'* he thought, *'I wonder if the Germans are involved, and if so, it seems they may have betrayed us.'*

George made his way back to the table and sat down opposite Maggie. He was nervous, and his face became ashen. He stared vacantly at Maggie.

"You look like you've seen a ghost," Maggie said, "What's wrong?"

George did not answer Maggie; his mind was elsewhere.

"George!" exclaimed Maggie loudly, "what's wrong?"

Maggie's persistence got George's attention, and he soon snapped out of the semi-trance.

"It's alright," George replied, "there's nothing wrong. I'm just tired and was thinking of the flight."

George tried to get back his composure and took a sip of beer.

"Who was on the phone?" Maggie asked.

George needed to think of some excuse quickly.

"Just the travel representative."

Maggie was not convinced and somewhat perplexed at the answer.

"At this time of the night? What did they want?"

George knew he had to fib some more to his wife, which he didn't like to do. She was unaware of the package he brought over to Brazil, and wanted to keep it from her, so that she would not have any concerns.

"They wanted to know if we arrived safely at the hotel," he said, "And if everything was ok."

Maggie was still not convinced of the answer.

"Hmm! Sounds dodgy to me," she said.

George did not wish to continue with the conversation and decided to change the subject.

"Let's eat," he said.

Maggie was reluctant to end the conversation, but did not want to make a scene in the restaurant, so she decided not to ask any more questions for the time being. The couple wandered over to the Buffet bar and helped themselves to food. Maggie selected a small amount and put it on her plate. She was tired and didn't want a large meal. George did not take much food either, but in his case, he was concerned about the phone call. They sat down and ate their food, not saying much to each other over dinner. Later, they returned to the room, did some more unpacking, and went to bed early.

Chapter 4 – The Abduction

George and Maggie arose early the next day and went down for an early breakfast. Afterwards, they headed to the activities desk located in the reception area to book local sightseeing activities. They were particularly interested in visiting Sugarloaf Mountain, a peak situated on a peninsula at the mouth of Guanabara Bay, which opened to the Atlantic Ocean. The couple, also keen to see the Carnival procession at the Sambadrome, where carnival schools exhibited glamorous outfits, and danced to samba music. They also wanted to visit Corcovado Mountain, which towered 710 meters above sea level. At the top of the mountain is the famous Christ the Redeemer statue, where Christ is depicted with outstretched arms. The monument is situated in the Tijuca Forest National Park, and from its summit, it offers exceptional views of Rio and the surrounding areas.

The hotel was fairly busy that morning; the next day was the main carnival day, and people were trying to book last-minute activities. The reception area was manned by three clerks serving behind the front desk, and two doormen attending the foyer. Three other couples, a young man, and two businessmen were seated in the reception lounge. One of the other couples seemed to be making an early start as well and waited eagerly to be served at the activities desk. George and Maggie joined the others in the reception lounge.
"Good morning," George said politely, so everyone in the lounge could hear him.
Most of the guests glanced up at George and reciprocated the greeting. One of the businessmen seated by the hotel entrance was of medium build and dressed in a dark suit. The other wore a light grey summer suit and sat near the activities desk. He was a large man, and being somewhat obese, his tight-fitting suit bulged at the seams. Both men tapped away on their laptop computers, while others seemed to be waiting for someone else. Nobody was serving at the activities desk, so George went over to the reception counter to find a clerk. He was soon accompanied back by one of the receptionists, who proceeded to serve the other waiting couple first. They seemed slightly

annoyed at the time taken to be served. George and Maggie sat down and waited for their turn, during which time they took the opportunity to be nosy. They watched other guests passing in the reception area, and as always, there was no harm in people watching.

After ten minutes, the booking clerk at the activities desk completed the dealings with the other couple and looked over to George and Maggie.

"Mr Peacock, I can help you now," she said.

George and Maggie went over to the booking desk and sat down.

"What can I do for you?" the clerk asked.

"We would like to book a few activities," George replied.

The clerk was about to say something when George interrupted her.

"Three trips, one today to Sugarloaf Mountain, and two tomorrow. In the morning, we would like to go to Corcovado Mountain to see Christ the Redeemer statue, and in the evening, we would like to go to the Sambadrome to see the parades."

"It sounds like you are going to have a full day tomorrow," the clerk said, "let's see what we can do."

The clerk selected some trips from a folder and discussed each with George and Maggie. They agreed on the trips, paid the booking clerk by cash, and were handed the tickets for the activities. Unbeknownst to George and Maggie, the man in the grey suit seated near the activities desk was paying attention to the couple's activity planning. Before the couple completed the transaction, the man got up and left the hotel. George and Maggie were now ready for the day's outing and had previously prepared a backpack with essentials.

"Let's go," George said to Maggie, "it's time to do some sightseeing."

George picked up the backpack, and the couple headed for the hotel entrance. They exited the hotel and were engulfed by a blast of warm air, for which they were not prepared. The temperature outside was 32 degrees centigrade, and, being acclimatised to the air conditioning in the reception area, the heat was unbearable for them. The doorman soon hailed a taxi, and the couple were pleased to enter the air-conditioned cab. They headed off towards Sugarloaf Mountain.

As they drove off, George noticed the man in the grey suit standing outside the hotel talking on a mobile phone. George did not know this at the time, but the man was Brazilian and a member of the gang who followed the couple to Brazil. He was sent to spy on them at the hotel and overheard their plans for the day. He was calling a colleague to inform them of the details.
"Can I speak to Marco? It's Eduardo," the man said.
Marco was another member of the gang, and Eduardo waited a few seconds until Marco came to the phone.
"Marco here, what's up, Eduardo?"
"You asked me to let you know when the British couple were on the move."
"Yes, I did. What's happened?"
"Well, they've just left the hotel and are going to Sugarloaf Mountain for the day."
"That's good news, Eduardo, we'll get on to it right away. Good work. Stay at the hotel in case the couple return."
"Ok, boss, will do."

George and Maggie's taxi drove through heavy traffic for about twenty minutes, and the couple arrived at the entrance to the cable car for Sugarloaf Mountain. The only way to reach the top of the peaks was by cable car, and a large crowd had gathered to queue outside the entrance. Rio was bulging at the seams with people because it was Carnival time. Foreigners as well as locals from all over Brazil travelled to Rio to participate in the festival.
"Oh my god!" George said while leaving the taxi, "Look at the queues, I hate queuing."
"We'll just have to do it," Maggie said, "it seems the whole world is in Rio this week."

The couple joined the queue and shuffled along with the other sightseers. They endured the 32-degree heat and often took sips of water to rehydrate themselves. George and Maggie queued for around twenty minutes before they reached the cable cars. The method to reach the top of Sugarloaf Mountain was by two cable cars, on the basis that when one ascends, the other descends. In fact, there were two sets of cable cars as Sugarloaf Mountain was comprised of two peaks. One set of cars transported people to the first peak, where passengers alighted. Another set of cars serviced passengers from the first peak to the second peak. Even though each car could hold 50-60 people, the volume of people that day meant the trip to the top was slow.

The couple eventually reached the first cable car, which was almost full. There was only room for two or three more people. Maggie stepped into the car and was followed closely by George, but before George could board, another couple pushed their way in front of him, and left him stranded on the platform. George tried to force his way on as well, but was obstructed by the guard, who stopped him from boarding.

"No more," the guard said, "the car is full, wait for the next car."

George felt he was unfairly treated and shouted at the guard.

"Hey! You've got to let me on. My wife is on board."

"Sorry, too late, wait for the next car."

"You must have seen the other couple push their way in. Why didn't you stop them and let me on?"

The guard was not concerned about the incident and ignored George's comments.

"Sorry, boss, next car," he said.

There was not much George could do now; he would have to wait for the next cable car. He looked at Maggie through the glass and noticed a terrified expression on her face.

"I'll see you at the top," he shouted.

George also indicated with his hands so that Maggie could understand in case she did not hear him, and she raised her thumb in acknowledgement. The cable car departed from the platform, and the couple were now separated. The cable cars ran every ten minutes, so it would not be long before they were together again.

George mumbled some expletives to himself and waited for the other cable car to arrive. He made sure he was the first to board and headed to the exit door of the cable car to be the first to disembark. Another male passenger noticed the whole episode and approached George to give him moral support.

"I sympathise with you," he said, "it was not good to separate you and your wife."

"No, I'm pissed off to say the least."

"I can see that," the man said.

The cable car departed from the platform, and George became calmer on the journey. At about the halfway stage, he saw the other cable car descending and looked at the packed passengers inside the returning car. To his surprise, he saw Maggie, pushed against the window. She was terrified and was being held firmly by the two Brazilians, Marco and Fabio. They saw George and derisively waved to him. George felt sick, and his heart began to pound quickly. He was powerless and could not do anything to help his wife.

"What the fuck!" he exclaimed loudly.

Other passengers turned and looked at him.

"That's my wife," George said, "They've got my wife."

"Who's got your wife?" the man who spoke to him earlier asked.

"The Brazilians."

The man looked a bit puzzled.

"What Brazilians?" he asked.

"Long story, you wouldn't understand," George replied.

George was now furious and scared. '*What were they doing? Where were they taking his wife?*' He could not think clearly and was anxious for the cable car to reach the top. He wanted to take the very next car to descend immediately, which ironically was the same car he arrived in. He asked the conductor if he could remain, but was told to disembark.

Another few minutes passed, and the cable car reached its destination. George was the first to alight and made his way over to the queue waiting to descend. The boarding was through a different door, and he pushed his way to the front of the queue.

"Hey! Watch it," a tourist shouted.

"Sorry," George said, "It's important I get to the front."

"We all want to get down first," the tourist said, "have some patience."

43

George ignored the man's comment and still pushed his way to the front of the queue to board and exit the car first. The passengers ambled aboard, which made George anxious. He wanted to descend as quickly as possible, but there was nothing he could do to speed up the boarding, and he stood there tapping his fingers on the handrail. The car eventually left, and George scanned the people at the destination, but it was too far to make out any detail. He remembered the binoculars in his backpack and scanned the base area for Maggie. Nothing promising could be seen at first, but when the cable car approached the destination, George spotted Maggie on the road below, being hurried along by the Brazilians. They headed towards a silver Mercedes parked nearby. George tried to get a closer view and zoomed the binoculars, but got a blurred result. He refocused quickly, only to see Maggie being bundled into the Mercedes. It started to move off, so George tried to identify the car's number plate. He was able to capture it just before the Mercedes disappeared into the traffic, and noted it on a piece of paper.

The cable car reached the bottom of the descent, and George speedily made his way to the location on the road where he last saw the Mercedes. The car was nowhere to be seen; it had already departed. He asked a few people if they had seen the kidnapping, but no one owned up, or they were more than likely unwilling to say. George felt despondent and sick in the stomach. He let his wife down by involving her in the delivery of the package, and now she had been abducted. What was he to do?

George's dilemma had become very serious; it had become a deadly scenario, and he was unsure what to do. The only person George knew in Rio was his contact, Antonio, who might be able to help him. He searched in his pocket for the piece of paper with Antonio's telephone number, and dialled it on his mobile phone. A man answered the call.

"Hello," the man said.

"Antonio, quickly please," George said.

Antonio had answered the call, and he recognised George's voice.

"This is Antonio. Is that George?"

George began to panic, and his hands were shaking.

"Yes, Antonio, I need help, I need your help urgently," George said.

"Stay calm, George. What's wrong?"

"My wife has been kidnapped."

"Kidnapped!" Antonio exclaimed, "Who would do such a thing?"

"The Brazilians."

"What Brazilians?"

"The Brazilians who followed us from England."

Antonio was surprised at George's comments and became concerned.

"You were followed from England?" he asked, "Why didn't you tell me before?"

"I didn't have time. Last time we spoke, I had to end the call quickly because my wife came into the room."

Antonio took a deep breath and calmed himself.

"Ok, this sounds serious. Tell me about the kidnapping."

George proceeded to tell Antonio about the Brazilians and the events that transpired up until now, while Antonio listened carefully.

"I think I know these men," Antonio said, "You said one had a scar on his face?"

"Yes," George replied, "can you help in any way?"

"Do you have any other information you can give me, like the colour of the car, or even the registration number?"

"Ah, yes, I forgot about that. I did make a note of the registration number. Have you got a pen?"

"Yes."

George gave the car details to Antonio, who scribbled them down.

"Ok, I'll see what I can do," Antonio said, "go back to the hotel and wait there until I contact you. I have your mobile number, but I don't have the details of the hotel you are staying at, or the room number."

George thought seriously about whether he should give the hotel details to Antonio. They had not met before, and he knew nothing whatsoever about the man. Was this the right thing to do? Could he trust this man? Who else could he trust? His wife was missing, and Antonio was willing to help. George felt uneasy about giving out the hotel details, but had no alternative but to do so if this guy was going to help him, so he gave Antonio the details.

"Oh, and one other thing," Antonio said, "have you still got the package?"

"Yes," George replied, "it is safe. Have you got the money?"

"Yes, that's all taken care of. I'll speak with you soon."

Antonio put the phone down and ended the call.

George walked for a while and pondered on the events of the day. He was bewildered and in a daydream state, accidentally bumping into people as he walked along. There was not much he could do now, so he decided to return to the hotel where he could rest for a while. George flagged down a taxi and was on the way back to the Othon Palace hotel. The taxi driver was talkative, in keeping with many taxi drivers worldwide.

"Are you from England, mister?" he asked.

"Yes," George replied.

George was not in the mood to talk and continued to look out the window.

"England has a good football team, yes?" the driver asked.

"Yes, but they could be better."

"Not as good as Brazil, though," the driver said in a perky voice. George looked at the driver in the rear-view mirror and noticed he was grinning with a big smile on his face. He ignored the driver's comments and remained silent. He looked out of the window once more and thought about Maggie, which brought tears to his eyes. Not wanting the driver to see, he quickly wiped them away. George was now feeling depressed, and it showed in his face. The driver looked at George in the rear-view mirror.

"Are you ok, mister? Are you in trouble?" he asked.

George looked at the driver again and wondered whether to partake in conversation. He thought it would not harm; at least it would stop him from thinking and worrying about Maggie.

"Yes, just a little."

46

"Maybe I can help you. We taxi drivers know all that goes on in the world."

George took a deep breath and wiped his eyes again.

"Gangsters have been following me," he said.

The driver could not believe his ears and laughed out loud.

"Ha! You are in Brazil now, mister. Plenty of gangs here. You need to be careful."

George became a little angry at the driver and his comments.

"No, you don't understand. My wife has been kidnapped."

"Oh my god!" the driver said, "You're not kidding, are you? You really are in big trouble."

"Tell me about it," George said.

"You seem to be a nice man, and I think I can help you."

"How can you help me?" George asked.

"My brother-in-law is a detective in the police force, and I'll give you his name."

"No, thank you, driver, I don't want to involve the police."

The taxi driver felt uneasy and assumed George did not want his help, so they both remained silent for the rest of the journey. After a while, the taxi pulled up at the hotel entrance.

"Here you are, man, Othon Palace," the driver said.

George checked the fare on the display, took a note from his pocket to pay for the fare plus a tip, and handed it to the driver.

"Thank you," George said.

He collected his bag and was about to leave the taxi.

"One moment," the driver said.

The driver then scribbled something on the back of a business card and handed it to George.

"What's this?" George asked.

He looked at the card, on which the driver had written a telephone number.

"It's my brother-in-law's number, and he will help you. You seem like a good man, and he is a good man, too. You should call him for help."

George thanked the driver and made his way into the hotel. He went directly to the lift and up to the room. He was tired and pleased to enter the air-conditioned building, leaving the exhausting heat outside.

The morning experience took its toll, and George was looking forward to a rest. He opened the door to the room and was not prepared for what awaited him. The room was ransacked, and George was utterly appalled at the scene before his eyes. At first, it seemed the chambermaid had not tidied the room, but he soon realised the room had been turned over. Someone had been in and searched the room. George peeped into the bathroom and noticed new soap and clean glasses, so he assumed the hotel staff had already been. The room was in a sorry state indeed, with pillows on the floor and the bed sheets turned back. All the drawers were open, and the contents strewn on the floor. The wardrobe was open, and the clothes were scattered at the base. The security safe was also open, and the contents were placed on the table. George searched around to identify any missing items and found that their passports were the only things missing. Everything else was accounted for, including cash from the safe. He knew it was a targeted burglary, and George thought about calling the hotel security or the police. He even thought about calling the police detective, the contact the taxi driver gave him on the way back from Sugarloaf Mountain. George assumed it was the Brazilian gang who followed them and kidnapped his wife, so he decided otherwise. He sat down to contemplate the situation.

George looked at the clock in the room, and it displayed 12:30. He thought deeply for a while and looked at the clock again. It was now one o'clock, and he did not realise the last half hour had flown by so quickly. There was not much he could do, so George waited for Antonio to call. For the first time, he felt all alone and vulnerable in Rio. How would his wife be feeling, having been kidnapped and in a strange city? George tidied the room and decided to go out for a light lunch. He exited the front of the hotel and crossed the road onto Copacabana promenade. It was festival time, and vast crowds of people were milling around, some with drinks in their hands, some waving banners. Many were dressed in bright coloured clothes, specific to the carnival season. Music sounded at almost every corner, mainly live samba bands, but sometimes from DJ sound systems. Everyone seemed to be enjoying themselves.

Many open-air bars and cafes on the promenade adjacent to the beach were packed, so George strolled along until he found a cafe with a vacant table and a sun umbrella. It was a hot day, and George was glad to be shaded from the blistering sun. He sat down and was lucky to find one with a view overlooking the beach. A few seconds later, a scantily dressed young woman approached him. He looked at her dismissively and thought, '*Here goes, someone on the make.*'

"Hello, my name is Gabriela. Anything to drink, Sir?" the young lady asked.

George was wrong about the woman because he thought she was a floozy. Instead, the young lady worked at the establishment, so George apologised to her in his thoughts.

"Ah, yes," he said, "I'll have a beer, a large beer."

"And to eat, Sir?" Gabriela asked.

George looked at the menu, but was not hungry due to his predicament.

"Can you recommend anything small?" A small meal perhaps."

"You can have the Nachos," Gabriela replied.

George thought for a few seconds while still looking at the menu.

"Ok, I'll have the Nachos. It sounds right for me."

The waitress scribbled the order on a notepad and walked away from the table. While George waited for his drink, he watched the people cavorting on the beach. A minute or so later, Gabriela returned with a large glass of ice-cold beer and placed it on the table in front of him.

"Here you are, Sir," she said.

"Thank you," George replied.

"Your meal won't be long," Gabriela added.

She walked away from the table, and George reached across to pick up his beer. He raised the glass and looked at the beer as if it were the last drink he was ever going to have. He took a long, slow sip and swallowed it in one gulp.

"Ahh!" George sighed loudly.

The noise drew the attention of other patrons, who just looked at him and smiled. George took another sip of beer and continued to watch the swimmers and surfers while he waited for lunch.

A few minutes went by, and George's mobile phone rang. He quickly answered it, thinking it was Antonio.

"Hello," he said.

The phone was silent at the other end.

"Hello," he repeated, "who's there?"

Then a weepy female voice spoke.

"George, it's me, Maggie."

"Maggie! My god! Are you ok?" George asked, "Where are you?"

"I don't know. I am being held captive, and I don't know where I am. You need to give them what they want, or else they said they will kill me."

There was emotion in Maggie's voice, and she began to cry.

"Please, George, please," she begged, "Give them what they want."

At that moment, the phone was snatched from Maggie, and a man spoke.

"Hello George, this is Marco."

Marco was one of the men who kidnapped Maggie, and George became infuriated.

"Where have you got my wife?" George shouted.

The outburst caused other patrons in the café to look around, embarrassed by George's comment.

"She's safe with us for now, and we are looking after her," Marco said, "No harm will come to her if you cooperate. Now, can we do a deal? Your wife, in exchange for the package. What do you say?"

George remained silent for a few seconds with thoughts swirling around his head. Then Gabriela returned to the table with the Nachos and placed them in front of George. She noticed George was anxious on the phone, but did not say anything.

"Are you still there?" Marco asked.

"Yes, I'm here."

"Well," Marco said in an urgent tone.

"Why do you need the package?" George asked.

"We have an influential buyer wanting to buy the package, and they are a large organisation."

"Large organisation!" George exclaimed, "I don't know of any organisations relating to the package."

"You see, George, you have got yourself into deep water, and are out of your league."

"That may be so, but I want my wife back."

"Well," Marco said again, "do we have a deal?"

"Yes, ok," George replied, "what now?"

"We'll contact you again in a while," Marco said, "We have some things to sort out first."

The line went dead, and George just sat there, puzzled. '*What is going on?*' he thought.

George hoped Antonio would call him soon with some news about his wife. He contemplated the dilemma over and over again while eating the Nachos. He recollected the time when he was first approached by a man in a pub in London, where he was having a few drinks with friends. He had gone to the toilet, and was followed by the man.

"I couldn't help overhearing the conversation with your friends out there, about your Brazilian holiday," the man said.

The man seemed friendly enough, and George did not mind talking to him.

"Have you been there?" George asked.

"No, but I have contacts there, business contacts."

"Where about in Brazil?"

"In Rio, where you are going. Isn't that what you said to your friends?"

"Yes, I did. It's my first time there, and I'm really looking forward to it, but it's expensive, though."

Both men finished in the washroom and returned to their respective friends.

About half an hour later, George went to the bar to buy drinks. While waiting to be served, he was approached by the man he had met in the toilets.

"We meet again," the man said.

"Yes, more drinks needed," George replied.

"I couldn't help thinking about what you said regarding your holiday."

"What did I say?" George asked.

"About the cost, you said it was expensive."

"Yes, I had to save up for this one. It's a long way away, and an exotic destination."

The man did not continue the conversation straight away. He looked over towards his friends and then back at George, who sensed the man was about to ask him something important.

"I am always sending things to my contacts in Rio," the man said, "and it's costing us a fortune. Would you be interested in making a few bucks?"

"What would I have to do?" George asked.

"Deliver a parcel to Rio."

George immediately raised his hand at the man.

"Whoa there!" he exclaimed, "I've heard about deals like this before. I'm not interested in that sort of thing."

"No, no, it's nothing like that. No drugs involved."

"What is it then?" George asked.

"It's a flat package, and will fit into your hand luggage easily."

"A package, what kind of package?"

"I can't really say."

"Then, no deal, I would need to know what I am taking with me."

The man now sensed George might have been enticed into the deal and decided to continue the conversation.

"Does that mean you are interested then?" he said.

"I might be, if I know what I'm taking, and if the price is right."

"Wait a moment," the man said.

He returned to the table where his friends sat and had a brief discussion with them. George looked across at the table and could just about make out the two other men seated there. One wore a grey suit and the other a brown leather jacket.

George ordered drinks and was awaiting them when the man returned.

"Ok, we will pay you £2000," the man said, "£1000 now, and £1000 on delivery of the package. But first, we need to know about you as well. We can't just hand over money and trust you without knowing more about you. Let's meet here again at the same time in two days, and we can have a chat."

The men agreed to meet, and two days later returned to the pub. After the initial greeting, they ordered a drink, and George was interrogated in detail by the other man. It was intimidating for

George, but he didn't mind; the £2000 would go a long way towards the holiday and pay off outstanding debts. Once the man finished questioning George, it was his opportunity to ask the man a few questions.

"What's in the package?" George asked.

The man looked around the pub to check if anyone was listening to their conversation.

"You must keep this under your hat," the man said, and whispered to George, "It's an electronic circuit board, but a very important one."

"What does it do?"

"It's used in a device to map the rainforest. It contains a special computer program that can identify different types of trees from the air and can also determine mineral deposits on the land. It is highly specialised, and not many people know of it. That's all you need to know at the moment."

George thought the man was very secretive, but did not think it was too much bother to take the electronic item for the sum of £2000.

"What about customs?" George asked, "Surely the item will be detected when my hand luggage passes through the scanner?"

"You don't need to worry about that," the man said, "it will be wrapped in a special material, and the scanner won't detect it."

George agreed to transport the item and shook hands on the deal. The man then surreptitiously handed George £1000 cash in exchange for the package.

"Thank you," George said, feeling a bit nervous, and was about to leave the table.

"One other thing," the man said, "here are the details of the contact in Rio to whom you must give the package. He will be waiting for you to contact him when you arrive."

The man handed George a piece of paper with a telephone number written on it and the name 'Antonio.'

"Take good care of the package," the man said, as George walked away from the table.

Back at the café on the promenade, George ate some more Nachos, sipped his beer, and then recollected the time when his hand luggage passed through security at Heathrow. He was very nervous about the package being discovered, and his heart stopped a beat when his bag went through the scanner. Then there were the many times he was intensely stared at by the Brazilians while they followed him from Heathrow to Rio. There was also the incident on the plane when one of the Brazilians attacked and punched him. Then there was the telephone call during dinner the previous night. And lastly, the kidnapping of his wife and the burglary in the hotel room today. A large organisation! What organisation? Was he delivering the package to a different organisation? Was there competition going on between them? Who were the Brazilian men, and for whom were they working? How did they know about the package? And, who was Antonio? Could he be trusted? All in all, there were many questions to be answered.

George's thoughts returned to the present, and he continued to eat his lunch slowly. He tried to ignore the festivities around him, but couldn't as the music was loud, and people were dancing nearby. He had almost finished lunch when Edouardo approached him, the man in the grey suit from the hotel. George immediately recognised him as one of the businessmen he saw seated in the hotel lounge that morning. Eduardo sat down next to George and looked out onto the beach.

"Hey Gringo," he uttered, "nice day for a swim."

George was in no mood for small talk and felt uneasy that the stranger sat next to him.

"What do you want?" he asked.

"Don't be like that Gringo. The sea is lovely for swimming. Your wife is safe, and all you need to do is give the package to me."

George was surprised the stranger knew about his wife, and paid more attention to the man.

"What do you know about my wife? Who are you?"

"Eduardo, my name is Eduardo."

"Go away, Eduardo, go away and leave me alone," George said, "I need to see my wife first before I hand over the package."

"Ok Gringo, you play it your way, but you will give us the package in the end, or your wife will die. Do you understand?"

Eduardo stood and faced away from the other diners. He pulled a handgun halfway out from the inside of his jacket and ensured George alone saw it. George immediately became alarmed and felt this was proof that these men were serious and really dangerous. The man returned the gun to his pocket, turned around and walked away from George. He soon disappeared into the crowd, and George remained seated, somewhat bewildered. George was unable to eat the remainder of his lunch and pushed the plate to one side. His stomach was churning at the sight of the gun, and his hands shook with fear.

He returned to the hotel soon afterwards and went to his room. There was not much he could do, and he waited for Antonio to call. At least Antonio was his last hope, and may have some good news for him, which George desperately needed. He remained in the room that night and tried to watch some television, but with so many things on his mind, he didn't absorb much. It was really for background noise. He decided to have an early night and hoped tomorrow would bring some good luck. George drank a couple of whiskies from the minibar, hoping they would make him sleep soundly.

Chapter 5 – Rescued at the Sambadrome

Carnival day was the next day. Several late revellers from the night before, as well as some early risers, gathered on Copacabana Beach to see the sunrise over the horizon. The bright sun rose above the sea and filled the distant sky with an orange glow, which, in turn, reflected on the diverse colours of the sea below. In a few minutes, the sun rose a further few degrees, enough to emit a blinding ray of sunlight, too strong for people to view with the naked eye. It was a public holiday in Rio, and not many people woke early. Most suffered hangovers from the night before and were sound asleep. Early morning mist rose from the buildings, caused by the overnight condensation evaporating from the heat of the sun. A few cars and motorbikes drove along the front at Copacabana beach, and the road was eerily calm without traffic. The hotels on the seafront were coming to life, and the general hum of air conditioning units emanated in the distance.

George did not rise early that day and was awoken by a knock on the door at 10 o'clock.
"Mr Peacock, room service," a female voice said from outside the door.
"One moment," George said, "just a minute."
George scrambled out of bed and donned some clothes. He was still bleary-eyed from sleep and wandered over to open the door.
"Good morning, Mr Peacock," the lady said.
George was confronted by a smiling woman dressed in a chambermaid's outfit.
"I'm here to clean the room."
The chambermaid looked at George and noticed he had just woken up.
"Is it a bad time?" she asked.
"No, it isn't," he said.
George was not properly dressed and was still half asleep. He became flustered and stood there looking at her, a bit puzzled, while running his fingers through his hair.
"Um, yes, this is a bad time," he said, "can you come back later?"
The chambermaid smiled at George.

"Ok. I'll come back, you take your time."
She gave another cheeky smile at George and walked away to clean the next room.

George closed the door, went over to the dressing table, and checked to see if there were any messages on his phone. As there were none, he opened the balcony doors to let in some fresh air and to view the throng of people gathering on the road below. There was not much George could do that day but wait for Antonio to call. He took a shower and went down to the restaurant, only to find he had missed the breakfast service. Luckily, coffee, bread rolls and cheese were still available. George grabbed them quickly and sat down to have breakfast. He returned to the room soon after, which had now been serviced by the chambermaid. George remained in the room for the rest of the morning, waiting for the telephone to ring. He kept looking at the clock every five to ten minutes, but no one called that morning. About 2 pm, he ordered a sandwich and some tea from room service, and after lunch, he sat on the balcony to wait for Antonio's call. The room phone rang at 15:30, and George rushed to answer it, hoping it was Antonio, but it was the receptionist dialling the room number by mistake.

Then, at about 17:30, George's mobile phone rang.
"Hello, George here."
"George, this is Antonio. I have some good news for you."
"Great! What have you found out?"
"Well, I had to call in favours from some of my contacts."
"And?" George asked.
"Well, the good news is that we have traced the car, the Mercedes. We have an address for it."
"That's great news, Antonio," George said, "is it a Rio address?"
"Yes, it's in Rio."
"What's the address? I've got a pen and notepad ready."
Antonio gave the address, and George wrote it on the notepad. The address was unknown to George, as he was not too familiar with Rio.
"Where is that?" he asked.
"Downtown, in the centre of the city, near the Sambadrome."

"The Sambadrome, that's where we were supposed to be going this evening to see the parade."

"There is not much more I can do on this issue now," Antonio said, "Maybe you need to go to the police."

"I'll have to think about that," George said, "and thanks, Antonio, thanks very much for your help, I appreciate it."

"No problem, as soon as you get yourself sorted, we'll meet up, ok?"

"Ok, Antonio, goodbye for now, and thanks once again."

George felt relieved he had an address and was feeling more confident. Maybe Maggie was being held at this location, and he needed to find out. He quickly searched for the street map he was given at reception and spread it out on the table. He scanned the list of road names in the index, but could not find the name of the road Antonio had given him. He located the Sambadrome and looked for the side roads radiating from it, but still could not find a road with that name. There were some smaller roads shown on the map, but they did not show road names. Maybe the hotel staff would know, so George slipped on his shoes, grabbed the map and notepad, and headed to the reception desk.

A male clerk was standing at the desk when George arrived.

"Excuse me," George said to gain his attention, "can you help me?"

"Yes, Sir," the clerk replied, "What can I do for you?"

George spread the street map of Rio on the counter and hurriedly flattened it with both hands. He put the notepad on the map and pointed at the address written on it.

"I am looking for this road. I think it's near the Sambadrome, but I can't find it on the map."

"Let me have a look," the clerk said.

He looked at the address on the notepad and searched the index for the name of the road as George had done.

"I've already done that," George said.

The clerk continued scanning the index and then looked up at George.

"No, it doesn't seem to be there. I've never heard of this road before."

"Is there anyone else here who could help?" George asked.

"Hold on, I'll call Raul. He might know."

The clerk looked towards the entrance of the hotel, where Raul, the doorman, was standing.

"Raul knows everything," the clerk said to George.

The clerk called over to the doorman and beckoned for him to come over.

"Raul, come over here, we need your help."

Raul raised one arm in acknowledgement and came over to reception straight away.

"Yes, how can I help?"

The clerk pointed to the address on the notepad.

"We are trying to find this address; we believe it's in downtown Rio."

Raul pondered for a while and then had an Eureka moment.

"Ah," he said with enthusiasm, "that's a side road off the Sambadrome."

"Great," George said, "Can you show me on the map?"

George shoved the street map of Rio in front of Raul.

"Now let's see," Raul said.

He studied the map and pointed at various places on it, while mumbling to himself.

"The Sambadrome is here, the main road is here, and..."

George and the receptionist both looked at Raul with anticipation, a look urging him to answer quickly.

"Ah, here we are," Raul said.

He pointed to one of the unmarked side roads on the map, which was at a right angle to the Sambadrome.

"It's this one."

"Are you sure?" George asked.

"Yes, definitely this one."

"Good," George said, "thank you, Raul."

"You're welcome, Sir," Raul replied.

George pulled the map away from Raul and marked the road on the map with his pen. Raul was about to walk back to the hotel entrance when George stopped him.

"Wait," George shouted.

George took a 5 Real note from his pocket and handed it to Raul.

"This is for you."

Raul was thankful and walked away with a smile on his face. George also thanked the reception clerk and made his way back to the room on the 27th floor. He was now poised to make his next move, so George sat down and planned what he had to do. It was imperative to find Maggie, and he needed to go to the address off the Sambadrome tonight.

George took a shower and dressed for the evening. He picked up a handful of brochures and an envelope from reception and left the hotel. It was around 9 pm, and George hailed a taxi from outside the hotel and headed to the Sambadrome. He wanted to reach the Sambadrome when the carnival procession was in full flow, to mingle with the crowds and not be easily recognised. He gave himself ample time to arrive at the address, allowing for the chaotic traffic that filled the streets on the main Carnival night. The journey took about an hour to reach the downtown area. A few blocks away from the Sambadrome, the traffic was at a standstill, and George decided to walk the rest of the way. He asked the driver to let him out and set off on foot to search for the address Antonio gave him. The area around the Sambadrome was packed with revellers, some in outrageous costumes, and all seemed to be having a good time. Music played and people danced in the streets. The noise of laughter and shouting created a colourful party atmosphere.

George pushed his way through the crowds and soon arrived at the Sambadrome. All he needed to do now was find the side road off the main drag. His hands became sweaty, his heart began to pound, and he was unsure what awaited him at the destination. The loud music and people shouting rang in his ears, and he could not concentrate properly. He eventually found the side road off the Sambadrome and entered it. The street was dimly lit and fairly dark, which made the buildings look somewhat dingy. He walked as close as possible to the buildings, so as not to be noticed, and soon came to the address for which he was searching. The house was nothing special, a two-storey building painted in cream, and had become grimy over time. He approached the large, brown wooden door to the house, and his heart pounded even faster. He looked up at the windows to check if anyone was looking out, but there was no one to be seen, not even from the other houses.

George knocked on the door with three loud taps. He waited for twenty seconds, which seemed like an eternity, but no one answered the door. He knocked on the door again, this time with four loud taps, and after a few seconds, he heard footsteps from within. He was nervous and tense while waiting for the door to be unlocked. The door opened slowly, and a bright light from the ceiling inside shone directly into his face. He could only make out the silhouette of a large man standing in the doorway. The man came forward to the edge of the doorway, and George was able to see his face, but didn't recognise the man. George stood on the doorstep, slightly trembling with the package in his hand. The man looked at George from head to toe and deduced he was a foreigner.

"Hello, you must be Mr Peacock. I see you found us," the large man said.

It seems the man was half expecting George to come to the house. The man looked down at the package, and George's mouth became dry, but he felt he needed to speak.

"And, who are you?" he asked.

"My name is Carlos."

George detected a Brazilian accent in the man.

"Is my wife here, Carlos?"

"Maybe," Carlos replied, "I see you've got the package."

George raised the package he was holding, so Carlos could see it.

"Now, where's my wife?"

Carlos leaned over and extended his arm to take the package, but George pulled it away. He had the impression that Carlos was not that clever, and continued with the deal.

"My wife first, where's my wife?"

Carlos thought for a moment about how he could turn the meeting to his advantage. The Brazilian gang were not expecting George to find them, let alone to have the package on him. He saw an opportunity that might put him in good standing with his bosses, Marco and Fabio. If he did the deal with George and swapped the package for his wife, it would show his bosses

61

that he could use his initiative, and it would give him some kudos as a gang member.

"Come in," Carlos said.

George entered the building, and Carlos shut the door behind him. It was much quieter indoors, and George sensed no one else was in the building, other than his wife, but could not be sure. He felt slightly relieved, but needed to be on his guard. He looked around and glanced through two open doors on either side of the hallway to check them out. The hallway extended to the back of the building, where there were doors to other rooms. A staircase rose from the hallway to a first-floor landing.

"Follow me," Carlos said.

He started to walk up the stairs, and was closely followed by George. Carlos was a big man, and his weight caused most of the stair boards to creak while he ascended the stairway.

"Where are you taking me?" George asked.

"You will see," Carlos replied.

Carlos reached the landing, where doors led off to three other rooms. The doors on either side of the landing were closed, but the door straight ahead was open and led to a kitchen-diner. Carlos stopped on the landing and unlocked one of the closed doors with the key that was already in the lock. He opened it slowly and walked in, followed closely by George. As soon as George entered the room, there was a terrific scream from a woman. It was Maggie.

"Oh my god," Maggie shouted, "it's you, it's you, George."

George quickly went over to Maggie and hugged her, while Carlos looked on with a smirk on his face.

"Oh, sweetheart, I thought I lost you," George said.

"Me too," Maggie said.

The couple continued to hug and caress each other's backs.

"Ok, enough," Carlos shouted, "that's enough. Now give me the package."

George released his hug on Maggie and threw the package directly at Carlos. Carlos fumbled to catch it and dropped it to the floor.

"Let's go," George said to Maggie.

George grabbed Maggie's hand and dragged her out of the room onto the landing. He looked back into the room and saw that

Carlos was about to open the package. With quick thinking, he shut the door and locked it with the key.

"Run," George shouted. "Quickly."

The couple hurried down the stairs as fast as they could and exited the building. Carlos eventually opened the package to find it contained various sightseeing brochures; there was no electronic circuit board inside. George duped Carlos by preparing a dummy package earlier that evening, using the brochures he collected from the hotel's reception.

Carlos realised George had tricked him, and that was why he locked him in the room. He took out his pistol and fired two shots at the door lock. The gunshots demolished the lock and resounded throughout the building. Carlos could now leave the room and was absolutely furious at the couple. At the same time, George and Maggie exited the building and onto the side street. They ran as fast as they could, and after a few seconds, Maggie became breathless and stopped running.

"Where are we going?" Maggie asked, while trying to catch her breath.

"I don't know, just keep running."

The couple headed towards the Sambadrome to mingle with the multitudes of people. This was the best place for them to hide from Carlos. The carnival was now in full swing, with the colourful parades passing through the Sambadrome. George and Maggie mixed with the people watching the parades and tried to blend in with the crowd as tourists. Carlos thumped down the stairs after the couple, but due to his obesity, he could not run as fast as they. He looked both ways when exiting the house and guessed the couple would have gone in the direction of the crowds, because it was the best place they could hide. He headed for the Sambadrome with a gun in hand and stopped at the edge of the Sambadrome. As he was a tall man, he was able to see over the top of most people and scan the crowds in all directions. He could not pick out the couple in the mass of colours confronting him. In his temper, he threw the gun down forcefully onto the road.

"Shit, now I'm in deep shit," he shouted in Portuguese.

The outburst caused the concerned crowd nearby to look at him, and they soon dispersed when they saw the gun lying on the ground.

"Shit, Shit, Shit," Carlos shouted.

The crowd stared at him with disgust, which made him feel uncomfortable.

"What are you staring at?" he shouted at them, "Piss off."

Carlos waved his arms in the air simultaneously to indicate the same sentiment. He picked up the gun and mingled with the crowd, in the hope of finding the couple, but George and Maggie had already wangled their way through the crowd in the opposite direction to Carlos.

"What was all the fuss about the package?" Maggie asked George, "What was in it? And why did you have to exchange it for me?"

"I'll explain later," George said, "let's get out of here to a safe place first."

Maggie was somewhat frustrated that George did not want to tell her about the package and huffed.

"Hmm!"

Then she remembered something else.

"The passports!" Maggie exclaimed, "The passports are in the house."

"Which house? George asked, "Do you mean the one we just came from?"

"Yes, they were in the kitchen, I saw them there."

George smacked his forehead with the palm of his hand.

"Oh heck! We'll have to go back and get them."

"That could be dangerous," Maggie said.

The couple knew it would be risky for them to return to the house, but because of their importance, they felt it necessary to recover the passports.

"Let's think about this," George said, "Carlos may be out looking for us, and there was no one else in the house."

"But it could still be risky," Maggie added.

The adrenaline was flowing heavily in George's body, and he was now feeling bullish.

64

"I know, but we need the passports; otherwise, we would have to go to the British Embassy," he said, "I'm willing to take the risk."

Maggie was uncertain about the risk and screwed up her face.

"Are you sure?" she asked.

"Yes, I'm sure. We'll have to do it."

"Ok," Maggie said, "in for a penny, in for a pound."

George and Maggie cautiously made their way back to the house. They continued to look for Carlos at the same time.

They agreed George should enter the house on his own, and Maggie should stand in the shadows of the doorway at the opposite house as a lookout. On returning to the house, George approached the front door, which was still ajar. Carlos must have left it open in the haste to chase after the couple. George peered inside the doorway and listened to see if anyone was in the house, but there was silence, apart from the music in the Sambadrome. He pushed the door slightly and swung it fully open. The lights in the house were on, so he tiptoed in and reached the bottom of the stairs leading to the first floor. He looked upstairs and listened for any sounds in case he was not alone in the house. Again, the only sound he heard was the carnival procession in the Sambadrome nearby.

George returned to the front door to check if anyone was approaching the house. He looked across the road to the spot where Maggie stood, but could not see her; she was well hidden in the shadows. He nevertheless gave the thumbs up to indicate everything was alright so far, and went back into the building. He partially closed the door behind him and started to ascend the stairs slowly and quietly. He became alarmed when he stepped onto the third stair, which creaked, and caused the sound to echo in the stairwell. George froze on the spot for a moment. Then, a sound of breaking glass came from the kitchen upstairs. His heart skipped a beat, and he was about to turn back to exit the building when a black cat came scampering down the stairs from the kitchen. The cat took no notice of George, exited the building, and disappeared into the side street. George slowly continued up the stairs and reached the landing. He peered into the room where Maggie was held, but no one was in there. He edged his way slowly into the kitchen and began to search for the passports. It was not long before he found them on the kitchen dresser.

George decided to leave immediately, having achieved his task. He left the kitchen for the landing and was about to descend the stairs when he heard footsteps approaching the house. The footsteps stopped outside the front door, and George remained stationary on the landing. It was Carlos approaching the house, and Maggie saw him outside, but it was too late to warn George. Doing so would have given her position away and endangered George. She was utterly terrified, but remained silent in the shadows.

Carlos entered the building, and as soon as he flung the door open, George dashed into the room off the landing, the room where Maggie was previously detained. He closed the door quietly and also heard Carlos slamming the front door. George became concerned when he heard Carlos thumping up the stairs, while mumbling a few words to himself. Carlos stopped on the landing and looked at the door of the room where George was hiding. George stood on the other side of the door and remained silent, while trying not to breathe heavily. He was unsure who was on the landing, and his heart pounded furiously. He guessed it was Carlos who returned, and wondered if there would be a confrontation. Carlos reached for the door handle and turned it a few times. Meanwhile, George got prepared in case he needed to defend himself against Carlos. He was not trained in the art of defence and was unsure how to protect himself against a big man with a gun. Carlos turned the door handle a few more times and then walked away to the kitchen. He was checking the damage to the door, damage caused when he blasted it with the gun. Carlos grabbed a beer from the fridge, turned on some music, and sat down.

George could not remain in the building and needed to get out somehow. Meanwhile, Maggie was gravely concerned; she had not seen or heard from George. No sounds were coming from

66

the house, so she assumed everything was alright. After a minute or so, George quietly and slowly opened the door to the landing. The music from the kitchen helped to disguise any incidental noises George may have made. He came out onto the landing and gradually peered through the crack in the kitchen door to see who was there, but he could see no one. George heard the slurping noise of someone drinking from a bottle, and as it was smashed down onto the table. It was the chance for which George was waiting. He slowly made his way down the stairs, but forgot the loose stair on the third step. As soon as he stepped on it, the creak from the board resonated in the stairwell.

Carlos jumped up when he heard the noise and came out onto the landing, only to see George disappearing out the front door. Carlos threw the beer bottle down to the ground and gave chase after George.

"You bastard!" Carlos shouted as he ran down the stairs, "I'll get you."

"Run, Maggie, run," George shouted as he exited the building.

"Have you got them?" Maggie asked, "The passports?"

"Yes, I have. Run, run, run, Carlos is after us."

The couple ran towards the celebrations in the Sambadrome, closely followed by Carlos. They entered the throng of people and tried to push their way through, but the crowd had become denser. Other revellers were still arriving to see the carnival processions. This slowed the couple's progress, and Carlos was catching up to them. A few people stood on the street corner all night and recognised Carlos as the man who threw the gun to the ground. They realised he was chasing the couple and that the couple were in danger. They instinctively moved towards Carlos to block his way by dancing and cavorting around him. This helped the couple, and they were able to get away. Carlos was furious because he lost the couple for a second time that night.

It was now about three o'clock in the morning, and the couple managed to escape the crowds. They hailed a taxi and headed back to the hotel.

"We can't stay in Rio now," George said to Maggie, "We have to go somewhere else."

George was concerned about being followed and constantly looked out of the back window of the taxi to make sure they were not being trailed.

"Where can we go?" Maggie asked.

"I don't know, but we need to get out of Rio quickly, or else they'll find us again."

Maggie was perplexed about how the situation arose. '*Kidnapping, guns, criminals,*' she thought. Maggie became angry at George and slapped him on the arm with the back of her hand.

"George, you've got to tell me what's going on," she said, "Who are these people? And, what have you got us into? Our entire holiday has been ruined."

"I'll tell you later," George replied, "not here."

George caught the taxi driver's eyes in the rear-view mirror.

"Can you go any faster?" he asked.

"Going as fast as I can," the driver replied, "much traffic tonight." The driver thought the couple were having a marital tiff and decided to remain silent. George and Maggie were both anxious and also remained quiet for most of the journey back to the hotel.

The couple needed to get away from Rio and get away fast to a place where they could not be found. On the way back to the hotel, George gave the problem some thought.

"I've been thinking," he said.

"What about?" Maggie asked with anticipation.

"Let's go to Iguassu Falls, I've always wanted to go there. It's one of the most spectacular waterfalls in the world, and no one would know we've gone there."

"Where is it?" Maggie asked.

"It's in the interior of Brazil, a long way away. We would have to go by plane."

"Isn't that going to cost us?"

"Yes, it will, but I don't think we should remain in Rio; it has become dangerous for us."

The taxi driver thought the couple were on speaking terms again and decided to join in the conversation.

"You would like Iguassu Falls," he said, "You will enjoy it there." The couple asked the driver a few questions about the falls and the surrounding area, and also asked about local accommodation at Iguassu. They were now convinced they should go to Iguassu Falls, but needed to go immediately. The taxi soon arrived at the Rio Othon hotel.

Meanwhile, Carlos returned to the house near the Sambadrome and decided to call Marco and Fabio.

"Marco, I've got some bad news," Carlos said in Portuguese.

"What's wrong?" Marco asked.

"The woman's gone."

"Gone!" Marco exclaimed, "What do you mean, gone?"

"She's gone..."

But before Carlos could say anything more, Marco shouted down the line.

"You idiot, you stupid idiot, you imbecile, what happened?"

Carlos explained to Marco the events of the night and how he lost the couple. It made Marco furious, but he tried to remain calm.

"Well, Carlos," Marco said, "You need to come good. You have to find them and find them quickly, or else you will be in serious trouble. There is a lot at stake here, and I need to get the package. Do what you have to do."

"Ok, boss."

Carlos wanted to end the conversation quickly; he was embarrassed and knew he had let his colleagues down.

"And another thing, Carlos," Marco said, "no excuses this time. You bring me the package, or failing that, bring me the couple. Do you understand, Carlos? Do you understand?"

Carlos was tired and nervous and wanted to finish the call.

"Yes, boss, I will start immediately."

Marco slammed the phone down on Carlos, who decided to go to the Rio Othon hotel, where the couple were staying. This was the obvious place for them to return to, and he needed to get there fast.

At the hotel, George and Maggie headed directly to their room. They wanted to check out the hotel and leave for the airport immediately, where they could book flights to Iguassu. They were hoping to find accommodation easily at the falls. As they entered the hotel room, there was an urgency to do things quickly.

"Hurry up, let's get packing," George said.

Maggie sneered at George, as if to say, *'Don't push me.'*

"Ok, ok, I'm hurrying," she said.

The couple did not speak much and bundled their belongings into the suitcases without due concern. There was no time to pack properly, and the cases ended up bulging at the sides. They retrieved the items from the room safe and hurriedly went to the reception desk.

"Yes, Sir, can I help you?" the clerk asked.

"We'd like to check out."

The clerk checked the time and looked up at George.

"At this time of the morning, it's just gone 5 o'clock."

"Yes, I know," George said, "we wanted an early start."

The clerk behind the desk looked at the couple strangely.

"Ok, what's your room number?"

George handed the room key to the clerk, who tapped the room number into the computer and perused the screen for a moment.

"You're booked for another three days with us," he said.

"Yes, I know."

George needed to think of an excuse quickly.

"We've received some bad news from home and need to get back to England urgently."

"I'm sorry to hear about that, Sir. It's too late for a cancellation refund, you realise."

"Yes, we know. We need to leave quickly."

"Ok, I'll prepare the bill."

The clerk then tapped a few characters on the keyboard.

"Anything from the room bar?" he asked.

"No, nothing," George replied.

George looked over his shoulder many times to make sure no member of the gang was at the hotel, while Maggie patiently remained silent next to him. She also looked over her shoulder a few times. The clerk tapped a few more characters on the keyboard and retrieved the bill from the printer.

"Nothing to pay," he said.

The clerk folded the bill and handed it to George.

"Great," George said, "that's what I like to hear."

"We hope you had a pleasant stay with us at the Rio Othon Palace," the clerk said to both George and Maggie.

"Yes, we have," they both replied.

"You'll have to come back and see us again sometime."

George and Maggie walked away from the desk quickly and dragged their luggage to the front door of the hotel.

"Taxi?" Raul, the doorman, asked.

"Yes, please, to the airport," George replied.

"Hope you have a pleasant trip home," Raul said."

"No, we're not going home. We've decided to go to Iguassu," George said.

George realised his answer was different to the one he had given to the clerk at the reception desk, but later thought it was not important anyway.

"Ah! Iguassu," Raul said, "I am from Iguassu. Where are you staying there?"

"Not sure yet," George replied.

"I can recommend the Hotel das Cataratas at Iguassu Falls. I worked there some time ago, and it is a good hotel. You will easily get a room there."

"That sounds ideal," George said, "We might take you up on it."

George and Maggie needed somewhere to stay in Iguassu, and the Hotel das Cataratas at Iguassu Falls would be ideal. It would also save them the time to search for another hotel. Raul hailed a taxi from the nearby taxi rank, and the couple were soon picked up. It drove away and travelled for about 50 metres when George shouted out.

"Stop!" He said, "I've forgotten something."

The taxi driver immediately pressed hard on the brakes, and the car came to a standstill at the roadside.

"What have you forgotten?" Maggie asked.

George was still not keen to tell Maggie about the package and ignored her question.

"Wait here," he said, opening the door to exit the car.

"What's wrong?" Maggie asked.

"Just wait here, I've forgotten to do something."

George left Maggie to ponder where he was going and ran back to the hotel. He went to the reception desk and asked for the package he had previously stored in the safe. It was lucky he remembered the package, as it was far too important an item to forget. On the way back to the taxi, he was crossing the foyer to the front door when he saw Carlos walking up the hotel stairs. Carlos did not see him, so George darted off in the direction of the lifts, from where there was a side door to exit the hotel. He left the hotel in the nick of time, just as Carlos entered the foyer. Carlos headed to the lifts to take him to the couple's room, while George ran back to the car quickly.

"Quick, let's go," he said.

"What did you forget?" Maggie asked.

"The package," George replied, and held it up.

"What package?" Maggie asked, "What's inside it?"

Maggie was keen to know what was in the package, and thought it was a good time to push George on it.

"It seems so important," she continued, "can you not tell me what's in the package?"

"I'll tell you later when we get to the airport."

George looked back to see if Carlos was following them, and was positive Carlos had not seen him at the hotel. The couple were in a pensive mood and remained silent on the journey to the airport.

They arrived at the departure area of Rio's domestic airport and set about searching for the booking desk of TAM, Brazil's internal airline. The airport was fairly busy that time of the morning, but luckily, it did not take them long to find the TAM booking desk, for it was right in front of them when they entered the building. There was a queue of about ten people waiting, so George and Maggie joined the queue. A small number of the TAM airline staff were on duty, and it was not long before the couple were served.

"Good morning, can I help you?" the female clerk behind the desk asked in Portuguese.

"In English, please?" George asked.

"Certainly, Sir, how can I help you?"

"We need to book return flights to Iguassu, leaving today."

The clerk tapped a few characters into the computer in front of her.

"Let's see," she said.

She quickly perused the screen displaying the results of the enquiry.

"I believe all the early flights are booked. Yes, fully booked, until 11:15 this morning."

George looked at Maggie, and they both felt disappointed, raising their eyebrows to show their dismay.

"Nothing earlier?" Maggie asked, "We need to leave before then."

"No, madam," the clerk replied, "no direct flights."

The clerk typed some more characters into the computer and waited for a response.

"We may have an earlier flight," she said, "but it stops at São Paulo for an hour."

"What time is that one?" George asked.

"Let's see," the clerk said, looking at the monitor, "It's at 8:30."

George looked at Maggie again, and they both nodded in agreement. The time suited them, and it was much better than waiting around at the airport in Rio.

"Ok," George said, "we'll book it, seated next to each other, yes?"

"Correct," the clerk replied, "When do you want to return?"

George thought about the return flight to the UK in a week. He also thought of spending the last two days of the holiday sightseeing in Rio, but it would be risky.

"We plan to spend two nights in Iguassu," George said, "have you got seats on a flight back the day after tomorrow?"

"Let's have a look," the clerk replied.

She typed some more details onto the keyboard.

"There's one at 9 pm, which gets into Rio at around 11 pm."

George looked at Maggie again, and they both nodded in agreement.

"Ok, that will do," George said, "can we book the flights?"

The clerk asked for their passports, proceeded to prepare the tickets, and checked in their luggage.

"You'll like it there," she said, "Iguassu is a beautiful place."

"Hope so," George and Maggie said together, and smiled.

George paid for the tickets by credit card and was handed them by the clerk.

The couple made their way to the departure lounge and tried to stay out of view as much as possible. It was about 7 am, and the couple were hungry. They had not eaten for a long time, so they headed for a café, sat down and ordered breakfast. George decided it was a good time to divulge the story about the package to Maggie. Afterwards, she was not impressed with him and became very angry.

"For heaven's sake, George, why the hell did you do it?"

"I thought the extra money would come in useful."

"Yes, but now we have to pay for the extra flights and accommodation. We're probably not going to have any money left over."

George leaned forward, rested his elbows on the table and put his head in his hands.

"It hasn't turned out the way I thought it would," he said, "I'm sorry for all the anxiety and inconvenience, sweetheart, really sorry."

Maggie realised George was trying to make some extra money to ease their debts back home, but she was frustrated at the situation. She soon calmed down, leaned across the table and rubbed George's hand lovingly.

"There is nothing we can do to change what's happened," she said, "let's try and enjoy the rest of the holiday."

George remained silent and held Maggie's hand across the table.

"What are you going to do with the package?" Maggie asked.

"Hmm!" George replied, "I still have to deliver it. Two thousand pounds is still useful. I've already been paid one thousand, so they're expecting me to deliver the package."

"One thousand pounds!" exclaimed Maggie, "you never told me about that."

"Yes, well. I'll deliver it when we get back to Rio. Antonio, the man I told you about, seems alright."

"Do you have to? Can't we forget about it?"

"We could, but if it only means we have to deliver a parcel for two thousand pounds, is it not worthwhile?"

"I guess so," Maggie replied.

The couple agreed to enjoy the two days at Iguassu and to keep a low profile at all times. They decided to deliver the package when they returned to Rio, and to do some sightseeing if they had a chance. They settled down to have breakfast.

After the couple left the Rio Othon hotel, Carlos went to their room in search of them. He knocked on the door, but there was no answer, so he took out a special kit from his pocket to unlock the door. He looked around to check there was no one nearby and proceeded to open the door with the thin wire tools from the kit. After 20 seconds, he succeeded and entered the room carefully. He realised from its emptiness that the couple had vacated the room.

Carlos hurried back to the reception desk and enquired about the couple.

"I'm looking for Mr and Mrs Peacock," he said to the reception clerk, "the English couple."

"They checked out about 10 minutes ago," the clerk replied, "they've left the hotel."

"Do you know where they've gone?"

"I believe they are returning to England. They received some bad news from home and had to leave immediately."

"Have they gone to the airport?" Carlos asked.

"I don't know. I believe they have; they caught a taxi outside. The doorman would know."

Carlos dashed over to the entrance of the hotel to find the doorman, but he was nowhere to be seen. He went outside and saw Raul talking to one of the drivers at the taxi rank. Carlos ran towards him, and because of his obesity, he resembled a bull charging down the road.

"Hey, doorman! I need your help," he shouted.

Raul looked up when he heard a voice calling, and waited until Carlos was close to him.

"What's up?" he asked.

"The English couple who left."

"What about them?"

"I want to know if they went to the airport."

"What for?"

"Don't play games with me," Carlos shouted, "I need to know if they are going back to England."

Raul was a fully experienced doorman and had encountered situations like this before. He became alarmed at the gangster figure standing and shouting in front of him, and decided to play Carlos at his game.

"Maybe I do know where they went," he said.

"Well?" Carlos asked.

Raul looked at Carlos with raised eyebrows.

"Well," Raul replied.

"Oh, I see."

Carlos took a 20 Real note from his pocket and shoved it under Raul's nose.

"Well?" Carlos asked again.

Raul looked at the note with disdain and shrugged his shoulders.

"Hmm!" he uttered.

Carlos realised Raul was playing hard to get, took out a 50 Real note instead from his pocket, and shoved it under Raul's nose.

"Ok, now tell me." He insisted.

Raul was satisfied with the amount and grabbed the note from Carlos's hand.

"I don't think they are going back to England," he said.

"Not going to England?" Carlos asked.

"No, I remember speaking to them about Iguassu, I think they are going there."

"Are you sure?"

"Well, I spoke to them about the hotel at Iguassu Falls, and they seemed keen on it."

"Which hotel is that?"

Raul looked at Carlos smugly and waved the 50 Real note at him. Carlos realised Raul wanted more cash for the extra information, and handed him the 20 Real as well.

"Ok," Carlos said, "what hotel?"

"Hotel das Cataratas at Iguassu Falls, that's all I know."

"It's good enough for me," Carlos said.

He slapped Raul on the back and hastened to his car parked on the road outside the hotel.

Carlos sat in his car and immediately telephoned Marco on his mobile phone.

"Boss, Carlos here."

"Yes, Carlos, what now?"

"The English couple have left the hotel."

"And do you know where they are?"

"Yes, boss, they are going to Iguassu."

Marco was somewhat surprised by the news, and it showed in his voice.

"Iguassu!" he exclaimed.

The conversation ceased for a moment, and Carlos overheard Marco on the other end of the line informing Fabio that the couple had gone to Iguassu.

"Do you know where in Iguassu?" Marco asked Carlos.

"Yes, boss, Hotel das Cataratas at Iguassu Falls."

"How can you be that sure?"

"The doorman of the hotel told me, and I paid him for the info."

"Ok, Carlos, I'll take your word for it. Come back here, and we can plan what to do next."

"Ok, boss, on my way."

Carlos ended the call and immediately drove over to meet with Marco and Fabio.

Meanwhile, back at the airport, George and Maggie rushed to catch their flight to São Paulo.

"Hurry, let's go," George said.

They drank the last of the coffee and grabbed their hand luggage.

"Yes, let's get out of here," Maggie said, "it's freaking me out."

The couple made their way to the departure gate for TAM Airlines. After a few minutes in the holding lounge, they boarded the plane to São Paulo. The aircraft was full of people returning home from the carnival the previous day. Some still seemed to be revelling, but most were trying to get their heads down to sleep through the journey. The seats in the plane were comfortable, and the couple were now able to relax. It was time for them to get some much-needed sleep after a gruelling 24 hours.

Chapter 6 – Iguassu Hotel

George and Maggie slept through the entire flight to São Paulo, missing out on beverages served during the journey, but they were not fussed; they had eaten breakfast at the airport before leaving. It was more important for them to catch up on some needed sleep. The flight took one hour, and the cabin crew woke them before landing. It was an uneventful touchdown at São Paulo Congonhas domestic airport, and they decided to remain on the plane in transit with other passengers travelling on to Iguassu.

Congonhas Airport was located in the centre of São Paulo. During landing, the plane seemed too close to the high-rise buildings, and the couple felt they could reach out and touch them.
"Did you know São Paulo has the largest population of any city in the Southern Hemisphere?" George asked Maggie.
"No, I didn't," Maggie replied, "How many people?"
"About 20 million, and did you know it is one of the most polluted cities in the world?"
"I think I heard that somewhere," Maggie replied, "Is this some kind of a quiz or what?"
"No, just some facts. Just thought you would like to know. I'll keep quiet now."
The plane came to a standstill, and when the doors opened, the cabin filled with hot, humid air, making the plane's atmosphere unbearable. The cabin crew were used to the occurrence and handed out bottles of water to the passengers while trying to comfort them. The passenger plane remained on the ground for about an hour, and eventually, more passengers boarded. They were soon in the air again on the way to Iguassu, and the next part of the journey would take an hour and a half. In that part of the world, Iguassu was locally known as Foz Do Iguaçu.

The landing at Iguassu airport was also uneventful, and the couple exited the airport building to hail a taxi. They felt relaxed travelling to the Hotel das Cataratas at Iguassu Falls. The surrounding vegetation was tropical, and the atmosphere was humid. Luckily, the car was air-conditioned, and the journey to the hotel was a pleasant ride. The Hotel das Cataratas was a short distance from the airport and located inside the Iguassu National Park, very close to the falls.

The exquisite Iguassu Falls are situated on the borders of Argentina and Brazil, on the Iguassu River. Apart from the main falls, there were separate, smaller falls and cataracts depending on the season and the water levels. The falls, numbering nearly 300 in total, are situated in both the Brazilian and Argentinian Iguassu National Parks, which are designated World Heritage Sites.

The Hotel das Cataratas was designed in a Portuguese colonial style and is constructed on two levels. It was one of the few hotels in the National Park, and it boasts a couple of restaurants and bars. The hotel was in an ideal location, and central to the falls and for excursions to the nearby jungle. It was located about 15-20 minutes from Iguassu town.

George and Maggie arrived at the hotel around 12:30 and headed for the reception desk.
"Can I be of assistance?" the clerk asked.
"Mr and Mrs Peacock," George said.
"Do you have a reservation?" the clerk asked.
"No, we don't. We took a chance in the hope there would be a vacant room; we were told we could get a room quite easily."
"Let me see," the clerk said, "How long do you intend to stay?"
"Two nights, only two nights."
The clerk entered a few details on the computer keyboard and scanned the enquiry results on the monitor.
"We have a vacant room overlooking the pool. Is that alright?"
"Sounds good to me," George said.
He looked over at Maggie, who had a broad smile on her face, and took it as a sign of agreement.
"We'll take it," he said.
The clerk asked for their passports and continued with the booking administration. After a few minutes, he handed the passports back and the room key to the couple.

"Here you are," he said, "room 236, one floor up. Enjoy your stay."

Before leaving the desk, Maggie stepped forward and caught the attention of the receptionist.

"I hope it's not too late, but can we still buy lunch?" she asked.

The receptionist smiled and pointed through the glass window towards the restaurant in another building away from the main hotel.

"Certainly, madam, you can have meals at that restaurant all day long."

The couple thanked the receptionist and headed for the stairway leading to their rooms.

George and Maggie began to climb the stairs to their room when a voice bellowed from the reception lounge.

"Hey, English!"

The callout caused other people in the lounge to look up, and George and Maggie looked in the direction from which the voice came.

"Hey, English!" the voice shouted again.

The couple recognised two men standing in the lounge waving their arms in the air, and knew the shouts were directed at them.

"It's the Germans!" Maggie said.

"So it is," George added, "what are they doing here?"

"Let's go and see," Maggie said.

The couple made their way over to the lounge where the Germans were standing.

"Karl and Helmut," George said, and held out his hand.

"George and Maggie," Karl said while shaking George's hand.

They were all pleased to see each other, shook each other's hands, and sat down to have a chat.

"What are you doing here?" George asked.

"Sightseeing for a few days, maybe do some trekking," Helmut replied, "what about you? How was Rio?"

"Rio was fine," Maggie replied.

George thought Maggie's reply was fairly modest, and they nervously looked at each other. They wanted to avoid any conversation about Rio, and George decided to change the subject.

"We saw the carnival, and now we want to see the falls. I hear they are spectacular."

"Have you seen them?" Maggie asked.

"No, not yet," Karl replied, "we only stayed in Rio for one day, and then came here. We wanted to do some hiking in the jungle."

"You should be careful," George said, "dangerous place, the jungle."

Helmut next directed a question to George.

"How long are you here for?"

"Two nights, then we go back to Rio."

"Only two, you will miss a lot," Helmut said.

"Two nights are enough for us; we just needed a short break from Rio."

"What room are you in?" Karl asked.

"236, what about you?"

"250, close to each other, eh!"

"Yes, just down the corridor from us," Maggie stated.

"It's good to see the two of you again," Karl said.

At that moment, a car horn sounded from outside the hotel, and both Karl and Helmut looked out the window.

"I think our coach is here," Helmut said, "we are going on a hiking trip today, and then taking a boat trip to the falls."

"Sounds terrific," George said, "I hope you enjoy the day."

All four stood and shook hands again before Karl and Helmut departed. The Germans headed to the hotel's front entrance, while George and Maggie made their way to the stairway. They all turned and waved goodbye to each other. The Germans exited the hotel and boarded the waiting coach, while the couple made their way up the stairs to find their accommodation.

George and Maggie entered the room and threw their bags on the floor. They flopped on the bed next to each other, stared at the ceiling, and remained silent for about two minutes, while contemplating the events that transpired over the last few days. The room was decorated in a colonial style, with dark wood furniture that blended well with the rest of the hotel.

"I know what we can do," George said, "let's go for a swim."

"Yes, good idea," Maggie said, "Let's have some kind of a holiday."

They got up and hurriedly searched for their swimsuits, and in their haste, everything taken out of the luggage was thrown to the floor.

They donned their swimsuits, dressed casually and headed for the pool area. It was hot in Iguassu, very hot, and many people were already enjoying the sunshine at the pool. Children ran around and played, while others jumped into the pool and splashed water onto the edge. There was a distinct holiday atmosphere at the poolside. The gardens looked lovely with manicured lawns, flower beds, and palm trees. A couple of gardeners were tending the plants. The warmth of the sun, the green vegetation, and people enjoying themselves created the atmosphere of a tropical paradise. George and Maggie searched for two vacant sun beds and rested their towels on them. It was not long before George stripped down to his swimsuit and dived into the pool, surfacing in front of the sun beds where Maggie was seated.

"This is lovely," he said, "You've got to come in."

Maggie also stripped down to her swimsuit and went over to the steps leading into the pool. She descended into the water, anticipating it to be cold, but it was at an ideal temperature for her. Immersing herself up to the neck, she swam over to George.

"It's really great," she said, "just what we needed."

They swam for about ten minutes and returned to the sunbeds.

"Would you like a drink?" George asked Maggie.

"I'm not sure," she replied.

"It's hot and I'm going to have a beer," George said.

"Sounds like a good idea, I'll have one as well."

George caught a waiter's eye and beckoned for him to come over.

"Two beers, please, nice and cold."

The waiter acknowledged George and repeated the order, "Two beers."

George was also feeling hungry and looked at Maggie.

"Shall we also have something to eat?" he asked, "maybe a sandwich of some kind?"

"Yes, just something simple. Maybe a cheese sandwich."

They ordered sandwiches to accompany the beer, and the waiter departed to fulfil the order, returning about three minutes later with the drinks. George and Maggie slowly sipped the beers and enjoyed the moment without a care in the world. For a short time, they forgot the recent events and enjoyed themselves.

"What shall we do while in Iguassu?" Maggie asked.

"I'm not sure. I would definitely like to see the falls. The Germans were going on a boat trip to the falls today, so maybe, if we see them tonight, we could ask them about the trip."

"Yes, I'd like to see the falls as well."

"We'll go to the reception and check out some trips when we leave the pool," George added.

The couple rested on the sun beds for about an hour, left the poolside, and headed back to the hotel reception area. It was a short walk along a path edged with hibiscus flowers and other tropical plants. The scented aroma from the flowers wafted through the air, which complemented the colours of the plants. They soon arrived at the reception and headed for the tourist information desk.

"Yes, sir, can I help you?" the lady behind the desk asked. "My name is Andrea."

Andrea was young, 21 or 22, and smartly dressed in casual attire, matching the other hotel staff.

"Yes, please," George said, "we're George and Maggie, and we would like to see the falls, but we're not sure of the different trips available."

"Well, you've come to the right place," Andrea said, "please sit down."

She pointed to the chairs in front of the desk.

"Do you want to see the falls from the air, or from the top, or from a boat which takes you very near to the bottom of the falls?"

George looked at Maggie, and they both raised their eyebrows, somehow knowing they were going to say the same thing.

"The boat trip," both replied.

"Something I always wanted to do," George added, "I did a similar trip when I was at Niagara Falls."

"Good," Andrea said, "we have just the tour for you. It includes a boat trip to the falls, and afterwards we take you by coach to the top of the falls. You can see it from a different perspective. Does that sound good to you?"

George and Maggie both nodded in agreement. Andrea then opened a folder containing details of the trips and turned the pages until she found the relevant one for the couple.

"Here we are," she said, and pointed to some pictures, "we have this trip twice a day, one in the morning, at 9 o'clock, and one in the afternoon, at 1 pm. Which time would suit you best?"

Maggie looked at George and said, "I think the one in the morning is best."

"I agree as well," George said, "can we go on it tomorrow morning?"

Andrea proceeded to check the available bookings on the computer.

"Yes, tomorrow is fine," she said, "tomorrow at 9 am."

George and Maggie looked at each other and nodded in agreement.

"So, are we settled on the trip?" Andrea asked.

"Yes, thanks," the couple replied.

Andrea typed the booking details into the computer.

"What is your room number?" she asked.

"236," Maggie replied.

Andrea typed some more, and while waiting, the couple took the opportunity to scan around the reception area. They hadn't forgotten the events of the last few days and were still apprehensive. The administration for the trip was almost completed.

"How would you like to pay? By card, cash or on the room," she asked.

"Ah!" George said, "On the room, please."

Andrea typed a few more details and printed the voucher for the trip.

"Here you are," she said, and handed them the voucher, "tomorrow at 9 am. Can you make sure you are in the reception area by 8:30 for the coach?"

George took the voucher and put it in his pocket. The couple, pleased they booked a trip, thanked Andrea and headed to their room.

On the stairway leading to the first floor, George looked across at the reception desk and saw a man standing there who looked familiar to him. The man was accompanied by two other men, who were dressed in cream-coloured suits and both wearing black shirts. George only saw the back of the man's head and thought it may have been one of the Brazilian men who followed them in Rio. His heart skipped a beat, and he was about to tell Maggie, when the man looked around in the direction of the couple. The man's eyes met with George's, and for a moment George felt sick in the stomach. The stranger smiled at George, and it turned out to be someone else. It was a false alarm, and George was thoroughly relieved.

The couple returned to the room and continued to unpack their luggage. It was late afternoon, and the heat in the room was unbearable. George turned on the ceiling fan and opened the window to allow fresh air into the room; he preferred it to air conditioning. The fan was effective in circulating the air and was in keeping with the colonial style of the hotel. After unpacking, George and Maggie rested on the bed and soon fell asleep. They were both tired, due to the early morning start and the long day of travelling. Around seven thirty that evening, the resident band in the outdoor restaurant began to play, and the sound of music echoed through the night air.

The music awoke George, which alarmed him and caused him to sit up in bed.
"What was that?" he said.
He looked over towards Maggie and realised he was speaking to himself; she was not in the bed. He got up to look for her in the bathroom, but she was not there either; she was not in the room. He went over to the window and looked out to scan the hotel grounds for her, but could not see her anywhere. George became concerned and was putting on his shoes to go in search of Maggie when the door to the room opened. He was apprehensive at first, but relieved to see Maggie coming through the door.
"Where have you been?" he asked.

"I went outside to phone home. You were asleep, and I took the opportunity to make the call."

"You scared me. I didn't know where you were, and was worried, especially with the events that occurred recently."

"I'm fine, everything is fine. There is nothing to worry about."

"Are the folks alright back home?"

"Yes, everyone's fine. They wanted to know if we were enjoying ourselves."

"And what did you say?"

"That we were having a good time. I didn't want to tell them about our problems."

The music from the band in the restaurant caught George's ear, and he decided to change the subject.

"The band sounds good," he said, "Can you hear it?"

"Yes, they sound excellent."

Maggie walked over to the window to view the band.

"Where are they?" she asked.

"In the restaurant below, have a look."

Maggie looked towards the restaurant and saw the band playing in front of diners. She was looking enviously at them when George joined her at the window.

"Let's get ready and go for dinner," he said.

"Ok," Maggie said, "maybe we could also have a dance."

Maggie immediately went to the bathroom to take a shower, while George selected the clothes to wear that evening. His shirt was creased from travelling, so he searched for the iron and began to iron it.

"Anything you want ironing?" George shouted to Maggie in the bathroom.

"Can't hear you," she replied, "the shower is too noisy."

George walked over to the bathroom and put his head inside the door.

"Is there anything you need ironing?" he asked.

Maggie's hair was full of shampoo, and she could not open her eyes, but thought about George's question for a while.

"Yes," she replied, "the green summery dress, the one with the white dots."

George took the dress from the wardrobe and proceeded to iron it while Maggie finished in the bathroom.

George went to take a shower when Maggie was getting dressed, and she noticed a piece of paper pushed under the door to the room. She was somewhat apprehensive, but picked it up. The note read, '*We found your room, and we'll see you downstairs!*'
'*What was the note all about?*' she thought.
Maggie immediately ran into the bathroom and showed George the note.
"I'm scared," she said, "really scared."
George got out of the shower and thought about the note, while Maggie continued to stare nervously at it.
"Let's be calm," he said, "First of all, we don't know who put the note under the door."
"It must be the Brazilians," Maggie said, "maybe they followed us here."
"How would they know we're here?" George asked.
"I don't know, I'm not feeling comfortable about this."
George pulled Maggie towards him and held her closely to comfort her.
"Let's say it was the Brazilians, what can they do? The hotel is busy, and they would not be able to do anything. We could make sure we stayed in a crowded area."
"Then what?" Maggie asked, "What would we do next?"
"We'll have to play it by ear, that's all we can do, unless we leave now. But we don't know who wrote the note, do we?"

George and Maggie dressed for dinner in silence and cautiously made their way down to the bar. They looked around but could not see anyone they knew. The barman soon approached the couple.
"Good evening, sir, madam," he said, "my name is Alfredo, what can I get you to drink?"
"I'll have a beer, please," George said, and then to Maggie, "What will you have?"
Maggie thought for a while.
"I'll have a glass of white wine," she said, "a small glass."

The barman acknowledged the order and went to prepare the drinks. George and Maggie scanned the bar again, and as they were unsure who the note was from, they had become nervous. The bar was full of people, chatting and having a good time, and there was nothing unusual. The barman soon returned with the drinks.

"Here you are," he said, "cash or on the room?"

"The room," George replied, "236."

George and Maggie picked up their drinks and were about to toast each other when they heard two male voices from behind.

"Got ya!" they shouted.

George and Maggie were startled, and in that split second, their hearts sank. But before they could turn around, one of the men spoke again.

"You didn't think you could get away from us, did you?"

Maggie was in fright, and dropped the glass of wine, which smashed on the floor and splashed its contents. The couple turned around to see who spoke and came face to face with Karl and Helmut. George and Maggie were relieved to see the Germans, who played a trick on the couple, and in jest put on false accents to disguise their voices.

"Did you get the note?" Helmut asked.

"It was you!" Maggie shouted, thumping Helmut on the chest, "You scared us dreadfully."

"Good joke, eh!" Helmut replied.

"I must say, you two seem pretty scared," Karl said, "anything wrong?"

George was about to answer Karl when the cleaning staff arrived to mop up the spilt wine.

"Let's go and sit somewhere," George said.

He looked for an empty table and saw one by the window. He pointed in the direction of the table.

"Over there, quick, before someone else takes it."

The Germans bought another glass of wine for Maggie as compensation for the joke played on the couple, and two beers for themselves. The foursome made their way over to the window seats.

"How was your day?" George asked, "You were going on a hike, and then taking a boat trip to the falls, how was it?"

The four friends sat and talked about the trips for about twenty minutes. The Germans spoke about their day's experience, and the couple about their anticipated trip the next day.

"Anyone for another drink?" George asked, "I'm going to have another one before dinner."

"Yes, please," Karl replied.

"Yes, thanks," Helmut added.

"I'll stick with this glass of wine," Maggie said, "I'm fine for now."

George got up and went over to the bar where Alfredo was in attendance.

"Hello again," Alfredo greeted George, "what can I get you this time?"

"The same again," George replied, "I don't know if you can remember."

"Three beers and a white wine," Alfredo said.

"That's correct," George said, "but no wine this time, just three beers."

Alfredo went away to prepare the drinks when a young, well-dressed man with a swarthy complexion approached the bar and stood next to George.

"Hey Alfredo," the man shouted across the bar, "any English in tonight?"

Alfredo returned with the drinks and pointed to George.

"This guy is English," he said.

"Oh, really," the man said.

He held out his hand to shake George's hand.

"I'm Pedro, what's your name?"

George was reluctant to shake hands with a stranger, especially at present, and paused for a while. Alfredo looked at George and sensed his reluctance to shake hands.

"He's alright, sir," Alfredo piped up, "he's just searching for English people to take on an evening tour to a restaurant and nightclub."

George felt easier and shook Pedro's hand, but was reluctant to give his real name.

"My name is Malcolm," George said, looking into Pedro's eyes, "I'm sorry to disappoint you, but we'll be eating in the hotel tonight."

George felt Pedro seemed a bit frustrated and sensed something was wrong. He felt uncomfortable in Pedro's presence and made his excuses to leave. George returned to the table where the others were seated and was closely observed by Maggie while he was at the bar.

"Who was that?" she asked, "I saw you talking to a man at the bar."

"No one special," George replied, "he was just touting for business."

Karl saw the funny side to George's comment.

"Oh! Was he a pro then?" he asked.

"No, not that type of business, he wanted to find English people to take on a night tour."

"You've got to be careful these days," Helmut said, "some strange people around."

"Yes, I agree," Karl said.

The foursome sat and chatted for another ten minutes when Karl said he was starving, and asked the couple if they were eating that night.

George and Maggie agreed to eat with the Germans; they thought it best to be with other people that evening. The four headed to the restaurant, which was separated from the main building by a cobbled path. On the way through, George noticed Pedro, the man he met earlier, talking to another couple in the bar. George overheard Pedro asking them if they were from England, and thought it a strange question to ask people, but he continued to the dining area. The foursome arrived at the restaurant and was seated almost immediately. The band played a variety of light music during dinner, mainly samba. The day's heat had subsided, and a cool breeze blew through the restaurant, creating a cooler ambient temperature, ideal for the evening diners. It was just after eight thirty, and many people were already eating, mainly families with children.

A waiter approached the table.

"Good evening, ladies and gentlemen," he said, "what a lovely evening for Al fresco dining. My name is Gustavo, and I will be your waiter for the evening."

"Good evening, Gustavo," the foursome said.

Gustavo handed out the dinner menu to each person.

"What would you like to drink before dinner?" he asked.

The foursome ordered drinks and began to peruse the menu. After a few minutes, another waiter brought the drinks over to the table, and Gustavo returned to take the dinner order. The foursome each ordered different meals from the exotic choices listed on the menu. They raised their glasses and clinked them together, toasting each other. About twenty minutes later, the meals arrived, and the friends settled down to eat dinner.

George was facing the main hotel building and could easily see the bar and reception areas. About halfway through the meal, while they were chatting and enjoying the evening, George glanced across to the reception area and saw Pedro, the man he had met at the bar, talking to two men. He recognised the two men as Eduardo and Carlos from Rio. Eduardo was the man in the grey suit who followed them from the hotel in Rio. Carlos was the man who held Maggie hostage in the house near the Sambadrome. They were both big men and fairly plump. George could not believe his eyes and glanced away for a moment. He looked back to check he was not having hallucinations, and confirmed it was definitely Carlos and Eduardo. George felt troubled, for he knew the gang had followed them to Iguassu. He thought about the situation for a while. '*How did they find us? Why were they talking to Pedro? Was his suspicion of Pedro justified?*'

George leaned over to Maggie and whispered in her ear.

"Don't look now, but I think we were followed from Rio."

The news was unwelcoming and sent a shiver down Maggie's spine.

"What!" she said, "What are you talking about?"

"I've just seen Carlos and Eduardo in the reception area."

Maggie was taken aback and was about to turn around to look, but George held her arm.

"No, don't look," George whispered.

Maggie also felt troubled, and her body began to tremble. Karl noticed Maggie's discomfort and that the couple were whispering to each other. He was concerned about their welfare.

"Is everything alright?" he asked, "Are you not well?"

"Everything is fine," George replied.

He then thought of an excuse to leave the table.

"The truth is, I'm not feeling well."

"Not well! Is it the food?" Helmut asked.

"I don't know what it is," George replied, "Maybe too much sun today. I'm sorry, but we will have to leave you on your own and return to our room."

"That's ok," Karl said, "we'll be alright. It's probably best you go back."

George beckoned to Gustavo, who came over to the table immediately.

"Can I sign for the meal, please?"

Gustavo looked at the half-eaten food on the couple's plates and was concerned they did not enjoy the meal.

"Is your meal not to your satisfaction, Sir?" he asked.

"Everything is fine, we're just tired and need an early night."

Karl and Helmut looked bemused at each other and remained silent. The waiter went away to prepare the bill and returned a few minutes later. George signed for the meal and apologised to Karl and Helmut again. He helped Maggie from the chair; she was still trembling with fear. The couple made their way through a side entrance to the hotel, away from the reception area, and headed to their room.

"Strange couple," Helmut said to Karl, "Do you think there is something wrong with their relationship?"

"Yes, very strange," Karl replied, "not all is right with them."

Meanwhile, Eduardo, Carlos and Pedro were still in conversation in the reception area.

"So, did you find the English couple?" Eduardo asked Pedro.

"No, I spoke to many English people, but did not find them."

"But we know they are here," Carlos said.

"Are you sure?" Pedro asked, "You may have the wrong information."

"We received the information from a good source," Eduardo said.

"Well, I believe I spoke to all the English residents here tonight, and none of them have the same names you want."

"Are you sure you spoke to all the English people?" Carlos asked, "Some of them may be out for the evening."

"Yes, positive. I first checked at reception for the number of English people staying in the hotel, and I spoke to all of them."

The three men contemplated the problem, and Carlos came up with a suggestion.

"Let's check the names at reception," he said.

"Why waste time?" Pedro asked, "I've already spoken to the English people and asked their names."

"What if they didn't tell you their correct names? What then?" Eduardo asked.

Pedro looked a bit sheepish and knew he could have made a mistake. He realised there may have been a flaw in his procedure and decided to be more proactive with his colleagues.

"The security is strict at the hotel," he said, "it may not be easy to get names. I know, I've tried in the past, especially at night when security is more rigid."

"Ok," Eduardo said, "we will wait until the morning when the day staff is on, and it might be easier."

The men couldn't do much until morning, and the conversation changed to their overnight accommodation.

"Did you arrange a place for us to stay?" Carlos asked Pedro.

"Yes, I did, it's only ten minutes away, let's go."

The three men left the hotel and headed for Pedro's car parked nearby. Eduardo and Carlos also came by car, but decided to leave their car at the hotel overnight.

George and Maggie made it back to the room without being noticed and were utterly terrified. Maggie became physically sick and rested on the bed.

"What are we going to do?" she asked.

"Let me think," George said, "they didn't see us, so they don't know for definite that we are here."

"But they are here, so they must know we are staying at the hotel," Maggie said.

"Yes, true. Now, let me think back. Pedro asked me for my name, and I became suspicious of him, so I gave him a false name, Malcolm. He has never seen us before, so he doesn't know us by sight."

"I'm still worried, though," Maggie said.

"Let's stay calm. No one has been to our room, so far, so good. If they knew we were staying here, they would have been to the room by now. I'm guessing that they don't know where we are."

Maggie sat up in bed, and George noticed the fear in her eyes.

"We can't stay here," she said.

"Yes, you're right, maybe we should go."

"Let's pack up and go now. We can call a taxi from the room and make a run for it."

George looked surprised at Maggie.

"And not pay the hotel bill?"

"Well, what are we going to do?" Maggie asked.

George paced around the room and thought for a while. He looked over at Maggie many times, saw the terrified state she was in, and was concerned for her. Maggie was lying in the bed, clutching a pillow close to her chest, and still trembling.

"This is what we're going to do," George said, "We'll go down to reception early in the morning to check out. Hopefully, the men won't be there at that time."

Maggie listened intensely as George continued.

"It would be a shame we came all this way and didn't see the falls, so we will get a taxi to take us there."

"What about the organised trip?" Maggie asked.

"We'll leave a note at both the reception and travel desks, informing them we will meet the tour at the falls. That way, we can leave early without anyone noticing us, and we can still see the falls."

"Sounds risky," Maggie said, "why don't we just go straight to the airport?"

"The men won't know where we are," George said.

"They found us here, didn't they?"

"Yes, that's true. The only person we spoke to about Iguassu was the doorman at the hotel in Rio. Maybe that's how they found us."

Maggie folded her arms and was becoming grumpy.

"I don't like it," she said.

"Look, we'll go to the falls and enjoy the day as best we can. Then immediately afterwards, we will go straight to the airport and catch a flight back to Rio. How does that sound?"

"Ok, I suppose, if you think it's safe."

George and Maggie settled into bed to get some sleep, but with so much on their mind, they stayed awake all night as the hours passed slowly.

Chapter 7 – To the River

George and Maggie were restless that night. They constantly tossed and fidgeted in bed, only speaking to each other a few times. The night was hot and humid, and the ceiling fan made no difference to the ambient temperature. The heat was unbearable, and their bodies became moist with sweat. The room was almost dark, and both kept a constant eye on the bedside clock, whose light partly illuminated the room. They were still awake at three in the morning, and George, frustrated at hanging around, sat up abruptly in bed.

"Right, that's it. I'm getting ready to go," George said.
Maggie was also eager to go and sat up in bed.
"I can't stand it any longer either. Let's get going."
George switched on the bedside light, and Maggie got out of bed to turn on the main light in the room.
"You'd better shower first," George said.
"Ok, I think I need it. I've been sweating all night."
The thought of Maggie sweating brought a smile to George's face, and he watched the clammy T-shirt stick to her body as she made her way to the bathroom. 'No time for hanky-panky,' he thought, and got out of bed to start packing.

Maggie was in the bathroom for about 10 minutes, and George hurriedly packed his bags. There was little or no tidiness to the packing; everything was picked up at random and shoved into the bag one way or another. George looked out the window a few times to check if the gang members were around, but the only person he spotted was the night watchman doing the rounds in the garden below. Maggie came out of the bathroom and joined George.
"All yours," she said, "it was good to have a shower, especially after such a humid night."
George quickly went into the bathroom without saying a word to her, and she sensed his nervousness as he walked by. He immediately turned on the shower.
"You ok, George?" Maggie asked.

There was no answer; the noise from the shower drowned out her voice. Maggie decided to ignore George for the moment and got dressed. She packed similarly to George, randomly shoving items into the bags. Maggie was now feeling paranoid and kept looking out of the window. As with George, she only saw the night watchman doing his rounds. It was a clear night with not a cloud in sight, and the only sound was the distant call of an owl, which echoed through the night air. George finished the shower and returned to the bedroom.

"Are we ready then?" he asked.

"Nearly there. You're not dressed yet anyway," Maggie replied. George dressed while Maggie finished packing, and they were both ready to go at 3:30.

They collected the bags and went to the door leading to the corridor. George turned to Maggie and raised a finger to his lips to indicate they should be silent. He switched off the light and rested his ear against the door to listen for any movement outside the room. There was silence, so George opened the door quietly and peered through the opening to see if anyone was around. He could see no one, and opened the door further to stick his head outside. The corridor was dimly lit at that time of night, and he looked in both directions, but no one was in sight.

"Come on," he whispered to Maggie, "let's go, but be quiet."

George left the room first, followed closely by Maggie, who closed the door quietly behind her. They edged their way along to the stairwell, paused at the top of the stairs, and listened for any movement. They chose to use the stairs rather than the elevator; it would have been too noisy at that time of night. George and Maggie gingerly descended the stairs leading down to the reception area, listening for any noises. There was no one in the lounge area, and they made their way over to the reception desk, where they found the clerk engrossed in reading a book. George could not help but notice the cover; it was the same book he had recently read, 'The Conflict Within' by Eddie Martin. George remembered that the book was a good read, and aptly so, it was set in South America, where they were now holidaying.

The clerk was surprised to see the couple standing there and jumped up from his chair.

"What the...?" he said, "You startled me. I didn't expect to see anyone at this time of the morning. How can I help you?"

George looked around the reception area to ensure no one else was there and spoke to the clerk in a quiet, subdued voice.

"We'd like to check out, if that's alright."

"Is everything ok?" the clerk asked.

"Yes, everything is fine, we wanted to see the sun rise over the falls before we left Iguassu, and thought we'd make an early start."

"Room number?" the clerk asked.

"236."

The clerk typed the number into the computer and paused while he read the details.

"You're booked in until tomorrow," he said.

"Yes, we know. We need to leave today."

"Ok," the clerk said, "I'll just make up your bill. Did you have anything from the room bar?"

"No, nothing."

The clerk typed some more details and printed the statement. Maggie was standing nearby and kept looking around the reception area, in anticipation that the gang members might appear at any moment.

"That will be 299 Real to pay," the clerk said.

George paid the bill by credit card and was keen to get going, but the clerk was eager to do his job properly.

"Hope you enjoyed your stay with us," he said, "we're sorry to see you go."

"Yes, it was fine," George replied, "can you book us a taxi right away, please?"

"Yes, sir, will do."

George and Maggie went to the reception lounge and sat down to wait for the taxi. They were both apprehensive while they waited and were constantly fidgeting with their hand luggage. George remembered he needed to leave a note at the travel desk to inform them they would join the tour tomorrow, later on at the falls. He sauntered over to the desk and wrote a message on a notepad. Hopefully, Andrea, the travel clerk, would see the note when she came in to work later that morning. But to ensure she received the message, George wrote a second note and took it over to the reception clerk, for him to pass on to Andrea.

The taxi arrived in 10 minutes, but it seemed like a lifetime for the couple. As it pulled up outside the hotel, the couple stood up, waved goodbye to the clerk, and headed to the taxi. The driver was already out of the car, opening the boot.

"Mr Peacock?" he asked.

"Yes," George replied.

"You get in the car, and I will put the luggage in the boot," the driver said.

George and Maggie did as the driver asked and slid into the back seat of the taxi, while the driver loaded the luggage into the boot. As soon as he finished, the driver got back into the car.

"Where do you want to go?" he asked.

George sat up and was about to answer when he saw the reflection of a car's headlight in the rear-view mirror. The car was approaching the hotel entrance, and George became apprehensive. He turned around to see who was in the car, and recognised the driver.

"It's Pedro," he shouted.

"What!" Maggie said.

George also noticed Pedro was not alone, and was accompanied by two other men sitting in the back of the car, Carlos and Eduardo.

"Drive on," George shouted to the taxi driver.

Maggie turned around to look at the other car, but was immediately smothered by George, who pinned her down on the back seat.

"Drive on," George shouted again.

The taxi driver was perplexed, shook his head, and tutted.

"Honeymoon couple, eh!"

"Yes, something like that," George said, "drive on quickly."

The taxi drove away from the hotel slowly, just as the other car pulled up outside the entrance. George raised his head to peer out the back window and saw the three Brazilian gang members walking into the hotel. It seemed the gang had not noticed the couple leaving, and George was immensely relieved. The driver shook his head from side to side while looking in the rear-view mirror.

"Where to?" the driver asked again. "Where do you want to go?"

"The falls," George replied.

He continued to peer out the back of the taxi while it drove away from the hotel. It soon disappeared into the distance.

Carlos Pedro and Eduardo entered the hotel, and they sat in the reception area. It was early in the morning, and the place was void of residents. The men arrived at that time, so they could check all residents coming and going, including those who rose early. They hoped most would pass through the reception area to the restaurant or leave the building. The reception clerk approached the men.

"Can I help you, gentlemen?" he asked.

"Three coffees please," Pedro replied.

The clerk acknowledged the order and went away to prepare the coffee. The three men were now on a stakeout mission and settled themselves in for a long session.

"Now listen up," Eduardo said.

The other two men leaned forward and listened intensely to Eduardo.

"This is the plan. If we see the English couple, we will escort them to the car without creating a fuss; there might be other people around. Once we've got them in the car, we will drive off immediately. Is that clear?"

Carlos and Pedro nodded in agreement, and Eduardo continued.

"No harm should come to the couple, at least, not until we get the package. We must retrieve the package from them. Is that clear?"

Carlos and Pedro nodded again, and Pedro raised one arm.

"Question," he said.

"What?" Eduardo asked.

"There is no need to harm the couple once we've got the package, is there?"

Eduardo looked at Carlos and recalled that Carlos was duped by George once before, at the house near the Sambadrome in Rio.

"Hmm! We'll see," Eduardo said. "Let's get the package first."

The men sat back in the chairs and remained silent, contemplating the task ahead of them. They were accustomed to long stakeouts and, having done many before, treated this one as second nature. The clerk returned with the coffees, and the three men chatted amongst themselves while sipping their coffees. They waited for residents to appear.

The taxi carrying George and Maggie drove through the darkness towards Iguassu Falls. The journey to the entrance of the National Park was short, only about 10 minutes, and the driver was about to enter the park to take the couple further on to the falls.

"Drop us here, driver," George said, "this will do."

"But you wanted to go to the falls," the driver replied.

"Right here is fine," George added.

The driver was somewhat perplexed at the request and insisted. "I will take you to the falls," he said, "it's only another 10 minutes away."

"No, here is fine, driver, we'll get out here," George said.

"Are we not going to the falls?" Maggie asked.

"Yes, we are," George replied, "I think this is the best place to meet our tour. They will have to stop here before going to the falls."

The driver stopped the car, and George paid the fare to the disgruntled driver, who had hoped for a longer journey with a higher fare. George sensed the driver's frustration and tipped him handsomely. The couple exited the taxi, collected the luggage from the boot, and stood on the pavement to get their bearings.

The entrance to the Iguassu National Park consisted of a complex of shops and a ticketing office, along with road and pedestrian access to the park. The retail shops were closed at that time of the morning, and the couple searched for an all-night café, which they soon spotted in the complex.

"Let's go and have a coffee," George said.

"What about the luggage?" Maggie asked.

"Ah, yes, we'll have to store them somewhere. There must be luggage storage nearby."

George and Maggie searched around the complex and eventually found storage lockers for their bags. The plan was to collect the luggage when they left the park later that day. The couple headed back to the café, where a few people were already seated. Most were dressed in hiking gear, and it seemed they spent the night in the café to avoid paying for accommodation. Some rested their heads on the tables and slept, while others chatted quietly and drank coffee. George and Maggie bought coffees at the counter and sat down at a table. Maggie was concerned about meeting up with the correct tour from the hotel.

"How will we know which coach is ours?" she asked, "I mean, will we be able to recognise the one from our hotel?"

"We'll ask when the tour coaches come through. I guess they all pass through one entrance for buses and coaches."

The time was 4:15 in the morning, and the coach was not expected until 9:30. It was going to be a long wait, so the couple sipped their coffees slowly to pass the time. Even though they needed to wait a few hours, it was far better to be there than at the hotel, where the Brazilian gang members were waiting. The café was fairly quiet, apart from a few people chatting and some passing by. The ambient temperature was mild for that time of morning, and a smell of coffee wafted in the air. The only drawback to the café was the overhead lights, which were full on and lit the café brightly.

George and Maggie finished the coffee, and both felt tired. The past day was stressful for them, and they just wanted to relax. They, too, put their arms on the table, rested their heads on them, and soon fell asleep. At around 6 o'clock, the couple were awoken by the engine of a delivery truck, which pulled up nearby. It was delivering goods to the complex, and did so first thing in the morning, to beat the tourist rush. The couple looked at each other, then at the other people in the café, also awoken by the engine noise. Everyone stretched their arms and legs, apart from one man in his early twenties, who was still fast asleep. The café staff anticipated a rush at the counter and prepared fresh coffee. The din in the café increased as people began to talk, and the staff became active with their duties.

A bleary-eyed Maggie stretched her arms, leaned back in the chair, and looked up at the ceiling.
"I could do with a cup of tea," she said, "English breakfast tea."
"Yes, I could do with another coffee," George said, and added. "How about some breakfast as well?"
"What have they got?" Maggie asked, "Do you know?"
"I don't know, I'll go and see what they have. You look after the bags."
George went to the counter where a queue of three people had already formed. He studied the menu on the wall, scanned the food available behind the glass counter, and returned to Maggie.
"Croissants, cheeses, frankfurter sausages, and I think eggs. The word 'Ovos' was on the board, which I think is eggs."
"Is that all?" Maggie asked.
"I think so. Maybe there was yoghurt as well."
"Did they have any fruit?"
"I am not sure. I didn't see any fruit."
"I'll go and see for myself."
Maggie went over to the counter, took a quick look at the food available, and returned.
"I'll have a croissant and yoghurt," she said.
"I think I'll have two eggs and a frankfurter," George said, "and some toast."
George stood up and remembered the beverages before going to the counter.
"Do you still want tea?" he asked.
Maggie nodded positively, and George made his way over to the counter, where the queue had reduced. He placed the order and went back to the table to await breakfast.

A little while later, a waiter brought the breakfast over to the table. The couple ate breakfast slowly to pass the time while watching the TV mounted high on the wall. It displayed local and international news, which slowly reduced the waiting time.

Occasionally, they got up to stretch their legs, as did many of the other people waiting, their eyes also glued to the TV. A stream of people came and went from the cafe, mainly backpackers setting out early in the morning. The sun rose rapidly in that part of the world, warming the ambient temperature. The skies were clear, but the weather forecast was for rain later. Hopefully, the couple would have good weather to see the falls that morning.

Meanwhile, back at the hotel, the Brazilian gang were still seated in the reception lounge and watched the tourists passing by. Every time a man and woman walked by, Eduardo would comment.

"Pedro, what about this couple?"

In all cases, Pedro gave the same reply.

"No, not them," or "They're not English."

"Well, they must be here," Carlos said.

Pedro looked at Carlos with a vacant expression on his face.

"Maybe not," he said.

"What do you mean by that?" Carlos asked, "Where can they be? We can't just sit here all day."

"You're right," Eduardo said, "I'll go and ask a few questions at the desk."

Eduardo ambled over to the reception desk and was served immediately by a clerk who had only just started the day shift.

"We are looking for an English couple, they are staying at the hotel," Eduardo said to the clerk.

"What is the surname?" the clerk asked.

"Peacock."

"Let's see," the clerk said.

The clerk tapped a few instructions into the computer, then paused for a while. He realised he should not be giving out secure information freely to anyone. He looked up at Eduardo.

"And who are you?" he asked.

The question caught Eduardo by surprise, and he needed to think of a solution quickly.

"The local police," he said.

The clerk was surprised the police were asking questions at the hotel, and now felt he should help Eduardo.

"We did have a Mr and Mrs Peacock staying with us, but they have checked out."
"Checked out? When was that?"
"Early this morning."
Eduardo pointed over to the spot where Carlos and Pedro were seated.
"My colleagues and I were seated in reception since early morning, and we didn't see them," he said, "We would have seen them leave."
"Well, all I can say is that they've checked out. They've gone. The records have been updated in the computer."
"Where have they gone?"
"I don't know, they have not left any forwarding details."
Eduardo turned around to look at Carlos and Pedro. He was perplexed and raised his arms in the air to show his frustration. The two men looked back with raised eyebrows, but could not understand what Eduardo was indicating. He joined his colleagues and sat down to discuss their next move.

In the meantime, Angela, the travel representative, arrived for work and overheard the conversation between Eduardo and the reception clerk. She went over to the reception desk.
"What was that all about?" she asked.
The clerk explained the prior conversation to Angela, and she became somewhat surprised.
"Police!" she said, "I wonder what this is all about. The couple were such nice people, and not the type of people to get into trouble with the police."
"Well, they said they were from the police," the clerk said, "it must be important."
Angela looked over to the three men, who stared back at her. She smiled at them and thought about the situation for a moment. Angela wanted to talk to them and made her way over to where they were seated.

When she arrived, the three men looked up at Angela with apprehension.

"Hello, my name is Angela, and I am the travel representative at the hotel. I understand you were looking for Mr and Mrs Peacock."

The men felt embarrassed because here was someone willing to help them in their criminal activities. They looked at each other, hoping for the others to speak, but none did, so Eduardo spoke up.

"Yes," he said.

"You are from the police, I believe?" Angela asked.

"Yes," Eduardo replied.

He kept his answers simple because he did not wish to give anything away.

"Do you have any identity?" Angela asked.

All three men were lost for words and looked at each other, unsure what to do next.

"Yes, we have," Pedro chipped in.

Eduardo and Carlos looked at Pedro in astonishment, and then at each other with raised eyebrows, because they were not sure of Pedro's intentions.

"Can I see it, please, if you don't mind?"

"Sure," Pedro said.

He took out an ID badge from the inside pocket of his jacket and showed it to Angela. Eduardo and Carlos were bewildered and remained silent. Pedro had shown a fake police badge, one that he carried at all times, in case an incident like this arose.

"Satisfied?" he asked Angela.

"Yes, it seems fine," she replied.

Angela was duped by the fake badge and was convinced by the men that they were from the police. She was unsure why the police wanted the couple; they seemed like a nice couple to her. Like the reception clerk before her, she felt obliged to help the Brazilian men.

"I believe I know the whereabouts of Mr and Mrs Peacock," she said.

"You do!" all three men said together.

The men's eyes opened wide with anticipation.

"Yes, I do. They've booked a tour to the falls today at 9 o'clock."

"Today?" Eduardo asked.

"Yes, they were booked on the morning tour from the hotel."

"Why did we not see them pass through here this morning?" Carlos asked, "We were seated here all the time."

"I believed they checked out early. It was about 3:30 this morning, and they left a note for me."

"3:30 this morning?" Pedro asked, "That's about the time we arrived at the hotel."

All three men looked at each other, and then at Angela, who sensed they were somewhat irritated.

"Is there anything else I can help you with?" Angela asked.

"No, that's fine," Eduardo replied, "you have given us enough information. Thank you."

"The tour starts with a boat trip up to the falls, and then they are taken to view the falls from above," Angela said, "just thought you would like to know."

Angela smiled at the men and casually walked back to the travel desk. The three men did not believe their luck and found it difficult to contain their excitement.

The elation from the unexpected luck lasted a few minutes, and Eduardo became serious again.

"Right, let's work out another plan," he said.

"Do you have an idea?" Carlos asked.

"Yes, I have. Hear me out," Eduardo said, "We know they are going on a boat trip, and we know they are going to the top of the falls, yes?"

Carlos and Pedro nodded in agreement.

"So, we have to check both locations," Eduardo said, "there are only three of us, and we might need some help."

Pedro raised his arm, scratched his head, and screwed up his face.

"I've got an idea," he said.

Eduardo and Carlos looked at Pedro, who remained silent in thought.

"Well," Eduardo said.

"Yes, what's your idea?" Carlos asked.

"I know someone who works on the boat trips," Pedro said, "He's called Manuel."

Eduardo and Carlos listened intensely as Pedro continued.

"I helped him out before, and he owes me a favour. He might be able to help us."

"In what way?" Carlos asked, "And can we trust him?"

"I've known him for quite a while, and he is trustworthy. As I said, I've helped him on many occasions, and it's about time he returned the favour."

Carlos looked at Eduardo, raised his eyebrows, and shrugged his shoulders.

"What do you think?" he asked.

Eduardo thought for a moment.

"Well, we need help now," he said, "and if Pedro feels we can trust this man, then I'll go along with it."

"Ok, boss," Carlos said, "I agree as well."

"He works every day on the boats," Pedro said, "so I'll give him a call."

"Hold on a moment," Eduardo said, "what do we want him to do for us?"

"Don't the tourists leave their bags in lockers when they go on the boats?" Carlos asked.

"Yes," Pedro replied, "very little is taken on the boats; otherwise, everything gets drenched."

"Well, why don't we get Manuel to search their bags?" Carlos asked.

All three men looked at each other and smiled. Carlos's idea seemed simple, but effective.

"Good thinking, Carlos," Eduardo said, "that's a terrific idea. Manuel needs to know in which lockers the English store their bags."

Carlos sat back in the chair and, pleased with himself, put his hands behind his head.

"I'm not just a pretty face," he said, "am I?"

Eduardo ignored the comment and turned to Pedro.

"Can you call your friend and see if he could help us?" he asked.

Pedro took out his mobile phone and searched for Manuel's number. He soon found it and called the number.

"Manuel here, who is calling?"

"Manuel, this is Pedro, your old friend, long time no hear."

"Pedro! My God. It's been a long time. What have you been up to?"

"Working hard, still working hard."

Pedro glanced over to Eduardo and sensed he wanted him to get on with the reason for the call, and not to make small chat.

"Listen," he said, "I need a favour from you."

"Ah! Business eh! I thought this was going to be a friendly call."

"It's friendly, alright, but I just need a favour from you, can you help?"

"I'll see what I can do, I owe you one, don't I?"

Pedro felt comfortable that Manuel wanted to help, and winked at Eduardo.

"We are looking for an English couple," he said to Manuel, "they will be going on one of the boat trips today, this morning."

Manuel detected the 'We' in Pedro's last comment.

"What are we talking about here?" he asked, "Who is We? Are others involved?"

"Just some friends, some close friends. The couple should be on their way there now."

"Yes, we are fully booked on the boats today. But how can I help?"

Pedro needed to think of a good reason to get Manuel to help him.

"The couple are called George and Maggie Peacock, and they stole a package from us."

"What package is that?" Manuel asked.

"It doesn't matter what the package is; we just need it back."

Eduardo and Carlos looked at each other with raised eyebrows, and both were impressed by how good Pedro was at ad-libbing.

"So, what do you want me to do?" Manuel asked.

"We wondered if you could identify the English couple for us, and when they are out on the boat, check their lockers for the package."

"And how would I recognise the couple?"

"Their names should be on the booking document, would they not?"

Manuel felt a bit embarrassed because he should have known that he could identify the couple from their names on the form.

"Yes, of course I can. I normally greet the tourist when they arrive and take their tickets. I can look for their names."

"Good, and hopefully you could follow them to see which lockers they use."

"I suppose so, it shouldn't be too hard. What do you want me to do if I find the package?"

"Just call me back, and let me know, we will come and collect it."

"Where are you going to be when I am doing this?"

"I'll come to see you at the marina anyway, and my colleagues will be looking for the couple at the top of the falls."

"Great, we'll talk soon. I've got to go. Another coach of tourists has just arrived, speak soon."

Manuel ended the call, and Pedro smiled at Eduardo and Carlos. He was pleased with the results of the conversation.

"All done, we've got some help, we should be fine now," he said.

"Good on you, Pedro," Eduardo said, "I didn't know you were so clever, well done."

Eduardo stood up immediately with a renewed zest in his manner.

"Right, let's go," he said, "we've got work to do."

"Ok, boss," the other two men replied.

Eduardo headed for the hotel door, closely followed by his colleagues. He and Carlos headed to their car, which was left at the hotel overnight, and Pedro to his own. They bundled into their respective vehicles and sped off quickly towards the falls.

Meanwhile, at the entrance to the National Park, George and Maggie left the café and went over to the entrance where the coaches stopped before entering the park. All coaches were requested to stop to complete the administration for security reasons, and it was the location where George and Maggie could join their tour if they found the right coach. It would not be easy, though, the Iguassu Falls were a very popular tourist attraction, and many coaches passed through daily. George and Maggie needed to be vigilant, or otherwise they could miss the coach. They anticipated the coach would pass through the entrance at about 9:15, and began to look for it from 9 o'clock onwards. Many coaches were already passing through.

110

"This is going to be hard," George said to Maggie, "I didn't expect to see so many coaches."

"Yes, there are quite a few," Maggie said, "let's keep looking anyway."

It was unfortunate that the display on most coaches stated the destination, 'Iguassu Falls' and not the location where the coaches originated. On many occasions, George popped his head into the doorway of the coach.

"Is this the tour from the Hotel das Cataratas?" he asked.

Many a driver shook their heads, but George persevered anyway. It was now 9:25, and the couple thought they had missed their coach.

"What are we going to do now?" Maggie asked.

"I can't see how we could have missed the coach," George replied, "I think we looked into every coach. Maybe they cancelled our tour."

George and Maggie became disillusioned and stood there mystified when a voice shouted from across the coach park.

"Hey, English! What are you doing here?"

George and Maggie recognised the voice and looked across to the other side of the coach park in the direction from which it came. They saw two men waving at them frantically; they were Karl and Helmut, the Germans.

"Hey, English, over here," Karl shouted.

He beckoned for them to come over.

"Hurry, or else you will miss the coach," he shouted.

It was music to George and Maggie's ears. '*Was that really their coach?*' they thought.

George and Maggie hurried over and were greeted by Helmut and Karl at the coach.

"What are you doing here?" Karl asked, "We thought you were on a coach tour today."

"Yes, we were, or should I say, we are," George replied, "we are definitely on a trip today."

He glanced behind the Germans and asked the driver if this was the tour from the Hotel das Cataratas. The driver nodded affirmatively, and the couple were relieved they found their coach.

The tour guide stepped off the coach and approached them.

"Are you Mr and Mrs Peacock?" she asked.

"Yes," the couple replied.

"We were looking for you at the hotel," the guide said, "Do you have your booking paper?"

George took the ticket from his pocket and handed it over to the guide.

"Sorry about that," he said, "we needed to leave the hotel early, and thought we could catch the coach here."

"Well, it's lucky we found you now, we were worried about you," the guide said, "Kindly join us on the coach, we are running a few minutes late."

She beckoned for them to enter the coach, and George and Maggie found two spare seats at the back of the coach, where they settled down for the journey. They were followed by the Germans, who promptly returned to their seats.

The coach drove into the National Park, and the guide proceeded to inform the passengers about the day's tour over the amplified microphone system.

"Welcome again, ladies and gentlemen. Now that we have a full complement, I will explain today's trip. First, we see the falls on the river. We stop off about two kilometres from the falls, and you will take a powerful speed boat up to the falls. I know some of you did the boat trip before. So, those people, please remain on the coach, and we will take you to the top of the falls. Later on, the people from the boat trip will be collected, and we will all meet up again for lunch at the top of the falls."

The coach drove for another five minutes and turned off the main road onto an unpaved lane. It was a narrow track, and branches scraped against the coach as it meandered through the lane. The coach stopped in a clearing, which housed a tourist reception building, where the guide beckoned for those on the boat trip to disembark from the coach. George and Maggie were among a group of eight people to disembark, but the Germans had already been on the boat trip and remained on the coach. The couple bid farewell to them and soon entered the reception building, where they met another tour guide.

112

"Good morning, ladies and gentlemen," the guide said, "my name is Manuel and I hope you are all fine."

"Hello, Manuel," a few people uttered.

"I know you all speak English," Manuel said, "so that makes it easy for me. Today you will have a wonderful, once-in-a-lifetime experience. It will be something you will cherish and remember for the rest of your life. Are you looking forward to it?"

"Yeah!" everyone shouted.

"Good. First, we take you down to the river on a trailer, which is pulled by a tractor. The lane is very steep and muddy, and the tractor is the best means to get down to the river. You could walk if you want to, but I don't recommend it. Lots of snakes and creepy crawlies."

"Ooh!" the group murmured.

Manuel liked to scare the tourists a little bit and laugh at them, then continued his patter.

"Not really, there might be the odd snake, but I'm sure they've already eaten today, they don't like tourists anyway."

The group of tourists burst out in laughter.

"Seriously, though, the lane is very muddy, and the walk would be difficult, so the tractor is the best way."

"Ok, boss," shouted one person from within the crowd.

"Now, there are some basic rules. When in the trailer, keep your head, arms and hands inside the vehicle. The lane is very narrow, and we will pass very close to some of the trees. It's a jungle out there, you know!"

"Ooh!" the crowd murmured again.

Manuel continued his deliverance.

"When we reach the river, we will issue you with life jackets. Please put them on, they are for your safety. Again, when in the boat, keep your arms, legs and body inside the boat. And, no standing in the boat, unless we say you can."

The crowd looked at each other with anticipation. Manuel raised his arm to get their attention again and spoke in a slow voice.

"One other thing," he said, "you will get wet today. I repeat, you will get very wet today. Are there any questions?"

He looked around the group, and no one wanted to ask anything.

"There are lockers at the marina," he added, "and you can change there."

Manuel looked around the group again to see if everyone was comfortable with the instructions.

"Right, let's go," he said, "follow me."

Manuel made his way out the back of the building to the spot where the trailer was waiting, and was closely followed by the group of tourists. The trailer was hooked up to a tractor, and a driver was already on board. The seats on the trailer were made of wood, and the trailer had open sides with a canopy supported by a metal frame. It was high off the ground, and most people needed help to climb onto the trailer. Some grumbled, while others laughed at the experience. Before the tourists boarded the trailer, Manuel collected the tickets for the trip and carefully scanned the names on the tickets, so that he could identify the couple. It was soon time for George and Maggie to board, so Manuel took and read their tickets.

"Ah! Mr and Mrs Peacock, welcome."

George thought it strange that Manuel greeted them in such a personal way and did not greet the other tourists in the same manner. The couple were helped aboard the trailer by Manuel.

"Hope you enjoy your trip," he said.

"Thanks very much," Maggie replied, "we hope so too."

They were soon on their way once everyone boarded the trailer and headed for the river.

At the destination, the tourists disembarked from the trailer and followed Manuel down the steps leading to the marina on the river. The marina was small and could only house about six boats. Only three were presently moored; the others were being used to take tourists to the falls and back. The side of the ravine was steep and engineered to house a tourist centre, which contained changing rooms and lockers, a tourist shop and a café. It was understood that tourists would get very wet when at the falls, so they needed to change into swimwear. At least wear a plastic raincoat, which coincidentally was on sale in the tourist shop. Manuel led the tourists to the changing rooms and asked them to be at the moorings in ten minutes. He needed to establish the locker numbers George and Maggie were allocated, so he followed them to the locker check-in area. He remained fairly close to them when they were given the locker keys and surreptitiously noted the numbers.

George and Maggie were the first to change their clothes and head to the mooring. They saw Manuel chatting with two men by the boats and paused for a moment before making the final descent to the mooring. Every time the couple saw strange men hanging around, it made them paranoid.

"Who are those men?" Maggie asked.

"I don't know," George replied, "let's go and see."

So far that day, the couple behaved like normal tourists, and the schedule was running smoothly. They temporarily forgot the events of recent days, and the sight of the two men made them suspicious. At that moment, Manuel and the two men looked up at the couple and beckoned for them to come down to the mooring.

"Come and meet my colleagues," Manuel shouted, "Jose and Fernando. These are the guys who will help you on the boat today."

George and Maggie felt they could trust Manuel, but cautiously descended the stairs to the mooring and were greeted by the other two men. The men were part of the tour and worked on the boats taking tourists to the falls. George and Maggie's suspicions were unwarranted.

"Well done!" Manuel said, "The first to arrive."

He pointed over to another section on the mooring.

"Go over there," he said, "and get fitted with a life jacket."

The couple went over to another colleague and were helped to choose the appropriate size of life jackets. They were now ready to embark on the boat.

Jose and Fernando escorted the couple to the boat, while the other tourists approached the mooring a few at a time.

"Sit anywhere you like," one of the men said.

George and Maggie chose the front seats on the boat, as they were the best seats for viewing, where no one could sit in front of them. The jet boat was a large rubber dinghy with twin engines and had seats for fifteen people. The motors were powerful, and needed to be, the flow of water on the river was powerful. The jet boat was capable of manoeuvring adeptly to avoid large rocks located at various points in the river.

The rest of the tourists boarded the boat, and it was now ready to venture out on the river. It departed slowly from the marina, and there was much excitement among the tourists on board. Many had not been on a trip like this before, let alone on a speedboat. The jet boat soon picked up speed as it approached the middle of the river, and needed to do so to combat the strength of the current. The much-needed power of the engines roared into action, making the journey upstream towards the falls seem easy. The driver swerved the boat from side to side to give the occupants a thrill of adventure as they headed to the falls. He deliberately steered near rocks in the middle of the river, which created a sense of danger for the passengers, but with safety in mind at all times. He had done this trip many times and knew exactly what he was doing. The idea was to thrill the tourists, and it became more exciting when water splashed over the side and onto the passengers. There were lots of 'oohs!' from the tourists each time this happened. On the way up to the falls, they passed another boat on the return journey, and the look on the faces of the passengers was that of great euphoria and satisfaction. On the contrary, the look on the faces of George and Maggie's boat was that of anticipation and nervous tension. They were travelling into an unknown adventure.

While the tourists enjoyed themselves on the river, Manuel remained on shore and went to the locker room to search George and Maggie's lockers. He was able to find a master key from the service counter and took it without anyone noticing. Other tourists were using the locker room, so to ensure the task looked official, he temporarily installed a maintenance sign outside the locker room to inhibit further tourists from entering. He was also dressed in a uniform, and no one would suspect him; no tourist would challenge him. He was careful, though, and waited until the locker room was vacant of tourists before performing the task. Manuel opened George and Maggie's lockers and searched through their belongings. Unfortunately for him, he couldn't find the package. George had left it in his suitcase, stored in lockers at the entrance to the Iguassu National Park. Manuel knew Pedro would not be pleased, but at least felt he had tried and had returned the favour owed to Pedro.

Meanwhile, the jet boat slowed down as it approached the falls. Iguassu Falls was not just one cascade, but made up of many individual falls, totalling nearly 300 in all. The central part of the falls was not accessible from the river. Large boulders blocked the way, and it was too dangerous to approach the bottom of the falls. However, many smaller falls cascaded down from the cliffs above, some only a meter across. The driver approached one of these smaller falls and manoeuvred the boat under it. Even though the cascade was small, a mighty force of water fell onto the tourists, drenching everyone from head to toe. It was the point Manuel made earlier about getting wet when he gave the safety talk to the tourists. The experience created excitement among the passengers and produced 'oohs' and screams from them. The driver completed the manoeuvre more than once, and again, there were 'oohs!' and screams each time, but everyone seemed to be enjoying themselves.

The driver then took the boat as near as possible to the side of the ravine to view the rock face and vegetation at close range. He cruised near the edge of the ravine very slowly, allowing the passengers to enjoy the scenery, and made it the ideal time for photo opportunities. Looking up from the river, the passengers could see other tourists on a walkway above that stretched to the edge of the falls above the ravine. The walkway was one of the attractions on the next part of the tour, which George and Maggie were taking later that day. Many people on the walkway waved to the tourists in the boats below, but their images were hard to make out; the atmosphere was slightly hazy due to the mist created by the falls. George took out a pair of binoculars to view the people and scanned the walkway above. The view through the binoculars was clearer, and after a few minutes, his mouth dropped open.

"Oh my god! I don't believe it," he said, loudly.

"Don't believe what?" Maggie asked.

"I can't believe what I am seeing."

"What are you looking at?" Maggie asked, "What is it?"

The other tourists in the boat overheard George and Maggie and looked around to see the reason for the remarks. George ignored them and continued to look through the binoculars at the walkway above.

"What is it? What are you seeing?" Maggie asked again.

George lowered the binoculars and sat there with his mouth agape. The excitement of the day drained from him, and he leaned back in the seat. Maggie was concerned at this point and took the binoculars from George.

"Let me see," she said, "where were you looking?"

George remained silent, while Maggie scanned the walkway above with the binoculars. She could not see anything unusual and turned to speak to George.

"What's wrong?" she asked.

"It's the Brazilians, they are up there on the walkway, the same place we are going to next."

"Are you sure?"

"Yes, I saw them; they stood out from the crowd in their suits, and they must be searching for us."

"I thought we saw the last of them," Maggie said.

George looked up anxiously at Maggie.

"Me too," he said.

Maggie soon realised the consequences and put both her hands to her face in desperation.

"Oh my god!" she exclaimed.

"Let's keep this to ourselves," George said.

The other tourists were perplexed at the couple's conversation and remained silent as they sat back in their seats. The driver sensed something was wrong and decided to return to the marina. The trip was almost at an end anyway, and the jet boat headed back to the moorings at high speed. George and Maggie remained subdued for the rest of the journey, and unlike the other tourists, did not marvel at any of the scenery. The journey from the marina back up to the coach stop was also unenthusiastic for the couple. They did not speak much, and although the other tourists were not aware of their anguish, they felt empathetic towards them. What were they to do now?

While George and Maggie were on the river, Pedro arrived at the tourist reception building near the marina where the coaches stopped for the boat trip, and waited for Manuel to call. He had not spoken to Manuel since calling him from the hotel, and sat nervously twiddling his thumbs. Each time a trailer returned from the marina, Pedro hid himself in the office to avoid being seen. He was unsure which trailer Manuel and the couple would arrive on. They eventually arrived, and the tourists disembarked from the trailer. The coach was already waiting to take them to the top of the falls, and the tourists boarded it immediately. Manuel searched for Pedro and found him in the office. After a joyous greeting, they got down to business.

"Any luck?" Pedro asked.

Manuel negatively shook his head.

"No luck, my friend. I searched the lockers, and there was no package."

Pedro was disappointed at the answer and scratched his head.

"Are you sure?" he asked.

"Positive. The only things we found were their personal belongings, you know, clothes, credit cards and cash."

Pedro looked around, rubbed his chin, and thought for a moment.

"They've obviously hidden the package somewhere else," he said.

"I don't know, I can't say. What's this all about anyway?" Manuel asked.

"The less you know, the better, trust me."

"Ok, it's your call."

Pedro thanked Manuel for his help and phoned Eduardo and Carlos to update them on the latest information. The two men were already at the top of the falls and waited for the couple to arrive.

Chapter 8 – At Iguassu Falls

George and Maggie followed the group of tourists to board the coach and remained subdued. They were anxious about the next part of the trip and felt as if they were being led to the lions. The same tour guide who escorted them before was on the coach, which soon departed for the falls.

"Everyone happy!" she asked.

The overwhelming reply from everyone, except George and Maggie, was 'Yes,' but the guide felt the response could be better.

"Everyone happy!" she asked again.

This time, the response from everyone, except George and Maggie, was much louder.

"Do you want to do it again?" the guide asked.

"Yes," most people shouted.

"Good, then you'll have to come back another time," the guide said, "We're off to see the falls from a different angle."

The journey to the top of the falls only lasted ten minutes, and the coach stopped outside the tourist centre, which contained restaurants, retail shops, and a small museum. The driver opened the door to the coach.

"Everyone off, please," the guide said, "We'll meet back here in three hours. That gives you plenty of time to have lunch and see the falls."

Everyone disembarked the coach and went their separate ways. Some of the tourists decided to have lunch first, then see the falls afterwards. Some headed directly to the falls; they did not want to waste any time seeing the spectacular Iguassu Falls. George and Maggie stood by the coach discussing their next move.

"Do you want to have some lunch?" George asked.

"I'm not hungry," Maggie replied.

"You have to eat something; it's been a long time since breakfast."

"I'm not hungry, and I don't think I can eat anything."

"Let's go anyway, there might be something suitable that you fancy."

George headed towards the cafeteria area, followed reluctantly by Maggie. They passed a few establishments before deciding on a cafe which provided light lunches. It was now about 1 pm, and the restaurant was filled with diners. The smell of food wafted through the air, and the café buzzed with people enjoying their lunch.

On entering the café, a waiter approached George and Maggie. "Good afternoon," he said, "how can I help you?"
"Hello," George replied, "table for two, please, away from the front."
"Certainly, sir," the waiter said.
He then guided them to a vacant table at the back of the café, where George and Maggie sat down. They immediately scanned the café to ensure there was no one about familiar to them.
"Drink, Sir?" the waiter asked.
"Yes, please, can I have a beer?" George replied.
"And for you, madam?"
"Err, Um, I'll have tea, please."
"Certainly," the waiter said.
He wrote the order on his notepad, but Maggie was feeling troubled and needed something stronger to drink.
"No, make mine a glass of white wine," she said, "I think I need some wine."
"Certainly, madam."
The waiter went away to get the drinks, and George perused the menu.
"Are you going to eat anything?" he asked.
Maggie picked up another menu and scanned it.
"I'm not sure," she replied.
Her mind was elsewhere, and she was not really concentrating on the menu.
"Have you still got the package?" she asked.
George was also feeling the tension and was short-tempered towards Maggie.
"Yes," he replied, "stop asking me about the package."
"Where is it?" Maggie asked.
"It's safe in the suitcase at the park entrance."

"I wish you had never agreed to deliver the package. It's been driving me crazy, and I've been on edge ever since I found out. The truth is, it has spoiled my holiday."

"You may be right, Maggie, and I'm sorry for this, but at the time, I thought it was easy money to make. We are always short of money, and I thought the cash would be useful."

The couple looked at the menus for a while longer, and soon the waiter returned with the drinks. They ordered food, which they ate in silence, and the next hour passed quickly. They scanned around the restaurant constantly, and anyone watching them would sense they may have had a domestic argument.

It was about 2 pm when the couple left the restaurant, and they headed for the falls. Iguassu Falls could be seen from different viewpoints, and as time was limited, the couple needed to decide quickly from which location to see the falls.

"Do we want to see the falls from above, or from the walkway lower down?" George asked.

"I'm not sure," Maggie replied, "both views would be spectacular."

"I agree, let's decide."

The couple procrastinated on their decision because they knew the Brazilian gang members were around somewhere,

"Which would you prefer?" Maggie asked.

"I think from the walkway below. Even though it would be great to see the falls from above, viewing the falls from below could be more spectacular, and we would see the back falls cascading to the same level as the walkway."

"I think so as well."

"I have a doubt, though," George said.

"What's that?"

"It was on the walkway that the Brazilians were standing when I saw them from the boat."

"Ah! Yes, that's true. What do you think we should do?"

George and Maggie thought for a moment.

"I would still like to see the falls from the walkway," George said, "The Brazilians may be no longer there. It's been quite a while since I saw them."

"Ok, let's go to the walkway below," Maggie said, "we've come this far, and it would be a shame not to have a good view of the falls."

The couple initially made their way to a viewpoint where they could see the falls from above. The falls were tiered by nature in some places, and a walkway was built on one of these tiers, from where people could also view the falls. Access to the walkway was from a platform built into the cliff above the cascade. It was constructed from steel and wood, and encircled with safety rails. It could support the weight of many tourists, and housed a lift which took them down 40 metres to the lower tier. A walkway was constructed on the lower tier, allowing people to stroll to the edge of the falls. This walkway, built on concrete pylons embedded in the rock, had sturdy handrails to keep tourists safe. Looking back from the walkway, you could see a section of the falls cascading from above, about 50 metres away. The cascading water dropped onto the same level as the walkway and flowed underneath it until it reached the end of the tier. It then cascaded again at least 100 meters into the ravine below. The water flowing under the walkway was not a full torrent, but it was forceful enough to feel the strength of the falls. The atmosphere was enhanced by the spray of water generated by the falls, which created a very damp mist, resembling a low cloud. The entire Iguassu Falls stretched across the ravine, and the roar from across the ravine, together with the misty air, created a dangerous and surreal atmosphere.

George and Maggie were on the upper platform above the falls, where many people were milling around. The tourists returning from the walkway below were completely soaked from the spray of the falls. Some of them looked miserable because they were drenched from head to toe, while others, not bothered by being wet, were elated with excitement.
"Seems we need to get raincoats," Maggie said.
"Don't be silly," George said, "let's go and experience the water."
"I'm not getting wet," Maggie said, "you can if you want to, but I'm going to get a raincoat."

Luckily for the couple, a tourist shop on the platform sold see-through raincoats with hoods. They were thin and light in weight, ideal for the wet conditions, so Maggie bought one. George realised his clothes would get completely soaked, and not wanting to travel back with damp clothes, succumbed to purchasing a raincoat as well.

The next stage of the experience was for George and Maggie to descend to the tier below. They approached the lifts to take them down to the next level, only to find long queues of tourists waiting. Two lifts were operating, and each carried about 15 people. George did not like to queue, and as it would take some time to catch the lift, he became displeased.
"I hate queuing," he said.
Several tourists turned around to look at George, and no doubt felt the same.
"You have to be patient," Maggie said.
The queue shuffled along, and after 10 minutes, the couple managed to get into one of the lifts, which took them quickly to the level below. They emerged onto the lower platform, which led to the walkway that would take them to the edge of the falls. On exiting the lift, they were met with a stupendous view of the water cascading down to their level from above.
"Wow!" George exclaimed.
He quickly made his way over to the rails with a camera in hand.
"Wow! Wow! Wow!" he said.
The noise of the cascading water was deafening, and Maggie had to speak loudly to be heard above the noise of the falls.
"Superb," she shouted.
They wasted no time in photographing the falls. Along the walkway, they noticed the spray from the water was intense, so they immediately donned their raincoats to protect themselves and the cameras.

In the meantime, Eduardo and Carlos, the two Brazilian gang members, were at the top level of the falls near the restaurants. They were last seen by George and Maggie on the lower walkway a couple of hours ago, when the couple were on the boat.

"We're not having much luck," Carlos said to Eduardo.

"No, we're not," Eduardo replied, "They are here somewhere, and we must keep searching."

"You're right there, the boss will feed us to the pigs if we don't come up with the goods."

"Let's retrace our steps," Carlos said, "We knew the couple were at the Hotel das Cataratas, then we found out they were coming to the falls for the day. We then searched around here and…"

Eduardo interrupted Carlos.

"Then we searched on the walkway, at the lower level," he said.

Carlos then interrupted Eduardo.

"Then we came back up here, and searched around again," he said, "we found nothing, absolutely nothing, a dead end."

"Let's go to a vantage point, where we will get a good view of the tourists to see if we can spot them," Eduardo said.

"Yes, good idea. We should go back to the upper platform, where we can see many people at once from the viewpoint."

The two men made their way from the restaurant towards the upper platform. They scanned in all directions as they walked along and soon reached the viewing area. The platform was packed with tourists, and as they approached the edge, the noise of the falls became louder and louder. Trying to pick out individuals from such a height was not easy, so they used their binoculars to scan the people on the walkway below.

By now, George and Maggie had ventured onto that walkway on the lower tier and slowly strolled towards the end with cameras in hand. The walkway was crowded with tourists of many nationalities, taking pictures of their companions and of the surrounding scenery. George looked back into the distance towards the main falls and felt excited when he saw the thunderous falls crash into the ravine below.

"I'm glad we came here," he said, "I can't believe it's so spectacular, the best thing I've ever seen."

"It's a bit scary," Maggie said. "Is this structure safe?"

"I guess so," George replied.

To Maggie's dismay, George leaned over the barrier to look at the water flowing underneath the walkway.

"What are you doing?" she shouted, "Be careful."

George ignored Maggie and continued to watch the torrent below, swirling around the posts supporting the walkway. The force of the water created moving whirlpools that eventually cascaded over the edge into the ravine.

Eduardo and Carlos were still searching for George and Maggie from the upper platform when Carlos stopped scanning with the binoculars and concentrated on something he had seen. He zoomed the binoculars into the location on the walkway where George and Maggie stood.

"Got them!" he shouted.

"Where?" Eduardo asked.

Carlos pointed towards the place where the couple stood on the walkway.

"Right over there," he said.

Eduardo quickly looked through his binoculars and saw George and Maggie.

"Right, let's go," he said, "We've got them now. They can't escape from us this time; the only way out from the walkway is by using the lifts."

Carlos and Eduardo quickly made their way over to the lifts and barged through the people waiting to get to the front of the queue.

"Hey! What are you doing?" one tourist shouted.

"Yes, get to the back of the queue," another said.

Carlos gave them both a nasty look and pointed his index finger at them.

"Shut up," he said.

The tourists were terrified of Carlos and soon backed down; they did not wish to get involved in a fracas.

"That soon told them," Carlos said.

Other tourists nearby decided not to say anything to the men but instead murmured rude comments in their own language. Eduardo remained nonchalant and also looked at the tourists with indifference. The lift arrived, and before the passengers disembarked, Carlos and Eduardo forced their way into the lift. Eduardo barred anyone else from entering, to the disgust of the queuing tourists. Carlos pushed the descend button before anyone else could enter, and the lift made a quick descent to the bottom level, the same level as the lower walkway, where the men hurriedly exited.

"Let's try to act like tourists," Eduardo said, "so we can approach them slowly, and not be suspicious."

"Ok, boss," Carlos replied, "But we're dressed in suits. Isn't that a giveaway?"

Eduardo tutted and ignored the comment.

The walkway stretched out over the water for about 100 meters and meandered until it reached the edge of the falls. Eduardo and Carlos slowly approached the couple, pretending to be tourists by snapping photos on their phones. The men did not wear raincoats, so their suits were dripping wet, which made them stand out from the crowd. George, however, was always vigilant and saw the Brazilians approaching.

"Oh, Shit!" he shouted.

Maggie looked over to George and was concerned at his remark. "What's wrong?" she asked.

George became frightened, and his voice turned croaky.

"The Brazilians are here on the walkway, and we're cut off," he said.

"Where?" Maggie asked.

"Approaching us."

George nodded in the direction of the Brazilians, which prompted Maggie to look along the walkway, and she saw the Brazilians heading towards them about 20 metres away. Eduardo and Carlos put the phones in their pockets and took out pistols from inside their jackets. One tourist standing nearby saw the guns and became concerned.

"Look out, they've got guns," he shouted.

Other tourists looked around, and when they saw the guns, they began to scream in panic. People started to run away, and chaos soon ensued on the walkway. The tourists in front of the men could not get by and cowered down, holding their heads in their hands. George and Maggie stood frozen, and the gleam in their eyes showed they were utterly terrified.

"What are we going to do?" Maggie asked.

The situation became serious when Eduardo and Carlos pointed their guns at the couple and blocked the exit.

"I don't know," George said, "let me think."

George and Maggie began to panic, and their voices became louder.

"Hurry up, do something," Maggie shouted.

"What can I do?" George replied, "I'm not sure what to do."

Eduardo and Carlos continued to walk towards the couple, and were about 10 metres away.

"I'll talk to them," George said, "I'll try to reason with them and ease the situation."

"Do something quick," Maggie said.

The men were now only 5 metres away and pointed the guns at the couple.

"Where is the package?" Carlos asked.

"I don't know what you are talking about," George replied.

"Don't be foolish," Eduardo said, "we know you have the package. Where is it?"

Carlos grabbed Maggie's arm and pulled her near to his body, and at the same time, pointed his gun at her head.

"Don't make me ask you again!" Carlos said to George.

Unbeknownst to the couple, the two Germans, Karl and Helmut, were also on the walkway and noticed the couple's predicament. They decided to help George and Maggie and approached the Brazilians slowly from behind. The Brazilians were unaware that the Germans were approaching them. They did not see them, and could not hear them either, through the deafening roar of the falls. The Germans were young, agile and strong, and crept up behind the Brazilians. Helmut was about to grab Carlos by the neck when Carlos turned around and saw him.

"What the...!" Carlos cried out.

He pointed the gun towards Helmut, who grabbed his arm and forced him to raise it into the air, when a shot was fired.

"Oh shit!" Helmut shouted.

He twisted Carlos's gun arm, and a struggle ensued. The two men exchanged blows and fought standing up. Helmut tried to disarm Carlos and forced the arm in which he held the gun between the two of them, when the gun discharged again. He let

128

go of Carlos and staggered backwards, out of breath, while holding his stomach. Looking down, he was amazed to see the front of his T-shirt covered in blood. Helmut rested against the barrier and looked over at Carlos, who dropped to the walkway. Carlos was shot in the abdomen and was bleeding profusely. He sat motionless on the walkway and groaned out loud while clutching his abdomen.

Meanwhile, Karl jumped on Eduardo from behind, hitting him with a thud on the head with his elbow.

"Ouch!" Eduardo cried out.

The hit on the head dazed Eduardo, who dropped his gun on the walkway and staggered for a moment. He regained his senses and turned around to see who had attacked him.

"You bastard!" he shouted, "I'm going to get you."

Eduardo composed himself and took the initiative by hitting Karl in the face with a closed fist. Karl staggered backwards, and Eduardo followed up the attack while Karl was still dazed. The men fell to the ground and exchanged blows, rolling over and over. At one point, Eduardo hit Karl with a mighty blow, which left him dazed again and lying on the ground. Eduardo stood up and took the opportunity to retrieve the pistol that had fallen onto the walkway. He pointed the gun at Karl, and was about to pull the trigger when George rushed forward and pushed him hard. Eduardo lost his balance, staggered towards the edge of the walkway, and fell over the barrier. He released the gun and tried to catch hold of the barrier, but it was in vain, and Eduardo fell screaming into the swirling water below. He tried to grab hold of one of the support columns and some rocks, but the flow of water was too powerful for him to get a grip. The couple and the Germans looked over the barrier to see Eduardo struggling in the strong current. His body was dragged by the torrent and swept over the edge of the falls. Eduardo fell 100 metres to his death, and his dying screams echoed across the ravine below, over and above the roar of the waterfalls.

"Oh my God!" George shouted, "What have we done?"

"It was unfortunate, but they would have killed you," Helmut said.

Maggie stood in silence, a blank look on her face and was numb with fright. Karl stood up and went over to comfort her by putting his arms around her.

"It'll be alright," he said.

Carlos was still alive, but was groaning in pain, and needed medical help immediately. Helmut knelt beside him to see if he could help him, but there was not much he could do, and he looked up to the others.

"We can't stay here," he said, "We have to go straight away."

"What about Carlos?" Maggie asked.

"We'll just have to leave him," Karl said, "Someone will come to help."

"We can't just leave him here, or else he will die," Maggie said.

George felt Karl and Helmut were right, and went over to convince Maggie.

"I think we should do as Karl and Helmut suggest," George said, "we can't stick around here."

For a few seconds, the couple and the Germans remained silent, looking perplexed.

By now, all the tourists on the walkway headed for the exit on the lower platform, where the lifts were located. Dozens queued to evacuate the platform, and there was a struggle to get into the lifts. The platform near the lifts was wider than the walkway and housed tourist shops and a small café. Two security guards pushed their way through the crowd and came running up to the foursome at the end of the walkway.

"What's going on?" one shouted.

The foursome remained silent.

"Quick, let's deal with the injured one," the second guard said.

They both knelt next to Carlos to see if they could help him.

"What's your name?" one guard asked.

Carlos was still in pain and just groaned at the men. The other guard realised Carlos was bleeding from the abdomen, and took off his jacket. He folded it and pressed it against the wound to stop the bleeding.

"Call for help," he said to his colleague.

His colleague grabbed his walkie-talkie and uttered a few words into it, while looking towards the upper platform. It now seemed the right time for the couple and Germans to depart.

While both guards were tending to Carlos, the foursome ran along the walkway towards the lifts, but were hindered by the crowd of people; they could not reach the lifts. Karl looked for another route by which to leave the platform and glanced over towards the shops.

"I know," he said, "let's go through one of the shops."

"Why?" George asked.

"There must be a service entrance to supply goods," Karl replied.

"That's true," George said, "It's a good idea."

Helmut quickly headed for one of the shops, closely followed by Karl and the couple.

"Here, let's try this one," Helmut said.

The Germans entered the building without hesitation, followed closely by George and Maggie. The shopkeeper was taken aback and stood terrified, holding her hands up to her face.

"Where is the service exit?" Helmut asked.

The shopkeeper was somewhat scared and pointed towards the back entrance to the shop.

"Over there," she replied.

The foursome made their way through the shop and exited by the back door. They found a passageway located behind the shops leading to a service lift. It was lucky for the foursome, for they could now make a quick getaway. Helmut pushed the button to call the lift and stood behind George and Maggie, allowing them to enter the lift first. When the lift doors opened, they were confronted by two police officers with guns in hand. The foursome thought they had been caught and put their arms up in a surrender fashion.

"Out of the way," one officer shouted.

He forced past George and Maggie, causing them to stumble backwards.

"Move it!" the other officer shouted.

He followed his colleague out of the lift, and both officers ran along the service passage, soon disappearing into one of the shops.

"That was lucky!" Maggie exclaimed.

"Sure was," Karl replied.

"We needed some luck," George added.

George looked at Helmut and pointed at his T-shirt.

"Lucky you were behind us, and the officers didn't see your bloodstained shirt."

"Yes," Helmut said, "I should really take it off."

George thought quickly about a solution to the T-shirt.

"Take off the T-shirt and throw it over the barrier," he said.

"What am I going to wear?"

"I'll give you my raincoat, I don't need it anymore."

Helmut did as George suggested, and the foursome entered the lift, which took them to the upper platform.

Many tourists had already ascended in the main lifts to the upper platform and were hastily vacating the area to get away from any danger. Some remained on the upper platform and mixed with the growing crowds to view the commotion happening below. The foursome took the opportunity to do the same and eased past tourists to reach the barrier. They also wanted to see the latest situation occurring below. They looked down onto the walkway and saw the police officers in conversation with the security guards. It was very crowded near the barrier on the upper platform, and people were jostling each other. A man in a brown leather jacket brushed past George and disappeared into the crowd. George took no notice of it at the time, but later realised it was the same man he had seen on the plane from the UK to Rio. It was also the same man George had seen in the café at Heathrow airport. At that moment, a siren rang out, and an ambulance arrived, dividing the crowd as it approached the platform. It was time for the foursome to leave the area, and they made their way quickly towards the coach stop.

"What are you going to do now?" George asked Karl and Helmut.

"Not sure," Karl replied, "I just want to get away from this place, and quickly."

132

"I think we should as well," Maggie interjected.

Helmut nodded his head in agreement.

"I think we'll catch the first coach out of here," George said.

"Yes, let's do," Maggie added, "And quickly."

"Wait," Helmut said, "We should not travel together. The police will be searching for four people."

"That's very wise," Karl said, "you two go first, and we will follow in a later coach."

George looked at Maggie, and they both nodded in agreement. He then turned to Karl and Helmut.

"We haven't had much time to thank you," George said.

"Yes, thank you very much," Maggie added.

"We're really grateful for your help," George said, "I don't know what we would have done if you hadn't shown up."

Maggie then gave Karl a big hug and did the same to Helmut.

"I'm sure you would have done the same for us," Helmut said.

George held out his hand to shake hands with the Germans, but Karl was having none of it. He grabbed George's hand and pulled him close to give him a man hug. Helmut did the same to George.

"I don't suppose we will see you again," George said.

"Perhaps not," Karl said.

"Let's hope for all our sakes we don't get caught," Helmut added.

Maggie became emotional, and tears filled her eyes.

"Let's hope so," she said.

Karl was a bit puzzled about something and wanted to challenge George before they departed.

"One thing I don't understand," he said.

"What's that?" George asked.

"Why did those men attack you?"

George was unsure whether to tell the Germans the whole story, and paused for a while. Karl sensed George's unease and that he didn't want to answer the question.

"I don't know," George said, "I really don't know. Maybe they thought we were someone else."

Karl raised his eyebrows, and the others waited for George to elaborate, but George remained silent to the enormous relief of Maggie.

"Ah, well, maybe we will never know," Karl said, "You two have a safe journey."

George and Maggie boarded the first coach to take them back to the park entrance, waved goodbye to the Germans, and watched them with sadness as the coach departed. Karl and Helmut returned the farewells and went to check the departure time of the next coach.

It was now about 4 pm, and the couple needed to get to the Iguassu airport as soon as possible. First, they had to collect their luggage from storage at the entrance to the Iguassu National Park. The coach drove for about 15 minutes before it reached the entrance, where George and Maggie disembarked. They collected their luggage from the storage and headed for the taxi rank.

"I think the journey to the airport would be quicker by cab," George said.

"What about our flights?" Maggie asked.

"What do you mean?"

"Our flight from Iguassu to Rio is not until tomorrow night, 9 pm. Is it not?"

"Oh yes, that's right. With all the commotion going on, I forgot about the flights."

"What are we going to do?"

"We'll go to the airport anyway, and see if we can change the flight to this evening. The sooner we get back to Rio, the better."

"Ok," Maggie replied.

George hailed a taxi from the rank, which came immediately.

"Iguassu airport, please," George instructed the driver.

The trip to the airport took ten minutes; the couple exited the cab and headed to the TAM Airlines booking desk. They were lucky; no one was waiting at the desk, and they were served immediately. The female clerk realised the couple were not locals and spoke in English.

"Can I help you?" she asked.

"Yes, please," George replied, "we have a flight booked to Rio tomorrow night, and wondered if we could change it for tonight."

"Do you have the tickets?"

"Oh yes, here they are," George said.

He handed the tickets to the clerk, who checked the details on them. She then typed a few characters into the computer.

"Yes, I've got you flying at 9 pm tomorrow."

"That's right," George said, "can you change it?"

"Let's see what we can do," the clerk said.

She typed some more letters into the computer and waited a few seconds for the response. Meanwhile, Maggie was vigilant and frequently looked around the airport. She wanted to make sure no one had followed them.

"The same flight at 9 pm tonight is fully booked," the clerk said, "but there is one at 7 o'clock with vacant seats."

George nodded positively to Maggie, who returned the nod. He then turned to the clerk.

"That's fine," he said, "that will do."

"Unfortunately, this flight is almost fully booked, and I can't allocate seats next to each other," the clerk said.

George looked at Maggie again.

"What do you think?" he asked.

Maggie seemed disappointed at the news and screwed up her face.

"I suppose it'll have to do," she said, "We need to leave as soon as possible."

George turned to the clerk again.

"Ok, that's fine, we'll take it."

The clerk typed a few details into the computer, printed the boarding passes, and handed them to George.

"Boarding is at gate 2, at 6:30," she said, "Hope you have a good trip."

"Thank you," George replied.

It was about 5 pm, and the flight to Rio was not until 7, so the couple decided to buy a snack before boarding the aircraft. They headed to the nearest cafeteria and waited for the flight to be called. The time went quickly, and the plane took off on schedule. The flight was uneventful and arrived in Rio two hours later.

Chapter 9 – Terror in the Favela

George and Maggie still had a few days remaining to spend in Rio before the flight back to England. They dared not return to the Rio Othon Palace hotel, in case members of the gang were looking for them, so the couple were unsure where to stay in Rio. After collecting the luggage, they went to the Arrivals lounge to discuss their next move. George and Maggie sat and looked blankly at one another, in the hope that the other would come up with a suggestion. George leaned forward towards Maggie and clasped his hands in front of him.

"The only contact I know in Rio is Antonio," he said, "maybe he could help us."

"Can we trust him?" Maggie asked.

"I think so. He helped us in the past, and it was Antonio who found the address near the Sambadrome where you were being held."

The remark reminded Maggie of the kidnapping ordeal, and her mouth went dry. She took a bottle of water from her hand luggage and drank some, while giving the problem some more thought.

"What about the Embassy?" she asked.

"Embassy!" George exclaimed, "What Embassy?"

"The British Embassy."

George seemed puzzled at Maggie's suggestion and scratched his head.

"Why should we involve them?" he asked, "It could make things more complicated, and create more trouble for us."

"It was just a thought," Maggie replied.

"I think we need to stay low-key," George added.

Maggie did not understand George and became unsure of his comment.

"Low-key!" she said, "What do you mean?"

"Well, not to make ourselves too obvious, by keeping out of sight as much as possible."

"How do we manage that? Every time we thought we escaped from the Brazilians, they found us again. I'm definitely not happy with the suggestion."

"What do you suggest then?" George asked.

"I don't know."

Maggie's answer infuriated George, and he knew from experience that she never suggested anything at a time of crisis.

"Well, there you are, you can't think of anything either."

"Look, let's not have another argument. We have enough on our plate to worry about at the moment."

"Well, you never come up with a solution. Every time I ask you what we should do, your set answer is always, 'I don't know.'"

The conversation between George and Maggie became fraught, so George got up and walked away to give them both some breathing space. He strolled around the airport lounge aimlessly for a few minutes and returned to Maggie.

"Look, I'm sorry," he said, "I know the whole escapade is not easy for you, but it is also difficult for me."

Maggie looked up at George with a smirk on her face and then patted the seat beside her with her hand.

"Come and sit next to me, George," she said, "come and sit down."

George sat down next to Maggie and held her hand. And in a loving response, Maggie laid her head on his shoulder. The couple were tired following the ordeal at Iguassu Falls, and just wanted to find accommodation where they could rest.

"I've been thinking about your suggestion," Maggie said, "I agree you should call Antonio, and see if he could help us."

George looked surprised at Maggie; only a few minutes ago, he thought she never took the initiative.

"Are you sure?" he asked.

"Yes, he helped us before, and I assume he can help us again."

"Ok, I will call him, but I could do with a drink first."

"Me too."

"Let's go to the bar."

George and Maggie dragged their luggage to the nearest bar and sat down to have a drink. They discussed the next steps to take and decided on a plan of action. They sipped their drinks slowly and felt happier with each other. They had thought of a way forward.

About twenty minutes later, the couple left the bar and found a quiet corner in the Arrivals lounge with no one nearby. George searched for the piece of paper with Antonio's telephone number on it, and dialled the number on his phone. The phone rang for a few seconds.

"Hello," a voice answered, in Portuguese.

"Hello," George said, "can I speak to Antonio, please?"

There was a pause at the other end of the line, and then the voice spoke again.

"Antonio speaking," the voice replied in English, "who is this?"

"It's me, George the Englishman, you remember, we spoke before."

"Ah, the Englishman! Yes, I remember. Where have you been? I was hoping to hear from you sooner, but you just disappeared."

George detected a change in Antonio's voice, and it sounded somewhat muffled.

"I've got a lot to tell you," George said, "but first, are you ok? You don't sound too well."

There was a slight pause at the other end of the line.

"I am fine, George. I've had a bit of a cold lately and am now getting over it. By the way, did you find your wife? Is she ok?"

"Yes, she's fine, but we've had a few problems..."

Maggie was listening to the conversation and raised her eyebrows at George. He got the message and decided to elaborate on the story.

"...Well, more than a few problems," George continued, "We are in deep trouble, and we need your help."

"What sort of trouble?"

"I think it's too much to tell you on the phone. Maybe we could meet, and I will explain it all."

There was silence on the phone, and a few seconds elapsed.

"Are you there?" George asked, "Are you still there?"

"Yes, I'm here," Antonio said, "I think it's a good idea to meet. Where are you staying?"

"Well, that's another problem. We are at the airport, and don't have anywhere to stay."

George sounded desperate, and there was another pause in the conversation. He felt he may be imposing on Antonio too much, and looked at Maggie with a wry smile.

138

"Ok, I have a solution," Antonio said, "take a cab to the address I'm going to give you, and I'll meet you there."

"Hold on, I'll just get a pen and paper," George said.

George beckoned to Maggie with his hand in a writing fashion. Maggie understood, took out a notepad and pen from her handbag, and handed them to George.

"Go ahead," George said.

Antonio gave the address where to meet, and abruptly ended the call. George was surprised at the abruptness and looked at the phone. He raised his eyebrows and felt he may have upset Antonio in some way, but was not sure.

"What's happening?" Maggie asked.

"We have an address where we can meet Antonio."

"Is that somewhere we can stay?"

"I don't know, Antonio just said to meet him there."

Maggie's intuition began to sense that something may not be right with the arrangement.

"This is sounding dodgy again," she said.

"Well, we agreed to ring Antonio, didn't we? We'll have to go along with it; we have no other options."

The couple collected their luggage and headed for the taxi rank outside the airport building.

George and Maggie took the first available taxi and instructed the driver to the destination address given by Antonio. They remained silent for most of the journey, only breaking the silence when the taxi driver asked a question. The address where they were heading was in one of the less salubrious suburbs of Rio, away from the coast, and situated on the edge of a favela. It was nighttime, the streets were dimly lit, and covered with rubbish discarded throughout the day. Loud music bleared out from houses and shops as they passed by. The music and the noise from the traffic created a constant din for most of the journey. People milled around, and while some worked at their businesses, others stood idly by. Many dogs and cats roamed the streets, taking a chance to dodge the traffic. The exhaust fumes from the vehicles and the smell of blocked drains created a mixture of toxic emissions for everyone to inhale. This was not a pleasant area for the couple to be in, and George and Maggie felt somewhat uneasy.

They reached the destination, and the taxi pulled up at a junction near the address.

"Here, boss, your address," he said.

"How much?" George asked.

"Fifty Real."

George paid the driver 55 Real, which included the tip, and the couple exited the taxi. The driver looked anxiously at the couple and spoke to them through the car window.

"You sure you want to be here, boss?"

George looked strangely at the driver and nodded positively.

"Ok, your choice. You be careful, boss."

The driver crunched the gears in the car before driving away slowly. George and Maggie, perplexed at the location they found themselves, stood glaring. Everyone around them, without exception, was staring at them. Two small children, about seven years old, ran up to the couple and tugged at their hands.

"Money, money," they shouted in Portuguese, "Give us money." George and Maggie ignored the children and scanned around the junction to get their bearings. The children then started to tug on the couple's clothes.

"Money, money," they shouted again.

A man seated on a chair on the pavement nearby, intervened and waved his arms at the children.

"Shoo!" he shouted, "leave them alone."

The children became scared of the man and ran away into the crowd. George acknowledged the man by nodding at him and held his hand up to thank him. He took the piece of paper from his pocket with the address and looked at the building opposite to see if he could match the name of the street with the address he was given. Unfortunately, there was no street sign, so George looked up to see if the street name was on the building behind them. There was no street sign on either side of the road, so George approached the man who helped them.

"Do you speak English?" he asked.

"What?" the man asked in Portuguese.

"English, do you speak English?"

The man shrugged his shoulders and shook his head from side to side.

"No English," he said.

George showed the man the piece of paper with the address on it.

"Do you know where this is?" he slowly asked.

The man looked at the paper, then at George, and smiled. He pointed diagonally across the road at the opposite corner.

"There," he said.

George turned around to look across the road and was confronted by a small crowd that had gathered around them. The people were interested in the couple and why they were there, especially in a place where tourists rarely ventured. George and Maggie were out of their comfort zone and felt a sense of unease. Maggie tried to listen to the conversation at all times, but made sure she held onto the luggage securely.

"Where is it?" she asked.

George pointed to the building across the junction.

"Over there," he replied, "let's go."

The couple pushed their way through the small crowd, dragging their luggage behind them. The road was busy with traffic, and could not be easily crossed. So, George turned his head to the man who helped them.

"Thank you," he shouted in Portuguese.

He waved at the man, who waved back in acknowledgement. Then a young man nearby realised the couple's predicament and stopped the traffic to allow George and Maggie to cross the road. Compliments were exchanged with the man, and the couple made their way to the establishment across the street.

The building happened to be a small hotel, looking somewhat dishevelled and in need of much repair. It could be a possible place for the couple to stay. George and Maggie approached the front door and peered in to see a man standing behind the counter at the back of the lobby. An Alsatian dog lay asleep on the floor next to the counter and was awoken by the presence of the couple. The dog barked loudly and ran to the door, where he blocked the entrance and stood there growling.

"What now?" Maggie asked.

"I don't know," George replied, "I suppose we go in."

They stepped forward to enter the building, but the dog growled again, making the couple retreat backwards.

"Shoo!" George shouted at the dog.

This made the dog angrier and caused him to growl even more. The man at the counter realised the couple were trying to enter the hotel, and decided to call off the dog.

"Here, boy," he said to the dog in Portuguese.

The dog obeyed the command and ran inside to lie down next to the counter. The man approached the door and saw George and Maggie standing on the pavement. He immediately detected from their appearance that they were not local and beckoned for them to enter.

"Come on in," he said in English, "he'll not harm you, come in."

The couple gingerly entered the lobby and saw the dog lying next to a well-dressed man standing at the bottom of some stairs.

"George?" the man asked, holding out his hand.

"Yes," George replied.

The man shook hands with George.

"I'm Antonio," he said, "at last we meet."

Antonio then turned to Maggie.

"You must be Mrs George?"

"Maggie," she replied, "my name is Maggie."

"I am very pleased to meet you both."

"Likewise," George said.

"Did you have a good journey from the airport?" Antonio asked.

"So-so," George said.

"Come, let's go and have a coffee in the lounge," Antonio said, "leave your luggage here, it will be alright."

He beckoned for them to go through a doorway into the lounge and allowed the couple to enter the room first. He then turned to the man behind the counter.

"Can you get coffee for us?" he asked in Portuguese.

The other man nodded, and Antonio followed the couple into the lounge.

George and Maggie scanned the room and noticed it needed decorating. In fact, since they approached and entered the building, they sensed the property was dilapidated. Antonio detected the couple's distaste.

"Let me explain," he said, "be seated, make yourself at home."

All three sat down, and the couple looked at Antonio for an explanation. He looked up at the surrounding room and then at the couple.

"I know it's not the Rio Othon, but it's somewhere you can stay, and it will be safe."

Maggie was surprised at Antonio's comment.

"Safe!" she uttered.

"Yes, safe. It would be better for you if you remained hidden for a few days."

"It's a bit unnerving being in this district," George said.

"Yes, it may seem so, but let me assure you, the people mean well. You will be safe here."

George looked at Maggie and shrugged his shoulders. He noticed she was disgusted and knew it was not what she expected. They both squirmed their faces, and in view of the recent escapades, reluctantly felt they should accept Antonio's advice.

"Oh, a word of warning, though," Antonio said, "We are on the edge of a favela, and although we are safe here, it is probably not wise to enter it. Well, at least, not on your own. It could be dangerous."

Maggie felt uneasy with Antonio's remark and clasped her hands nervously.

"What sort of danger?" she asked.

Antonio sat forward in the chair to clarify himself.

"Let me explain," Antonio said, "there are many gangs in the favela, and they fight each other for dominance."

"Gangs?" George asked.

"Yes, gangs. They have many guns and shootouts, and many people get killed each year. It seems to be a way of life for them in the favela."

"So, are we definitely safe here?" George asked.

"Yes, I believe so," Antonio replied, "there seems to be an unwritten code that the people live by within the favelas, a gang culture code, you could say. The police, to an extent, leave the favelas to run autonomously, and will only intervene if the fighting spills out onto the streets outside the favelas. So, the gangs all over Rio stick to the code rigidly, and only fight within the favelas, which makes us safe here."

"If you say so," George said.

The conversation was interrupted when coffee was served. He placed the coffee on the table in front of the trio and left the room without saying anything. Antonio continued with the conversation.

"Now tell me you two. What trouble are you in?" he asked.

George proceeded to tell Antonio about the escapades of the last two days, Antonio interjecting occasionally. It lasted for about half an hour, and at the end, all three sat in silence. Antonio contemplated the next move. He was keen to know about the package, and looked at Maggie, then at the ceiling, and finally at George.

"Do you have the package?" Antonio asked.

"Yes, I do," George replied.

"With you?"

"Yes."

"Can I have it now?"

"Yes, of course you can, but first the money."

"What money?" Antonio asked.

Antonio seemed surprised at George's request, and George was confused as to why he would ask such a question. George thought about Antonio's comment and rubbed his chin in bewilderment.

"The money, you know, the money for the package," George said.

Antonio remained silent, a little bemused. He seemed unaware of the exchange of money for the package, and George sensed something was wrong. He looked over to Maggie, who was also bewildered. George recalled a conversation with Antonio about the exchange of the package when speaking to him on the phone at the Rio Othon hotel a few days earlier. George thought it strange that Antonio was unaware of the exchange, and it put doubts in his mind about the man. Was the person sitting across from him really Antonio? George looked at him and noticed that his body language seemed uncomfortable. George decided to change the story.

"Well, Antonio," George continued, "When I said I had the package earlier, I didn't mean I brought it here."

Antonio looked surprised at George.

"What!" he exclaimed, "What do you mean?"

George was not telling the truth; the package was in the travel bag next to him, but he felt there was something untoward and was unwilling to hand over the package to the man sitting opposite him. Maggie was unsure what George was up to and looked at him anxiously.

"I placed it in a luggage compartment at the airport for safekeeping," George said.

"Why?" Antonio asked.

"I wanted to be sure I got the money, that's why."

Antonio felt George was using delaying tactics and stood up in disgust. He cuffed his right hand and shook it in the air.

"Oh! for crying out loud," he uttered in Portuguese.

He pointed and waved his index finger at George and reverted to English.

"You're beginning to annoy me, Mr Englishman," he said, "You're beginning to annoy me."

George and Maggie realised the meeting was not going well and both stood up. Antonio stormed out of the lounge and into the hotel lobby, where he could be heard shouting in Portuguese at the man behind the counter. George and Maggie thought it was time to leave and grabbed their hand luggage. They exited the lounge through a door at the rear of the room, which led along a passageway towards the kitchen, where they found an old woman with a knife in her hand. She was chopping vegetables and was alarmed to see the couple, but did not say a word to them. The couple brushed past her and exited the building by the back door. They entered a dimly lit street and ran away as fast as they could from the hotel.

"What about our luggage?" Maggie asked.

"We'll have to forget them," George said.

"But they contain all our belongings."

145

"Do you want to go back there? I think it would be dangerous, and I don't think that man was Antonio."

Maggie agreed with George, and the couple continued running away from the hotel.

The man calling himself Antonio was not the real Antonio and turned out to be an imposter. His name was Julio, one of the gang members, and he posed as Antonio. Julio returned to the lounge to find the couple gone and immediately ran back out to the lobby.

"The couple have gone," he shouted at the man behind the counter, "Quick, phone Marco and Fabio, and let them know what's going on."

Marco and Fabio were the two Brazilians who followed the couple from England, and it was Fabio who accosted George on the plane to Brazil. The man behind the counter telephoned them immediately, while Julio ran towards the kitchen, and was fuming when he entered it.

"Where are they?" Julio asked the cook in an angry voice.

She looked up, shrugged her shoulders, and pointed to the back door. Julio went to the door and popped his head outside, but could not see the couple.

"Shit!" he shouted.

He ran back to the lobby, just as the man behind the counter finished the call.

"What did they say?" Julio asked.

"They are coming over," the man replied, "They reckon the couple can't get far on foot, so we should wait for them here."

Julio anxiously tapped on the counter and looked around the lobby. He noticed the couple's luggage in the corner and made his way over to it.

"Let's see what's in here," he said.

He tried to open one of the cases, but it was secured with a padlock.

"Shit, it's locked," he said, "bring me a screwdriver."

The other man searched under the counter and found a screwdriver, which he handed to Julio.

"You open the other case," Julio said to the man, while grabbing the screwdriver.

Julio wrenched at the lock with the tool until he opened the case. The other man took the screwdriver and opened the other case in the same way. They threw all the items from the cases onto the floor until all were strewn in a mess. The men did not care about the couple's belongings; their ultimate aim was to find the package. The cases were completely emptied, but the package was not found.

Meanwhile, George and Maggie headed towards the favela and were noticed by people loitering on the side of the streets.

"You don't want to go in there," a passer-by shouted in Portuguese.

"You're asking for trouble," another shouted.

George and Maggie did not understand much Portuguese and entered the favela anyway. Most favelas were built on the side of hills that surrounded Rio, and on land inappropriate for building houses. Favelas were an assembly of small shacks, mostly attached to or on top of each other. The thoroughfares were small passageways and stairs which ascended the hills, and some criss-crossed each other horizontally. George and Maggie ascended one of these stairways, closely watched by surprised inhabitants out late at night, who did not expect to see tourists in the favela. The passageways were dimly lit, and it wasn't easy to identify people passing by. The couple ran without knowledge of the surrounding area, and soon found themselves completely lost. The time was now around midnight.

"Where are we going?" Maggie asked.

"Just getting away," George replied.

The couple continued to ascend the stairs in the favela, but were somewhat exhausted.

"Stop! I'm tired," Maggie shouted.

George and Maggie were out of breath and stopped running. They were breathing heavily and took a couple of minutes to recover from the gruelling climb. Dogs were barking in the distance, and the sound of music could be heard across the favela. There was the sound of a car backfiring in the distance, but in truth, it was probably gunshots from the gangs in the favela, who were becoming active for the night. George and Maggie felt scared and hugged each other for mutual comfort.

"Let's think about this," George said.

"What do you mean?" Maggie asked.

"Well, the Brazilians don't know where we are, do they? That's to our advantage, but on the negative side, we've entered the favela, which is a dangerous place."

"So, what do we do now?"

"I don't know, let's think. Any suggestions?"

"No, I can't think of any."

"I can't either."

George and Maggie looked around in all directions to determine which way to go when someone spoke from a dark corner.

"Need some help, Boss?" the voice said in English.

The voice startled the couple, who turned to see a young man coming towards them. He was holding hands with a young lady, and they both smiled at George and Maggie as they approached. The young couple were snogging in the dark corner for a while, and were interrupted by George and Maggie's presence.

"Need help?" the young man repeated.

"Yes, we do," George replied, "we're lost, can you help us?"

"You shouldn't be in here," the young man said, "no tourists here, very dangerous."

"We're trying to hide from a criminal gang," George said.

"In here?" the young man asked sarcastically, "Very clever, gangs all over."

The young man then scanned the couple from head to foot.

"You, the English people everyone is talking about?"

"I guess so," George replied.

"Can you help us?" Maggie asked.

"I don't know," the young man replied, "Maybe you can help me out."

George immediately detected that the young man was hustling for money and put his hand in his pocket to withdraw some cash. The young lady with him did not understand English, but realised her boyfriend was trying to extort money from the couple. She hit her boyfriend solidly on the arm.

"What are you doing?" she asked him in Portuguese, "can't you see these people are scared and need some help."

The young man looked at his girlfriend coyly and smiled at her. He looked back at George and raised his hand, as if to say, 'No, I don't want your money.' The young man then pointed across the favela.

"Go in that direction, you don't want to go back in the direction you came. Much safer this way."

The young man grabbed his girlfriend's hand, and they wandered off into the darkness. George and Maggie were perplexed at the meeting and stood there contemplating where to go next. They followed the young man's instructions and headed off across the favela.

Meanwhile, Marco and Fabio arrived at the hotel and were greeted by Julio in the lobby.

"What a mess!" Marco said to Julio, What a fucking mess?"

"Sorry, boss," Julio said.

Marco shook his head from side to side and tutted to indicate he was not pleased with Julio's actions.

"Which way did they go?" he asked.

Julio felt embarrassed that he lost the couple and wanted to make up for the mistake. He was overly keen to help Marco and Fabio find the couple.

"Not sure, boss, they ran out the back door, and onto the streets."

"Well, someone must have seen them. Did you go and ask?"

"No, boss, we waited here as you said."

Marco was disappointed at the reply and tapped his hand on his forehead in disgust.

"Idiot," he said, "What are you? A fucking idiot."

Julio stepped back nervously and bowed his head in shame.

"Yes, boss," he replied.

Marco was angry at Julio and wanted him to know it.

"Have I got to do your work as well?" he asked.

"No, boss, my mistake."

Marco and Fabio headed outside to the street, and were followed by Julio. They searched the vicinity in the hope of finding the couple. They also asked a few people if they had seen them, but without luck. They walked further along the street and were approached by an old man.

"I know the direction in which the couple went," the old man said.

"Where?" Fabio asked.

The old man waited a few seconds, stared at the threesome, and opened one of his hands.

"Life's tough here, mister, very tough."

Marco realised what the old man wanted, and nudged Fabio.

"Ok, old man, you better be right," Fabio said.

He handed a 20 Real note to the man, which surprised him, and produced a big smile on his face. The man was keen to inform the threesome where he had seen the couple, so he pointed towards the favela.

"In there. They've gone in there," he said.

The threesome, happy with the information they needed, pushed the old man aside to get by. The old man was pleased, though, and waved the 20 Real note in the air as he watched the men rush towards the favela.

The three men entered the favela and asked people along the way if they had seen the English couple. It worked out well for the threesome, and they got the answers they wanted. Most people were scared of gangs and were afraid to lie. The men slowly followed the trail of the couple into the depths of the favela. By now, George and Maggie instinctively made their way through the narrow passages and were unsure which way to go, so they proceeded slowly. The three men came upon the young couple who spoke to George and Maggie earlier and stopped them to ask a few questions.

"Have you seen an English couple walking through here tonight?" Marco asked.

The young couple did not want to answer and tried to dodge the question by walking away.

"Hey! I'm talking to you, you little prick," Marco said.

Marco ran after the young couple and grabbed hold of the young man's arm.

"Where do you think you are going?" Marco asked, "I asked you a question."

The young man was scared and realised the men might be the gang following the couple, whom George mentioned earlier. The men had serious intentions, and the young man knew they would persist in their questions.

"I know nothing," he said, "nothing."

Fabio detected that the young man might not be telling the truth and pointed the pistol at his head.

"You sure?" Fabio asked, "I think you're lying."

Fabio pushed the gun barrel into the man's head, which made him cower down. His girlfriend tried to get Fabio off of him, and was soon pulled back by Julio.

"Yes, I'm sure," the young man said.

Fabio then released the safety catch on the gun, which made a loud click, causing the young man to tremble.

"No!" he shouted, "no!"

His girlfriend, being held by Julio, became concerned.

"Tell them." She shouted. "Tell them, it's not worth it."

Fabio tightened the grip on the young man and pushed the gun even harder against his head.

"Ok, ok, I know where they've gone," the young man said.

"Well?" Marco asked, "Where are they?"

"Over there," the young man said, "over there."

The young man pointed across the favela in the same direction he had given to the couple. Fabio then pistol-whipped the man on the head for not providing the information in the first place, and the young man soon fell to the ground. Julio released his hold on the girl, who immediately knelt beside her boyfriend. She began to sob and tried to comfort him.

"You bastards!" she shouted at the men, "you bastards."

The three men ignored the girl's comment and headed off quickly in the direction of the English couple.

Meanwhile, George and Maggie inadvertently strayed into the territory of one of the favela gangs and were approached by four gang members. The four men were surprised to see tourists in the favela so late at night, and wondered why they were there. One of the men walked up to the couple, waved a pistol towards them, and looked them up and down from head to toe.

"What are you doing here?" he asked in Portuguese.

"Yeah! You got no home to go to?" another asked.

A third man was brandishing a machete and came near to the couple.

"Little children out late at night," he said sarcastically.

George and Maggie's hearts began to beat quickly, and they felt they were in immediate danger, so they held on to each other.

"We want no trouble," George shouted, "We just want to get out of here."

The gang members detected that George spoke English and continued to speak in the language.

"No trouble," one of the men said, mimicking a child, "what are you doing here then?"

Maggie was almost in tears and trembled with fear.

"We got lost," she said.

"Ooh! The lady speaks," one of the gang members said sarcastically, "the pretty lady can talk."

The three gang members drew nearer to George and Maggie and brandished their weapons around their heads. The fourth gang member stood back and listened to the conversation.

"Wait!" he shouted in Portuguese, "we have no quarrel with this couple, and they seem lost, let them go. We don't fight tourists, only our rivals."

The fourth member of the gang spoke with authority and seemed to be the leader of the group.

"Let them go?" one surprised gang member asked, "This is an opportunity to make some money, and we could cash in."

"No, let them go," the leader said, "it's not our style."

"But…," the gang member said.

And before he could continue, he was interrupted by the leader. "But what?"

The leader then pointed his gun towards his colleague in a threatening way.

"Who is the leader here, you or me?" he asked.

The gang member backed down, and the others remained silent.

George and Maggie looked on with fascination, and even though they did not understand Portuguese, they appreciated that the gang leader was trying to stamp his authority on the gang. The leader turned towards the couple and waved his gun.

"Go," he said, "Go now, go back from where you came, tourists not welcome here."

All the gang members began to fire their pistols into the air to scare off the couple, while they laughed and shouted expletives. The couple took heed and ran back in the direction from where they came.

Unbeknownst to them, the couple were heading back in the direction of Marco, Fabio and Julio, who were approaching the other way. The three men heard the gunfire in the distance and readied their guns. The passageways and stairways were dimly lit, and the lighting created strange illusions as the couple ran along. It was on one of these long passages that the two groups saw each other from a distance. The couple stopped in their tracks, about forty metres away from the men.

"Oh shit!" George said, "It's the Brazilians, let's go back."

George and Maggie turned around and started to run in the opposite direction. The men soon gained on them, as they had the momentum of running in the direction of the couple.

"Hey! Stop!" Marco shouted.

"Stop, you bastards," Fabio shouted.

The couple kept running, and Julio decided to try another tactic. He stopped running, took aim at the couple with his pistol, and fired a shot. The bullet flew close to Marco's head and hit George in the shoulder. George stumbled for a moment but picked himself up to continue the getaway. Marco and Fabio stopped running and turned to Julio.

"You idiot!" Marco shouted at Julio. "You stupid idiot, you could have killed me, we want them alive."

"Uh!" Julio responded.

All three were out of breath and puffing heavily. Marco walked up to Julio, slapped him on the face with the back of his hand, and took a deep breath.

"You stupid idiot, how are we going to get the package if we kill them?" Marco asked, "Answer me that."

Marco was furious with Julio because he knew they could have lost the couple.

"Sorry, boss," Julio replied, "I didn't think."

In the meantime, Fabio kept an eye on the couple disappearing into the distance.

"Quick, they are getting away," he shouted, "let's get after them."

The three men began to chase George and Maggie again. By now, the couple had a bit of a head start and found a small alley off the passageway.

"Quick, down here," George said.

He shoved Maggie ahead and held his wounded shoulder with the other arm. They were both out of breath, and it was the adrenaline flowing through their bodies that gave them the strength to continue. The alleyway came to a 'T' junction after about thirty metres. They turned right, then left after a few more metres, and continued to run past the homes where most people were asleep. They were now in the depths of the favela, and passed a couple of dogs chained to the walls of houses, causing them to bark and snarl as they ran by. George and Maggie ran past a few people still awake at that time of night, who gave them strange looks. An old man dressed in a green nightshirt came to the doorway and looked outside when he heard the commotion. The couple could hear the voices of the three Brazilian men shouting in the distance, but kept on running. After five minutes, they stopped for a rest, and it was the first time Maggie noticed the blood on the front of George's shirt.

"Oh Crikey!" Maggie cried out, "You've been shot!"

Maggie looked at the wound and noticed the bullet went straight through George's shoulder. George held his arm and slumped against a wall to rest. He was in obvious pain, and at first Maggie seemed unsure what to do, but then her instincts took over.

"Give me your handkerchief," she said.

George reached into his back pocket and handed Maggie the handkerchief. She looked carefully at the wounds on both the front and back of the shoulder, and decided the front was bleeding more than the back. Maggie folded the handkerchief to make a pad and pressed it against the wound on the front of the shoulder.

"Careful!" George cried out in pain.

"Sorry," Maggie said, 'I'm just trying to stop the bleeding."

"I know, but it hurts."

"We have to get you to a hospital."

George and Maggie then heard footsteps coming from the direction they had come, and looked up, but could see no one.

"Let's go," George said.

The couple continued to meander through the favela, but George began to stagger. His strength was draining away, and they were slowing down.

"Hurry up," Maggie said, "we've got to hurry."

They went down the small alleyways, turning left and right at will, not knowing where they were going. They soon realised they went in a big circle when they passed the same doorway with the old man dressed in green still standing in it. They stopped and looked anxiously at him when the man noticed the wound in George's shoulder. He saw the Brazilians run past his home a few moments earlier and assumed they were after the couple. Realising their plight, he beckoned them into his small one-roomed home, and said something in Portuguese. George and Maggie did not understand him, but entered the house and shut the door behind them.

"Thank you so much," Maggie said.

"Yes, thanks," George added.

The old man waved his hand in acknowledgement and beckoned for them to sit on the floor. His home was basic, with two cabinets near the door, and a straw mattress on the floor in the far corner of the room. A few clothes items hung on a line stretched across the room. There was a candle on one of the cabinets, which was the only source of light, giving off a dim flame. George and Maggie felt uneasy in the surroundings, but knew they were safe, at least safer than being in the open. They could hear people running outside, and the voice of Marco shouting as the Brazilians passed the house again. The old man put his index finger to his lips and indicated for the couple to be quiet. Marco, Fabio and Julio passed the house and headed off into the distance.

George and Maggie were desperate, not knowing which way to turn for help. The old man did not have any medical aid either; he had few provisions in the home. He sat down, closed his eyes, and clasped his hands as if in prayer. Maggie tore off a part of her dress and tended to George's shoulder as best as possible.

"Help us," Maggie said to the old man.

The old man opened his eyes, shrugged his shoulders, and looked at the couple blankly. He did not understand English, so Maggie pointed at George's wound.

"You have to help us," Maggie repeated.

The old man understood they wanted him to help with the wound.

"No medicine," the old man said in Portuguese.

He opened his arms to show around the room.

"No medicine."

Maggie understood the man because he shook his head from side to side, and the Portuguese for 'medicine' was recognisable. George grimaced due to the pain in his shoulder and remained silent. He made the effort to stand up.

"I think we need to get going," he said.

"Wait," Maggie said, "you shouldn't move at the moment."

"No, don't move," the old man also said.

"We can't stay here; you have to get me to a hospital," George said.

Maggie looked over to the old man.

"Hospital," she said very slowly.

"Ah! Hospital!" the old man said.

He recognised the word; it was the same in Portuguese as it was in English. In fact, the old man spoke in Portuguese all the time. He stood up and went over to the door.

"I'll show you," he said, "come."

He beckoned for the couple to come over, so Maggie helped George as he hobbled over to the door. The old man opened the door slowly and peered out. He could not see anyone, so he went outside and looked around again to see if anyone was nearby. As no one was around, he beckoned for the couple to come out and indicated that they follow him along the alleyway.

"This way," he said.

George and Maggie slowly followed the man along the meandering paths. There was no haste; the old man was frail and walked with a limp. He took them through different alleyways, which seemed to the couple like a rabbit warren, but the old man knew the quickest way out of the favela. He lived there for most of his life and knew the passageways like the back of his hand. They passed no one on the way and eventually emerged from the favela onto a brightly lit street. The old man beckoned to the street with his hand.

"You can get a taxi here," he said.

Again, the couple recognised the word for 'taxi' and Maggie shook the old man's hand to thank him for his help. George tried to get some money from his pocket to pay the old man in gratitude for his kindness, but the old man waved his hands from side to side.

"No, no money," the old man said, "It is a pleasure to help you. It makes me feel good to be of assistance."

George and Maggie smiled at the old man and waved goodbye as they hobbled along the street. The man waved back and soon disappeared into the dimly lit favela.

George and Maggie walked along the road for about five minutes when they heard a car approaching from behind. They were hoping it was a taxi and tried to flag it down, but the car was privately owned, so the driver ignored them and drove on. They walked further and came to a junction where there was a greater chance of hailing a taxi. Unsure of their location, they waited for one to pass by. As luck would have it, an off-duty taxi was approaching, and Maggie jumped out in front of it. The cab screeched to a halt and almost hit Maggie, but she was determined to stop it. The driver put his head out of the window and shouted in Portuguese.

"What the fuck are you doing, woman?"

Maggie was adamant about keeping the car there and remained in front of it.

"We need help," Maggie replied, "We need to go to a hospital."

The driver understood Maggie and replied in English.

"I'm off duty, woman, can't you see, no taxi lights on."

He pointed to the light on top of the taxi, but Maggie wasn't having it and pointed at George standing on the pavement.

"My husband is hurt," Maggie shouted, "we need to go to a hospital urgently."

The driver looked over at George, leaning against a lamp post and saw the blood on George's shirt.

"No way," he said, "I don't want any trouble. I go home."

"Please help," Maggie said, "he's losing blood fast."

The driver waved for Maggie to move away from the front of the car, and revved the engine a few times, but Maggie stood her ground.

"Move woman, move out of the way," he shouted.

At that moment, George passed out and slumped onto the concrete pavement. Maggie quickly ran over to help him, and the taxi driver saw his chance to get away. He revved the engine and, with screeching tyres, sped off quickly down the road. After a few seconds, the driver slammed on the brakes, and the car screeched to a halt. He then reversed the car to go and help the couple. No one knew what changed his mind, but maybe he felt compassionate and realised they really needed some help. As soon as he reached them, he jumped out of the car and went over to help.

"I know a hospital nearby," he said, "I'll take you."

"Thank you so much," Maggie said.

The driver and Maggie lifted George into the back seat of the taxi, and Maggie also sat in the back of the car with George's head on her lap. The driver hurriedly drove to the nearest hospital.

The taxi approached the emergency entrance to the hospital, and the driver honked the car horn furiously. This had the desired effect, and two medics hearing the noise immediately ran out to help. They looked into the back of the car, saw the state of George, and without hesitation summoned a stretcher. George was lifted onto the stretcher and taken into the hospital with Maggie constantly by his side. The taxi driver, not wanting to be involved, decided to leave and sped away immediately. George was treated for the gunshot wound with no questions asked about the incident; the medics just carried out their professional duties. The treatment for a gunshot wound was a normal occurrence at the hospital; it was the closest medical centre to the favela, where gang fights were always happening. George was kept in the hospital overnight, and Maggie slept in a single bed, specially assembled for her in the same room as George.

Chapter 10 – Finding Antonio

The next morning, at about 8 am, the couple didn't appreciate that someone was in the room and were abruptly awoken by a woman who brought them breakfast. She was an overweight woman with a bubbly character who spoke in Portuguese.

"Here you are," she said, "breakfast time."

The woman served the breakfast and left the room before George and Maggie could thank her. Maggie sat up in bed, stretched her arms, and looked over at George. He was awakening from a deep sleep induced by medication.

"How's your shoulder?" she asked.

"It feels good, but it still hurts," he replied.

Maggie went over to George to check the bandages on his shoulder and was surprised by the excellent job done by the medical staff. The couple were hungry and spent the next twenty minutes eating breakfast. It was the first time in ages they were able to feel relaxed. After breakfast, Maggie went over to take in the view from the window, while George sat back in the bed to rest. The room was situated on the first floor and fitted with all the modern technology you would expect in a large city hospital.

Soon after, a doctor entered the room, accompanied by another man in a grey suit.

"Good morning, Mr Peacock," the doctor said.

He turned to Maggie and acknowledged her with a nod of the head.

"Mrs Peacock," he said.

George and Maggie both responded to the greeting.

"And, how are we today?" the doctor asked George.

"Much better, thanks."

"Good, that's what I like to hear. Now let's have a look at your bandages."

The doctor went over to George to check the bandages and was satisfied they were ok. He then turned and pointed to the man in the grey suit.

"This is Inspector Fernandes," the doctor said, "He is from the local police, and would like to ask you a few questions."

George and Maggie looked at each other, shocked to know that the police were involved so soon. George knew the inspector would inquire about the shooting.

"What sort of questions?" George asked.

"I want you to tell me how and why you were shot," the inspector said. "Is this a good time to speak to you?"

George and Maggie remained silent for a while and looked at each other again.

"I guess so," George replied.

The doctor felt his tasks were completed and decided to leave the room.

"I'll leave you to it then," he said.

He bid his farewells, waved goodbye, and left the room. The inspector sat down next to George and took out a notepad.

"Now, what can you tell me? Start at the beginning," he said.

George needed to think up a false story quickly; he did not want to tell the inspector the real story. He remained silent for a moment, contemplating a story.

"Well?" the inspector asked.

"Well, it's like this," George said.

He looked over to Maggie and noticed her concern; she was unsure what he was going to say next. George looked the inspector in the eyes.

"We were foolish," George continued, "very foolish. We were warned not to go to the favelas on our own, but as we are quite adventurous, we decided to ignore the warning. We were advised to go on an organised trip, but we wanted to experience the favelas for ourselves. So, we went into the one just down the road."

"I see," the inspector said, "continue."

"Well, we came to this area from the hotel…"

The inspector interrupted George.

"And what hotel is that?" he asked.

"Er, the Othon. The Rio Othon."

"The Othon Palace," the inspector repeated, "the one at Copacabana beach."

"Yes," George said, "that's the one."

The inspector wrote the details in the notepad, and George continued.

"Then we got lost..."

The inspector interrupted George again.

"Hold on a moment," he said, "Why did you come all the way from Copacabana to this favela? It's quite far, and there are others closer to the hotel."

The question caught George off guard, so he needed to think of an answer.

"Er, um, this was the one we were taken to."

"Taken to? Who by?" the inspector asked.

Again, George needed to think of an answer and looked towards Maggie for inspiration.

"The taxi driver," Maggie said, "the taxi driver brought us to this favela."

The inspector looked at the couple and seemed unsure of their replies.

"Hmm! I see. Why did he bring you to this one?"

"I don't know," George said, "he just did. We asked him to take us to a favela, and he brought us here."

The inspector then wrote some more notes in the notepad.

"Go on," he said.

"We went into the favela and got lost," George continued.

"Got lost?" the inspector asked.

George did not want to tell the inspector that they were being followed by the Brazilian criminals and continued with the false story.

"Yes, we managed to find our way into the favela, and then we got lost in there."

"I see," the inspector said.

He then turned to Maggie.

"Is that your recollection as well, Mrs Peacock?"

Maggie was caught unawares by the question.

"Yes, yes," Maggie stuttered.

"Go on, Mr Peacock," the inspector said to George.

"Well, there is not much more to tell you. We came upon a group of men with guns..."

"What men? Do you mean a gang?" the inspector asked.

"Yes, that's right, a gang. They were waving their guns all around and were shouting at us. We ran away, and they shot at us, and that's when I got hit by the bullet."

The inspector continued to write his notes, and George looked over to Maggie with his eyebrows raised. She gave George the thumbs up without the inspector noticing, to indicate the story sounded plausible.

"Is that all?" the inspector asked.

"Yes, we then ran out of the favela back to the lighted streets, and hailed a cab which brought us here."

The inspector wrote some more notes and then rubbed his chin while looking at George intensely.

"So, how did you find your way out of the favela?" he asked.

George needed to think of an answer quickly, but this time he could tell the inspector the truth.

"We ran away from the gang and came across an old man..."

Maggie then piped in with a comment.

"Yes, and he showed us the way out of the favela."

The inspector wrote some more notes and rubbed his chin again, while looking up at the ceiling.

"So, I can check you are staying at the Rio Othon Palace?" he asked.

George knew he needed to lie to the inspector again, for they had checked out of the hotel days earlier.

"Yes, sure. We're registered there."

The inspector closed the notepad and stood up.

"Ok, that's all for now," he said, "I hope you feel better, Mr Peacock."

"Thank you," George said.

The inspector made his way to the door and seemed unconvinced by the answers the couple gave. He turned around to face them.

"If I need to talk to you again, you will be here, or at the Rio Othon, yes?"

George nodded affirmatively, and the inspector left the room. The couple were somewhat dumbfounded and looked at each other.

"Phew!" Maggie exclaimed.

George then rubbed his forehead a few times.

"Phew is right," he said.

Maggie then ran over to George to give him a big hug for the excellent performance he had just given.

They knew they had to leave the hospital immediately, before any more questions were asked.

"What are we going to do?" Maggie asked.

"We've got to sneak out of the hospital without anyone seeing us," George said, "we can't stay here any longer."

Maggie placed her hand gently on George's damaged shoulder. "Are you up for it?" she asked, "A gunshot wound is a serious thing, and you've only just had your shoulder bandaged."

George looked at his shoulder and rubbed it to see if there was any pain.

"I don't know, we'll have to try," he said.

"Where shall we go?" Maggie asked.

"Let's decide on that when we get out. We need to leave soon. Quick, pass me my..."

At that moment, the door to the room opened, and the same doctor who treated George entered the room, which took the couple by surprise.

"Hello again," the doctor said, "Did everything go all right with the inspector?"

"Yes, fine," George replied.

"Good, I just wanted to talk to you about payment for your treatment. Do you have medical insurance?"

The couple had medical insurance coverage, but George did not want their personal details to be known. He looked at Maggie and thought he would continue the conversation to appease the doctor.

"Ah, Am, yes. Yes, we do," he stuttered.

"Good, I just wanted to make sure. We'll probably keep you in for a day or two until you are fine."

"Is it going to take that long?" Maggie asked.

"Yes, we need to make sure Mr Peacock is well before he can leave the hospital."

"Ok by me, if that is necessary," George said.

"Good," the doctor said, "That's settled."

The doctor headed for the door, but stopped in his tracks and turned around.

"One other thing," he said, "someone in administration will come to see you about the payment of your bill. I hope that's alright. Bye for now, I've got to see other patients."

The doctor left the room, and in view of the circumstances, the couple decided to leave the hospital immediately.

George eased himself out of the bed slowly, grabbed his clothes, and got dressed. The hospital had given him a new shirt in exchange for the one covered in blood. Maggie, on the other hand, slept in her clothes, which were slightly crushed, but they were the only clothes she had with her. Maggie quickly brushed her teeth with a toothbrush provided by the hospital, and George did the same. They grabbed their hand luggage, which they always kept close to them at all times, and went to the door. Maggie opened it slowly and looked out to check if anyone was around. A nurse passing by in the corridor noticed her.

"Good morning," the nurse said.

Maggie was not expecting to see anyone and was taken aback. "Good morning," she replied.

Maggie quickly closed the door and waited a few seconds. She opened the door again and looked outside once more. This time, no one was around, so the couple left the room and walked along the corridor slowly, but with extra attentiveness. They listened out for other people, and as they approached the administrative area for that floor, they heard voices.

"What shall we do now?" Maggie whispered to George.

"Keep going," he said.

The couple shuffled along further and heard footsteps approaching in another corridor. They paused in their tracks and looked at each other. Luckily for them, there was an exit door about two metres away, and the couple dashed for it. The door would not open at first, and the footsteps were getting closer. The couple were panicking, and both shoved hard on the security bar of the door. It eventually opened, and the couple rushed through, closing it shut in the nick of time. The person approaching soon came around the corner and stopped on the other side of the door. All the couple could do was to stand still and remain silent. Their hearts pounded quickly when they heard the person on the other side test the push bar for the door. George and Maggie were terrified, but soon relaxed when the person walked away. The door led them into a stairwell, which happened to be one of the emergency exits.

"Let's go," George whispered.

He took Maggie's hand, and the couple made their way down the stairwell to the ground floor, where there was an exit door to the car park. The couple left the building, walked quickly across the car park, and into a busy street. They were relieved to get away from the hospital and felt free once again as they walked along.

The couple were on their own once again, and the only possessions they had with them, apart from their hand luggage, were the clothes they wore. Their suitcases were left at the hotel near the favela, where they met Julio, the man who called himself Antonio. It would not be wise to return to the hotel to collect the luggage, however tempting. Nevertheless, their hand luggage contained their personal belongings, including the travel documents, cash, and most importantly, their credit cards. They also had the package with them, the dreaded package that caused all the problems in the first place. What were they to do now? And, whatever happened to the real Antonio who helped them before? He was the only friendly contact the couple knew in Rio.

George and Maggie strolled along the street in search of a taxi.

"We need to get settled somewhere," George said.

"What do you mean?" Maggie asked.

"We need to find a place to stay, and we need to buy some clothes."

"Where are we going to do that?"

"I don't know. Let's get a taxi and head back to Copacabana."

"Why there?"

"Well, it's an area we know, and it's safer than where we are now."

George and Maggie walked further and came upon a taxi rank. They were approached by one of the taxi drivers.

"Taxi boss?" the driver asked.

"Yes, please," George replied.

The couple entered the back of the taxi and were driven to Copacabana. George asked the driver to stop outside a department store near the destination, allowing them to buy some clothes and other personal items, including hats and sunglasses. Exiting the store, they asked a security guard if he knew of bed and breakfast accommodation nearby. They thought it best not to return to the Rio Othon Palace hotel on Copacabana beach. The guard suggested a location, not far away, where there were Bed and Breakfast accommodations at reasonable prices.

The couple walked in the direction the security guard suggested and found a house advertising itself as Bed and Breakfast. It was situated two blocks inland away from Copacabana beach. They rang the doorbell, and after a short time, a well-dressed middle-aged woman opened the door.

"We're here about the accommodation," George said.

The lady remained silent and looked at the couple from head to foot in a snotty sort of way. George was unsure if she understood him.

"Do you speak English?" he asked.

"Yes, I do," the woman replied. How can I help you?"

"We are here about a room."

The woman looked over the couple again, ensuring she was happy with their appearance. Sometimes, first impressions can indicate a person's character.

"Ok, come in," the woman said.

She led them into the lounge and beckoned for them to sit down.

"How long do you wish to stay?" she asked.

"Just two nights," Maggie replied, "we fly out the day after tomorrow."

"Oh!" the landlady said, "where are you from?"

"England," George and Maggie replied.

"Ah! A lovely country. I've been there many times."

The landlady now felt a lot more comfortable with George and Maggie knowing they were tourists.

"I charge 165 Real per night," she said, "is that alright?"

George and Maggie looked at each other, and not knowing the rates for Bed and Breakfast in Rio, they nodded their heads in agreement anyway.

"That's fine," George said, "we just need a place for two nights, and the rate will be fine."

"Oh, good," the landlady said, "the room is ready, let me show it to you."

She took George and Maggie to the back of the house and up some stairs to the room on the first floor. It was a large double-bedded room with an en-suite bathroom. The landlady showed them around and informed them of the time breakfast was served. She sensed the couple were somewhat jaded.

"You both seem very tired, and I guess you must have been very busy. Can I make you some tea?" the landlady asked.

"Oh, yes, please," Maggie replied. "That would be nice."

The landlady left the room, and the couple threw the bags onto the bed.

"So far so good," George said.

The couple sat down on the bed to rest their weary legs.

"What next?" Maggie asked.

"We need to find the real Antonio, but we can't use the telephone number I was given."

"Why not?"

"Well, we rang the number at the airport, and got through to the fake Antonio, so the gang must have found the number somehow."

"Yes, that's true. So, what can we do?"

"We'll have to find another way to get in touch with him."

"How do we do that?"

George scratched his head and thought for a while.

"The Brazilians must have found Antonio somehow," he said, "Let me think."

George lay back on the bed, his hands behind his head, and looked up at the ceiling.

"The only lead I could think of was the house where you were being held," George said.

"What about it?"

"We need to go back there to see if we can find out anything."

Maggie was furious at George's suggestion.

"You must be joking. I'm not going back there," she said.

"Well, can you think of anything better to do?"

"No, I cannot, but I'm not going back to that house, period. Can we not forget about the whole thing and go home?"

"We can, but what about the money?"

Maggie became angrier at George, and it showed in her raised voice.

"Is the money worth it? Was it worth the traumas we've been through? For Christ's sake, George, you were nearly killed."

"I see your point, but the money will help to pay off our debts back home."

Maggie then folded her arms to show her indignation.

"Hmm!" she said, "I don't like it."

The landlady returned a few minutes later with the tea and was let into the room by Maggie.

"I've brought you some Brazilian biscuits as well," the landlady said, "to remind you of my country. I hope you like them."

The landlady departed, and the couple sat silently for a while. After a few minutes, Maggie decided to go along with George's suggestion and jumped up from the bed.

"Right, let's do it," she said, "let's not waste any more time, let's go now."

The couple agreed to take basic items with them, cash and credit cards, and to leave everything else in the room. They took the map of Rio and their hats and sunglasses, which would at least help with a disguise. George made sure the package was well hidden at the back of the wardrobe in the room. The couple left the accommodation soon afterwards and caught a taxi to take them to the house off the Sambadrome where Maggie had previously been held.

George and Maggie arrived at the Sambadrome about 20 minutes later. They put on their hats and sunglasses and exited the taxi, about 50 metres walking distance from the house. It was a warm sunny day, and the hats and sunglasses were appropriate, if not only for a disguise.

"Right, let's go," George said, "we have to be extremely careful."

"Wait, hold on," Maggie said, "what are we actually trying to achieve here?"

"Well, this is the only place we know that might give us some information as to the whereabouts of Antonio. The last time we rang him, we were set up, so we need to find anything that can give us a lead to him."

"Ok, but we'll have to be careful."

"Too right. Let's go and check out the place first."

The couple walked along the Sambadrome towards the house. The main Carnival days were over, and a few street parties were still ongoing, but the Sambadrome was almost devoid of people. The couple reached the side road off the Sambadrome, where the house was located, where Maggie was confined.

"Let's pass by the street first and make out we're tourists, we can nonchalantly glance down the road to check the house," George said.

He took Maggie by the hand, and they walked past the side street, looking in all directions, pretending to be tourists. No one could be seen in the street where the house was located, so they turned around and walked back. They stopped at the top of the street to get a better glimpse of the house, and at that moment, two men came out from the house and stood in front of it. George and Maggie felt nervous and continued to walk past the street.

"We need to get into the house somehow," George said, "but there are people there, and we don't know how many; we only saw two men."

"I know what we can do," Maggie said, "Why don't we create a diversion to get them out of the house?"

"A diversion!" George exclaimed, "That's a good idea, what kind of diversion?"

"I don't know. Maybe we could think of something."

George thought Maggie's idea was a good one and began to think of what they could do to create a diversion.

"It could be risky," he said.

"I know, but we've been taking risks all along. What's another one?"

George was surprised at Maggie's comment and looked at her strangely.

"That's bullish of you!" he said.

They walked further along the Sambadrome and turned around after a few minutes. As they approached the side road again, George noticed a heap of rubbish on the ground at the junction with the side road, which gave him inspiration for an idea.

"What do you think about this?" George asked.

"What?" Maggie replied.

George pointed to the rubbish on the ground.

"It would be risky, but we could set fire to this heap of rubbish," he said.

This time, it was Maggie who was surprised at George.

"Set fire to it!" she said. "Isn't that going to be dangerous?"

"Yes, it is, and as I said before, whatever we do would be very risky."

"Sounds too risky to me. What if it causes a big fire?"

"We'll have to take the chance, maybe in all the commotion, the men will come out of the house."

"So how are we going to set fire to the rubbish?" Maggie asked.

"We need some matches, we need to find a shop," George replied.

They both looked around the Sambadrome, and Maggie noticed a kiosk about 100 metres away. She pointed in the direction of the kiosk.

"Maybe there," she said.

The couple went over to the kiosk and purchased a box of matches. They returned to the rubbish heap and waited until no one was around before setting it on fire. The couple walked away quickly as the flames took hold, and the rubbish began to burn. They turned around to look at the burning debris.

"Fire!" George shouted, "Fire!"

Other people were now close by and also shouted 'Fire' while one man used his mobile phone to call the emergency services. By now, a large crowd had gathered around the fire, and the plan seemed to be working. About five minutes later, fire sirens could be heard in the distance, and they were louder as they got closer to the Sambadrome. Many people now surrounded the fire, and their shouts and the sounds of the sirens created a terrific din. It had the desired effect the couple wanted, and three men came running from the house on the side street. They went to investigate the commotion and allowed the couple to approach and enter the house without being seen.

"Quick, let's go," George said.

He took Maggie's hand, and they slowly walked down the side street towards the house. The couple glanced back a few times to make sure the men were still occupied at the fire. George and Maggie carefully approached the house and noticed the door was open. It must have been left open when the three men left the house in a hurry. George knocked on the door and put his head inside the doorway.

"Anyone there?" he asked.

There was no reply.

"Anyone there?" he asked again in a louder voice.

There was still no reply, and George turned to Maggie.

"You stay at the door and let me know if the men are coming back," he said, "and I'll go inside to search for anything relevant."

"Ok," Maggie said, "I'll shout if I see them returning."

George stepped inside the ground-floor lobby and entered the room on the left. Maggie, meanwhile, hid in the doorway to the house so as not to be seen. George opened the drawers of a sideboard and rummaged through some papers, but could not find anything useful, so he returned to the lobby.

"Everything ok?" he asked Maggie.

"Yes, they're not coming back yet," she replied.

George opened the door to the room on the other side of the lobby and stood at the entrance. He glanced around the room and could not see anything worthwhile to search; the room was only filled with furniture, so he closed the door and returned to the lobby once more. He popped his head outside the front door, and both he and Maggie looked towards the Sambadrome to check if anyone was coming. There was nothing to worry about; the fire was still ablaze, and a crowd, including the three men, were still looking at it. George ascended the stairs and went into the room where Maggie had previously been held. There were a couple of cabinets, each with three drawers, which George set about to search. In his haste, the sound of rustling papers could be heard all the way to the front door.

"Everything alright up there?" Maggie shouted.

There was silence, and Maggie became anxious.

"George, is everything ok up there?"

This time, the door to the upstairs room opened, and George came out onto the landing.

"Is something wrong?" he asked.

"No, I didn't hear from you, and thought there may be a problem."

"No, everything is ok. The door to the room was closed. I couldn't hear you."

"Ok, I was just checking."

Maggie popped her head outside the door again to check on the men, while George entered the kitchen diner, the room at the back of the house, where Carlos was sitting the last time they were there. George found a few papers on the dining table and searched through them, but did not find anything of use. He looked at the kitchen worktops where there was a phone, amongst other kitchen utensils. Nothing of use there either, and George became disappointed that he did not find a link to Antonio. Then Maggie shouted with urgency from the doorway.

"George, hurry up, hurry up, the men are coming back."

George became nervous, and his heart began to pound quickly.

"Ok, I'm coming," he shouted, "give me a few more seconds."

"You haven't got a few seconds. They are on their way."

George looked around the kitchen-diner again and spotted a notepad on the counter. He grabbed it in case it revealed anything and headed down the stairs.

"Where are they now?" George asked.

He popped his head outside the door to check where the three men were, and they were casually walking back to the house about 50 metres away. A few people had gathered in the side street, which blocked the men's view of the front door to the house. This was the chance for George and Maggie to escape.

"Let's go," George shouted.

They left the house, headed in the opposite direction to the men, and walked as quickly as they could. The men arrived back at the house and did not notice anything inappropriate. The couple had escaped just in the nick of time.

George and Maggie walked for about 20 minutes and found a café. They sat down, ordered coffee, and George proceeded to look at the notepad taken from the house. The first few pages were covered in doodle drawings, and other pages contained lists of shopping items. The couple scanned through the pages quickly, but could not find anything pertinent to them, so George threw the notepad on the table. They were both disillusioned and sat in silence sipping their coffee. After a while, Maggie perked up.

"Ok," she said, "what are we going to do now?"

"I don't know," George replied.

The couple remained silent for a bit longer, thinking about the next steps to take. Maggie then picked up the notepad and began to scan through the pages again. She noticed some of the pages were missing, and only the tabs remained.

"Here, look at this," she said.

"What?" George asked.

Maggie showed George the tabs in the notepad.

"Some of the pages are missing," she said.

George took the notepad and flipped through it until he found the tab of the first missing page. He looked at the page beneath to check if there was any indentation from writing, but unfortunately, the page was covered in a doodle, and he could not detect anything.

"I can't make this out," he said, "What do you think?"

George showed Maggie the page with the doodle and handed the notepad to her. She looked at it, but couldn't make out if there was anything written on it. She flipped through the notepad to the next tab with a missing page and looked at the page beneath. It contained a shopping list, but there was also some indentation of written words. She scrutinised the page, but could not decipher the writing, and handed the notepad back to George.

"What do you think?" she asked.

George took the notepad and looked at the indentation of the words, but could not make them out either. He turned the notepad in different directions to try to decipher the writing, but it was of no use. He eventually held the page up to the light to look through it, and to his amazement, he could clearly see the hidden writing on the page. It was an address, and the name

174

Antonio was written on the page. He felt they were onto something.

"Got it," George shouted.

His voice was overheard by the café's patrons, causing most of them to look at the couple, making the couple feel slightly embarrassed.

"Have you found something?" Maggie asked.

"Yes, an address, and the name Antonio is also written on the page."

"So, you think we have a clue now?"

"Yes, definitely, this is something we can follow up on."

The couple high-fived and felt pleased at their findings. It was just after midday, and they decided to have lunch at the café. They could relax over lunch, and go to the newly found address in the afternoon.

They used the map they had with them to find the address, which was in downtown Rio, near the business district. After lunch, George and Maggie hailed a taxi and headed to the address. The area was busy with people going about their business, and at that time of day, they were mainly office workers dressed in suits and formal attire. George and Maggie exited the taxi and headed directly to the address, a suite of rooms in an office block on the fifth floor of the building. The door to the office was closed, so George knocked on it, and there was no answer. So, he tried a few more times, and there was still no answer.

"What are we going to do now?" Maggie asked.

"I'm not sure," George replied.

George knocked on the door again just as a young lady walked by, and she noticed the couple were trying to access the suite.

"There's no one there," she said in Portuguese.

"English," George remarked.

"Ah, sorry," the young lady said, "there's no one there at the moment; they left two days ago."

The couple were surprised at the young lady's comment.

"Left!" George exclaimed, "Do you know where they have gone?"

"No, not really, they left suddenly."

"Oh dear!" George said. "Thank you for your help."

"You're welcome," the young lady replied.

She then continued along the corridor.

"Now what?" Maggie asked.

George looked up and down the corridor, waiting until another office worker passed by. He then tried the door handle and, to his surprise, found the door unlocked. The couple quickly entered the office suite and shut the door behind them. It was a typical small office with desks and computers on top. Cabinets were neatly aligned against the walls, but there was something amiss; papers were strewn all over the desks and on the floor.

"What a mess," Maggie said.

George agreed with her, and while searching, they found an adjoining room. It was a lounge area, and accessed by a door from the office. The lounge contained a settee, two armchairs and a coffee table. A small kitchenette was off to one side and opened to the lounge area. The couple entered the adjoining room and again were confronted with a mess. Crockery, cutlery and glasses were strewn over the work surfaces, and it was obvious someone had ransacked the office suite. The couple searched for a few minutes, but could not find anything useful. They eventually sat down on the settee in the lounge area to rest.

"Nothing much here," George said, "I thought we would at least find someone here."

Maggie scratched her head and sat back in the settee, looking disappointed.

"Yes, me too," she said.

George and Maggie sat pondering for a while, and then they heard the main door to the office suite being opened. They were unsure who entered the office, and were startled, so they stood up immediately and went over to the lounge door. The door to the lounge was closed, and the couple could not be seen from the front office, so they remained silent. They heard someone shuffling through the papers in the adjoining office and were concerned to find out who had entered it. They opened the lounge door to find a man kneeling on the floor searching through papers. The man was startled when he saw the couple; he did not expect anyone else to be in the office suite.

"What the hell!" the man said in Portuguese.

He stood up and faced the couple.

"Who the hell are you?" he asked.

The man was dressed in a dark suit, and the top of his head was wrapped in a surgical bandage. George and Maggie were taken aback and stood there in silence.

"Well," the man said, "who are you? And what are you doing in my office?"

The couple did not understand Portuguese, and George felt he needed to say something.

"Who are you?" he asked.

The man detected English and spoke back in it.

"This is my office, what are you doing here?" he asked.

"Your office!" George exclaimed.

"Yes, my office," the man said forcefully.

George detected that the man was angry and thought it better to explain the reason why they were there.

"We were looking for Antonio," he said.

The man noticed the couple were nervous and eased off the forceful dialogue.

"Why do you want Antonio?" he asked.

"We need to speak to him urgently."

"About what?"

"I can't really tell you, it's confidential."

"Are you the English couple that made contact with Antonio?" the man asked.

George and Maggie looked at each other, not sure how to respond. Was this man genuine? Or was he another member of the Brazilian gang? The man looked at the couple and smiled, for he recognised George's voice from previous telephone conversations. He realised their predicament and eased their nervousness.

"I needed to be sure about you guys," he said

The man held out his hand to shake George's hand.

"My name is Antonio, and I am very pleased to meet you, eventually."

George shook the man's hand.

"George Peacock is my name."

Antonio also shook Maggie's hand.

177

"Pleased to meet you too, Mrs Peacock."

The couple were cautious and still unsure about the man. He was polite, but was he the real Antonio?

"How do we know you are Antonio?" Maggie asked.

"Ah! I see what you mean. You've never met me before, and with all the fuss going on, you want to be sure."

"Yes," George said, "give us some proof."

The man divulged the telephone conversations he had previously had with George, and the accuracy was enough to satisfy the couple.

"Right, I'm satisfied," George said, "you seem genuine enough. But before we continue, what happened to your head?"

George was referring to the bandage tightly wound around the top of Antonio's head.

"It's a long story, but I suppose you'd better know about it," Antonio said, and continued, "I was here working alone late one evening, when three men entered the office. They ran over to my desk, but before I could stand up, they pounced on me and punched me to the ground."

"Oh my god!" Maggie exclaimed, "How horrendous."

Antonio waved his hand in acknowledgement of the sympathy and continued.

"I managed to get up and tried to fight back, but I was hopeless against all three. They eventually overpowered me and tied me to a chair."

Maggie could not believe the story and held her hands up to her face.

"Oh my god!" she repeated.

George was also concerned about Antonio's misfortune.

"Bastards," he said, "why would they want to do such a thing? Do you know the reason for it?"

"Yes, it was all about the package..."

"...The package!" George interrupted.

"Yes, the package, the one you have for me, they were looking for it."

"Why is this package so important?" Maggie asked.

"It's a long story and I will fill you in later, but let me tell you what happened to me next," Antonio said. "The men then ransacked the office and the lounge area, as you can see. They could not find the package or anything of use to them, so they set about to pistol-whip me on the head, hence the bandage."

George was anxious and began to feel guilty because he still held onto the package, and somehow felt he could have averted the attack on Antonio. He became very sympathetic towards him.

"My god!" he said, "I am very sorry to hear your misfortune; somehow I feel guilty, and could have avoided the attack on you."

Maggie was also concerned about Antonio, but was keener to hear the rest of the story.

"So, what happened next?" she asked.

"They asked many questions about both of you, and then tied me to the chair. They were here when you rang the other night and took your call. That's when one of the men pretended to be me. I couldn't say anything; they had covered my mouth. They eventually left empty-handed."

Antonio's recollection of the encounter with the men made him pause for a moment, and he held his head with both hands.

"So how long were you here for?" George asked.

"Overnight. There was nothing I could do, and I was found by the cleaners the next morning."

George and Maggie looked at each other in bewilderment; they could not believe the story they had just heard from Antonio.

"Let's go to the lounge where we can sit comfortably and continue to talk," Antonio said.

He ushered the couple to the lounge area, where George and Maggie sat on the settee, while Antonio went to the kitchenette to make coffee. The couple remained silent, waiting for him to return. He sat down in a chair opposite them.

"First of all," Antonio said, "do you still have the package?"

"Yes, it's in a safe place," George replied.

"Good, that's something," Antonio said.

He then glanced over to Maggie, then back to George.

"Does Mrs Peacock know?" he asked.

"Know what?" Maggie asked.

"Obviously not," Antonio said, "did you not tell her about the package?"

"Yes, she knows about the package," George replied.

"This package seems very important," Maggie said, "what's so important about it?"

Antonio looked at the couple again and paused for a while. He thought it best to tell them the truth about the package.

"The package contains a Printed Circuit Board…"

It was the first time George heard about the contents of the package, and he interrupted Antonio.

"A Printed Circuit Board!" he exclaimed.

"Yes, that's right, a PCB."

"So why is this PCB so important?" Maggie asked.

"I really can't tell you all the details right now, until I receive the board from you. It is top secret," Antonio said.

"Top secret! What do you mean by top secret?" George asked.

"As I said, I can't tell you any more at the moment."

George turned to Maggie, and they both looked puzzled at each other. He then contemplated Antonio's comments.

"Is this some kind of a joke?" he asked.

Antonio was reluctant to tell the couple the full story at this stage and convincingly looked at George.

"I can assure you. This is genuine. If it was a joke, then why would we agree to pay you money?"

George rubbed his chin and screwed up his face. He looked at Maggie and then back at Antonio.

"I guess it sounds real, but something doesn't seem to add up. I think we are being kept in the dark, and I don't like it," he said.

"Everything will be alright," Antonio said, "you'll see, when we exchange the package for the money."

George was not entirely pleased with Antonio's answers and knew Maggie was also not pleased.

"Ok, let's leave this for now. We have to move on," George said.

"Yes, I agree," Antonio said, "let's discuss what we have to do next."

Maggie was not happy with George's reluctance to find out more from Antonio. She folded her arms, crossed her legs, huffed and turned away from the men in disgust. She still wanted to hear the discussion, though, and remained seated in the lounge.

"Ok, George," Antonio said, "do you have the package with you?"

"No, I don't," George replied.

"So, when can you let me have the package?"

"As soon as I get the money," George replied, "the deal is still on, isn't it?"

"Yes, of course, but I just can't hand over the money without receiving the package at the same time. We'll have to meet again to do the handover."

"Ok, that sounds fair," George said.

Antonio thought for a moment about a convenient time and place to meet.

"What say we meet again tomorrow at café Blanco. Do you know it? It's on the sea front at Copacabana beach, about one o'clock?"

"I don't know it, but we'll find it."

The men shook hands in agreement and smiled at each other. George then remembered he and Maggie were leaving Brazil in a day or two, and wanted to inform Antonio about their schedule.

I don't know if you realise this," he said, "but we leave for the UK in a couple of days."

"No, I didn't know about your flight," Antonio replied, "Maybe we should meet earlier in the day. How about 11 am. Is that alright for you?"

George nodded his head positively, and the men shook hands again in agreement. Antonio then stood up to indicate the conversation was over. He had work to do and prompted the couple to leave.

"I've got some tidying up to do here, so I'll see you tomorrow," Antonio said.

The couple instinctively stood up and bid farewell to Antonio. They left the office and exited the building onto the busy street.

George and Maggie stood on the pavement for about five minutes to determine their next move.

"I think I need a proper drink," George said.

The couple searched for a bar nearby, but there was none in the vicinity, so they walked for a short while before they found a cocktail bar. George and Maggie sat at a table in the window and were soon served by a waiter. Antonio finished tidying the office about 30 minutes later and was passing the cocktail bar on the way to his destination when he saw the couple through the window. He waved at them and went into the bar to have a chat.

"Hi, Antonio," George said, "anything wrong?"

"Hello again," Antonio said, "No, everything is fine. I saw you through the window, and just wanted to remind you about tomorrow. Eleven o'clock, don't forget."

"We'll be there, don't worry," George said.

Antonio shook hands with George again and exited the bar.

"He worries a lot," Maggie said.

"Yes, I suppose he's got a lot on his mind."

Chapter 11 – The Man in Black

During the drinks interlude, Maggie made her excuses to go to the washroom. As soon as she left the table and was out of sight, a well-dressed man in a black suit came to the table and sat down opposite George, who was surprised to see the man.

"Don't worry," the man said in a soft tone, "there is nothing to worry about. I guess you are the English couple everyone is searching for."

"Who are you?" George asked.

"It doesn't matter what my name is," the man said, "I have a proposition for you."

George accepted that the man knew his identity and wanted to find out more. He looked around the bar to establish if the man was alone and if Maggie was out of sight. In the circumstances, George tried to remain calm.

"What proposition?" he asked, "What kind of proposition?"

"My organisation has been chasing you for a while now…"

George raised his hand to interrupt the man.

"What organisation?"

"You don't need to know who or what we are; we just want the package from you."

George raised his eyebrows and was somewhat puzzled at the man. Who was he? And how did he know where to find them?

"What do you know about the package?" George asked, "And how did you find us?"

The man did not want anyone else in the bar to hear the conversation, so he leaned forward towards George and put his elbows on the table.

"It was quite easy," the man said, "we have been following Antonio, and saw him talking to you a few minutes ago. We lost you in the favela last night, and it was only luck we found you again so soon. You see, there can't be many English couples speaking to Antonio."

George sat back uneasily in the chair, realising the man knew much about him.

"What do you want from us?" George asked.

"We want the package, of course. But, before you say anything else, hear my proposition."

The man paused for a while and looked around the bar again to check if anyone was listening.

"I guess you are being paid to deliver the package, yes?" he asked.

George gazed blankly at the man and did not want to give any indication of the deal arranged with Antonio.

"Well, we are prepared to pay you double the amount you are getting," the man continued.

The comment lit up the 'cash register' in George's mind.

"Double!" he exclaimed.

"Yes, double. We want the package, and chasing after you has gone on far too long. Too many people have been injured, and we wish to bring this to an end. We are prepared to pay you double the amount you are getting now. What do you say?"

George now realised the package must be of huge importance, and was excited at the prospect of doubling his money. He pondered a while longer, '*Was he being greedy if he took the extra money? What was there to lose? What difference would it make where the money came from? They could easily take the money, and knowing they would be leaving Brazil soon, it wouldn't matter.*' The man waited for George's reply and looked around in the direction of the washroom to make sure Maggie was not returning yet. He turned back to speak to George.

"I tell you what," he said, "I'll give you some time to think about it. Here is my number."

The man passed a piece of paper with a telephone number on it to George and was keen to leave before Maggie returned.

"Give me a call soon," he said, "don't leave it for too long."

The man got up and exited the bar, leaving George somewhat perplexed. He looked through the window to see the man disappearing into the crowd on the pavement outside. George was still holding the piece of paper when Maggie returned to the table.

"What's that you've got there?" she asked.

George looked at the piece of paper and quickly put it in his pocket. He was reluctant to tell Maggie about the meeting with the man in black.

"Um, it's only the bill."

Ten minutes later, George and Maggie finished their drinks and left the bar. But before doing so, George went to the washroom and paid for the drinks on the way without Maggie noticing. They hailed a taxi and returned to the area where they stayed, spending the rest of the afternoon perusing the local shops. George was unenthusiastic about shopping and had a vacant expression on his face for most of the time. His mind was elsewhere, contemplating the latest offer from the man in black. Maggie noticed George's lack of enthusiasm many times and thought he may be feeling slightly depressed, a consequence of the recent ordeals. She let him be, but the extra agony of George being shot had taken a toll on them both. It was time for them to relax.

The couple returned to the Bed and Breakfast and rested on the bed. Maggie dozed off immediately, and George remained wide awake, his eyes fixed on the ceiling. What was he supposed to do? Should he hand over the package to the man in black for double the money? Or should he stick to his agreement with Antonio? He did not wish to let Antonio down, but greed was getting the better of him. The couple had many debts back in England, and the extra money would come in useful. George was nervous at the thought and the repercussions it could bring. An hour passed, and after many deliberations, George made a decision.

He nudged Maggie on the arm to awaken her.
"Wakey, Wakey," he said.
Maggie woke instantly and sat up in bed.
"What! What's going on?" she asked.
Maggie was in a deep sleep, and the sudden awakening must have disturbed a dream. She rubbed her eyes and held her face in her hands.
"God! That was scary," she said.
"Bad dream, eh?" George asked.
"Yes, really frightening. I was..."
George felt he needed to interrupt Maggie and rubbed her arm.
"Sorry to stop you there, sweetheart," he said, "It's almost 7 pm, and I think we should get ready for dinner."

"Yes, you're right."

"We could continue the discussion about the dream over dinner."

"Ok, it wasn't so important anyway. What shall I wear tonight?"

George ignored the comment; it was customary for Maggie to ask that question before they went out. The couple prepared for dinner and were about to leave the room when George took the package from the back of the wardrobe. Maggie was somewhat puzzled at George's action.

"What are you doing?" she asked.

"I'm taking the package with us."

"What for?"

"I think it will be more secure if we have it with us."

Maggie was surprised at George's comment and became confused.

"More secure than here?" she asked.

"Yes, think about it. We were seen by..."

George was about to say that he spoke to the man in black today, and realised Maggie did not know anything about it, so he paused.

"Seen by who?" Maggie asked.

"Err, Um. We may have been seen by someone when we went to Antonio's office today."

"By who?" Maggie asked.

George needed to think of an answer quickly; he did not want to let on that he had been approached earlier by the man in black.

"I don't know, anyone could have seen us. They found Antonio before, and beat him up, did they not?"

"I suppose so."

"Ok, let's go. I'm starving."

The couple did not venture far for dinner and strolled onto the promenade at Copacabana Beach. They found an Italian Bistro and were shown to a table. George laid the package on the table, so it was visible to both of them. The Bistro was small, about ten tables, with subdued lighting, and a candle on every table. The evening was warm, and the front of the Bistro was open to the elements, which allowed a gentle breeze to flow through the restaurant. A resident guitarist sat in one corner and played Italian music. The restaurant was nearly full with other diners, and as it was almost the couple's last night in Rio, they wanted to have a memorable dinner. They decided to choose the speciality dishes from the menu, accompanied by a good bottle of red wine.

While they waited for dinner, the couple looked around at the other diners, again for a bit of people watching. Maggie always checked out the people in restaurants sitting nearby, and being nosy, wanted to see how they were dressed. Before it was too late, George needed a reason to get away from Maggie for a few minutes; he needed to ring the man in black he had met earlier that day. George had decided to take the extra money and wanted to exchange the package that night if possible. George did not want Maggie to know his plan, so he kept the decision to himself.

"Excuse me for a moment, sweetheart," George said, "I have to go to the washroom."

George stood up, and Maggie gave him a loving smile as he walked away from the table. He found a telephone in the corridor at the rear of the Bistro near the washrooms, and dialled the number on the piece of paper which the man in black had given him.

"Hello," a voice answered in Portuguese.

"Ah, yes, hello," George said, "Er, I am George, and I met someone today who gave me this number."

There was silence at the other end of the phone for a few seconds.

"Hello, who is this?" another voice asked in English.

"Hi, I am George. I met someone in a bar today who gave me this number."

"Ah! The Englishman, it was me you met earlier."

"Are you the man in black?" George asked.

He immediately realised it was a stupid question to ask; the man on the other end of the phone had recognised his voice, and he felt slightly embarrassed at the comment.

"Yes, it's me. Are you ready to do a deal?"

"Yes, I think so."

"Think so! Do you want to exchange the package or not?"

George detected that the man seemed a bit anxious at his indecision and became nervous. His hands began to sweat, and he thought he should be more positive.

"Yes, I do," he said.

"Where shall we meet?" the man asked.

George thought for a moment. He wanted to exchange the package without Maggie knowing, but then changed his mind; it probably would not make any difference if she knew about it.

"Well?" the man in black asked.

"We're at an Italian Bistro on Copacabana beach."

"What's the name of the Bistro?"

George looked around to see if he could find the name of the Bistro, and found it on a menu pinned to the wall.

"It's the La Fiducia Ristorante."

"Ok, I know it," the man said, "Do you have the package with you?"

"Yes," George replied, "and can you make sure you bring the money?"

"Yes, ok," the man said, "how much are you being paid for the package?"

George thought for a moment, and wondered if to up the price, because the man was unaware of how much money he was getting from Antonio. He thought otherwise; he did not want to create another problem.

"They are paying me two thousand pounds," he said.

The man in black did not seem concerned about the price.

"Good, I'll bring the equivalent of four thousand pounds in Brazilian Reals. I'll be there in an hour."

The man then put the phone down and ended the call. George hurried back to the table where Maggie was looking out for him. She seemed a bit concerned.

"You've been a while," she said.

George sat down, stretched across the table, and held Maggie's hands in his.

"Yes, I've got something to tell you."

Maggie reciprocated and held his hands in what seemed like an intimate moment. She felt loving toward George and was eager to hear some good news.

"What have you got to tell me?" she asked.

George nodded towards the package on the table.

"I'm going to exchange the package tonight."

Maggie was somewhat disappointed at the comment, hoping to hear some good news for a change. She felt uneasy and sat back in her chair.

"Is Antonio coming here tonight then?" Maggie asked.

"No, he's not, let me explain."

George began to tell Maggie about the meeting with the man in black earlier, and how he agreed to exchange the package for double the amount of money. Maggie could not believe George was willing to do something else, and nodded her head from side to side.

"You are full of surprises, aren't you? When is this going to end?" she asked.

"Hopefully, tonight, we can then enjoy the rest of the evening."

The couple were interrupted by a waiter who came to serve the starters.

"Who's having the soup?" he asked.

Maggie raised her hand.

"I am," she replied.

The waiter placed the soup bowl in front of Maggie.

"And the crab salad for you, sir," the waiter added.

He placed the salad in front of George and walked away from the table.

"What about Antonio?" Maggie asked.

"What about Antonio?" George asked rhetorically.

At that precise moment, the wine waiter approached the table and presented the bottle of Valpolicella to them.

"Would you like to taste it, sir?" he asked George.

"No, just pour it, please," George replied.

The waiter poured the wine into the glasses until they were about a third full.

"Enjoy your meal," he said.

He then walked away from the table, and the couple were left alone for a while.

"You promised to meet Antonio tomorrow," Maggie said, "what are you going to do about that?"

189

"We don't have to meet him. We could spend the last two days elsewhere and leave for England without him knowing."

"I think that's so unfair."

"So, what, we'll have our money."

"Hmm!" a disillusioned Maggie uttered.

Over the next hour, the couple ate their meal, and the conversation was sparse. The dishes were cleared and the table was dusted clean by the waiter in preparation for the dessert course.

Before the dessert course was served, the man whom George had spoken to entered the restaurant and came over to the couple's table. He was still dressed in a black suit and shook hands with George. A waiter immediately came over and offered the man a chair. He acknowledged Maggie and sat down.

"Well, my friend, I see you have come to your senses," he said. He looked at the package on the table.

"Is that it?" he asked.

George gently put his hand on the package.

"Yes, it is."

"Good," the man said, "let's do some business."

He put his hand inside his jacket to extract something, which instantly made the couple nervous. The man sensed their concern and raised his other hand as a gesture of surrender.

"No, don't worry, nothing to worry about," he said, "It's only the money."

The man scanned around the restaurant to check if anyone was looking, and pulled out a brown envelope from inside his jacket. He put it on the table and slid it over. George moved his hand over the envelope to pick it up when the man slammed his own hand down on the envelope.

"Not yet," the man said, "pass me the package first."

Maggie looked on in amazement, thinking this could have been a scene in a James Bond film, and smiled to herself. George then passed the package over to the man in black.

"Thank you," the man said.

He released his hand on the envelope, and the man proceeded to open the package. At the same time, George opened the envelope to count the cash inside. The man pulled the printed circuit board from the package and scrutinised it. This was the first time any of them had seen the contents of the package.

"Is that it?" Maggie asked, "Is that what all the fuss has been about?"

The man and George both looked at Maggie, then at each other, and shrugged. George pulled the notes halfway out of the envelope he was holding and noticed they were all in the Brazilian currency, the Real. He flipped through them and tried to count the cash, but it was awkward to do so in the restaurant while the money was still in the envelope. He flipped through the cash again and attempted to count the notes, which he assumed to be correct. George then looked over to Maggie with a broad smile on his face. In return, she raised her eyebrows and nodded, as if to ask, 'Was it correct?' George nodded positively back to Maggie. The man in black completed a visual check of the circuit board and returned it to its wrapping.

"Is the money correct?" he asked George.

George was reluctant to answer, for he had no idea how much money was in the envelope, and acted nonchalantly.

"Yes, everything seems fine," he said.

"You will find it's all there," the man said, "Business is business."

The man held out his hand to shake George's hand.

"Pleasure to do business," he said.

George shook the man's hand in return.

"Likewise."

The man stood up, bid farewell to the couple, and walked out of the restaurant without looking back.

George held out his trembling hands towards Maggie.

"Phew!" he said, "I am shaking like a wobbling jelly."

Maggie was also shaking nervously.

"You're shaking!" she said, "I am utterly terrified."

George immediately put the envelope in his trouser pocket and sat with his elbows on the table. He looked around the restaurant to see if anyone had noticed the transaction, and then back to Maggie.

"We've done it," he said, "We've got the money."

"Did we get four thousand pounds?" Maggie asked.

"I hope so. It was hard to count the money in the envelope."

"Then let's celebrate," Maggie said, "let's have some champagne."

"Yes, what a good idea."

George turned around and beckoned the waiter to come over. He ordered the champagne, and the couple drank the bubbly while they ate their desserts.

George and Maggie were genuinely happy during the remainder of the night. Later, they ended up in a nightclub and enjoyed the rest of the night in Rio. It was 2 am, and the effects of the carnival had not ended in the city. Many people were still dressed in the bright colours for the carnival. Scantily dressed women were showing off their shapely bodies while dancing to the Samba all night long. The men tried their best to keep up with the women, but could not match the movements of the female body. Everyone was having a good time without a care in the world. The atmosphere was entirely different to the escapades the couple endured over the last few days.

Chapter 12 – Downtown Rio

The couple arrived back at the Bed and Breakfast in the early hours of the morning and slept until 10 am the same day, and were awoken by a knock on the bedroom door.

"Yes, who is it?" George asked.

"Breakfast," a voice from outside the door said, "you missed breakfast, so I brought you some."

"Oh, right," George said, "hold on a moment."

George got out of bed and went over to the door, wearing just shorts and nothing else. He opened the door to be greeted by a young woman holding a breakfast tray in her hands. She was surprised to see George half-undressed and became embarrassed.

"Oh dear," she said.

The young woman's face went a pale shade of red; she did not expect to see a half-naked man in the room. She turned her head away and held out the tray for George to take.

"Breakfast," she said, "we thought you would like something to eat."

George took the tray from the young woman, who turned around quickly and walked away. The woman's embarrassment brought a smile to George's face, and he ogled at her until she disappeared. George then closed the door and returned to bed with the breakfast.

The couple were scheduled to meet Antonio at the Blanco cafe around 11 am, but as the package was handed over to the man in black, they remained in bed for another hour. They were tired from partying the night before, but more importantly, felt drained from the recent ordeals of the last few days. They decided to spend a few hours on the famous Copacabana Beach to relax, and departed the accommodation at 12 o'clock to head down to the seafront. Hordes of local people were already at the seaside, taking the opportunity to go there during the carnival holiday. It was traditional to go to the beach at that time. Tourists from all over the world mixed with the locals, and Rio buzzed with joy during that time of year. Many people were already swimming in the sea, and others enjoyed being at the water's edge. Women dressed in scanty bikinis walked on the beach and revealed their bronzed figures, while most of the men watched on with pleasurable interest. The men, on the other hand, displayed their masculine physiques to the utter delight of the women. Most people, though, both young and old, could be described as having normal body shapes. Some men, women and children were overweight and bordered on obesity, but all in all, the scene could be described as the norm worldwide. George and Maggie found two spare deck chairs and settled down to relax in the hot sun for the next few hours.

At about 12:30, their peace was disturbed by Antonio's voice.
"Hello, my friends," he said.
The couple were startled and looked up to see Antonio standing in front of them. He stood with his back to the sun, and his silhouette was surrounded by its rays, which beamed directly into the couple's eyes.
"We agreed to meet at 11 o'clock," Antonio said. "What happened to you?"
George needed to think quickly of a plausible excuse.
"Er! We had a late night," he said, "we got up late, and needed to recover."
Antonio sensed George was not telling the truth, and perhaps something was untoward.
"We had an agreement, though, it was important."
"I know, I'm sorry, but we just forgot."
"Forgot! How can you forget about something like this?" Antonio asked.
Maggie thought to give George some moral help to try to ease the situation.
"It was my fault," she said, "I caused the delay. You know what women are like."
George looked over towards Maggie and smiled to thank her for the interjection. Antonio felt there was no further need to pursue the reason why the couple did not meet him.
"Ok," he said, "I don't suppose you have the circuit board with you."
"No," George said.
George and Maggie remained silent.

194

"Well! Where is it?"

George didn't want to confess that he sold the board and needed to think up another plausible excuse.

"You see, Antonio, I have some bad news for you."

"What news is that?"

George paused for a moment; he was unsure of the excuse to give to Antonio.

"Um," he said, and paused once again.

"Well?" Antonio asked.

"Well, we've misplaced the board."

"Misplaced the board! What do you mean? How can you lose the board?"

Antonio was frustrated with the conversation, raised his arms and looked up to the sky in disgust. George tried to buy some time and waffled on a bit more.

"The cleaners must have moved it, or maybe taken it," he said.

Antonio was now confused at the couple's remarks and scratched his head in disgust. He looked at Maggie, and then at George, shaking his head from side to side.

"You need to find the board quickly," he said, "It's important you do, or else you won't get your money."

"I understand," George said, "No board, no money."

Maggie listened to the conversation and remained silent; she could not add anything constructive. Antonio was now annoyed and became firm with the couple.

"You go and find the board," he said, "and I'll meet you in two hours at the café where we were supposed to meet this morning. Do you understand?"

"Yes, we understand," George said.

"Ok, I'll see you later with the package," Antonio said.

He walked away from the couple, who looked at each other with grim faces. But as soon as Antonio was out of sight and hearing distance, the couple burst out laughing.

"I think we'd better go and pack, and find somewhere else to stay for the last day," George said.

"Good idea," Maggie added.

She collected their personal items from the beach, and the couple left the seaside to head back to the Bed and Breakfast.

Unbeknownst to the couple, they were being followed by one of Antonio's men, Felipe, who kept himself well hidden from them. The couple arrived back at the Bed and Breakfast to pack their belongings.

"We should tell the landlady we're leaving," Maggie said.

Yes, I agree, it would be the correct thing to do," George said, "I'll go and tell her now."

George took some cash to pay the bill, left the room to find the landlady, and returned about ten minutes later.

"Everything alright?" Maggie asked.

"Yes, fine, everything is fine. She only charged us for one night."

"Ah, good, she needn't have, but it seemed the decent thing to do."

George and Maggie completed the packing, left the accommodation, and hailed a taxi on the road just outside the building. They thought it best to stay in a hostel for the last night, and headed for the centre of Rio, which was the best place to find a hostel. Felipe watched them constantly and also hailed a taxi to follow them to the city. The couple arrived at a hostel recommended by the taxi driver about fifteen minutes later. They exited the cab, made their way into the hostel, and booked a room. The hostel was basic, but it had all the necessary facilities, which suited the couple. It was an ideal place for them to hide from their pursuers for the last night, so they thought.

Felipe followed closely and waited for a few minutes to allow the couple to settle into their room. He then needed to confirm they were definitely booked in, so he went to the front desk to check that they actually booked into the hostel, and it was not a deception to give him the slip. After completing the task, Felipe found a café on the other side of the road and settled down by the window to watch the couple's movements. He telephoned Antonio once he had established himself in the cafe. Antonio recognised Felipe's voice on the other end of the phone.

"Hi Felipe, this is Antonio. What is it?"

"The couple have left the Bed and Breakfast," Felipe said.

"Where are they now?"

"In downtown Rio."

196

"Ah, good, you need to track them everywhere, even when they go back to the Bed and Breakfast. I need to know all their movements."

"I don't think they will be going back there, boss," Felipe said.

Antonio was a bit surprised and puzzled at Felipe's remark.

"Why is that?"

"I think they have checked out of the Bed and Breakfast."

"They've done what!" he exclaimed, "What do you mean?"

"They took their belongings with them when they left, and they've checked into a hostel in the centre of Rio."

"Are you sure?" Antonio asked.

"Positive, boss, positive. I've checked with the hostel, and they have definitely booked in."

Antonio pondered on the couple's change of accommodation and wondered what they were planning now. He became concerned about losing them again.

"Do you know why they moved accommodation?" he asked.

"I don't know, boss, they seem a strange couple."

"Ok, keep a close eye on them, and I'll be there as soon as I can. Where's the address?"

Felipe gave Antonio the details and waited in the café for him to arrive.

About twenty minutes later, George and Maggie left the hostel to go for a stroll. Felipe followed, and he was determined not to let them out of his sight. The couple walked through the central business area and down to Guanabara Bay, the bay on which Rio was built. It was now about 3 pm, and the couple walked along the promenade fronting the bay.

"I don't know about you, but I'm feeling peckish," George said to Maggie.

"Me too," she replied. "We've missed lunch, and I'm starving."

They looked for somewhere to eat, and Maggie pointed to a cafe across the road from the promenade.

"Look, let's go there," she said.

George scanned across the road at the café.

"Ok," he said, "that will do, it looks alright."

The couple headed across the road, while Felipe remained on the promenade and sat in the shade under a palm tree. He telephoned Antonio to inform him of the couple's location. George and Maggie were shown to a table and were handed a menu by the waiter.

The couple were pleased to retire from the heat of the sun and into the cool environment of the cafe. The outside temperature became very hot in the afternoon, but the café was air-conditioned and comfortable. They scanned the menu and were served iced cold water by the waiter. The smell of cooking wafted through the air, and a few patrons were still in the café having late lunches. The couple waited to be served.

"What do you want to eat?" George asked Maggie.

"I don't know yet," Maggie replied, "I can't quite decide. Have you chosen?"

George scanned the menu again and decided on a meal.

"I will have the pasta salad," he said, "something light for the time of day. What about you?"

Maggie scanned the menu and deliberated a while longer.

"Hmm!" she said, "I think I will have the pasta salad as well."

"And beer?" George asked.

Having just come in from the sun, Maggie was feeling the heat and wiped her brow with her hand.

"Yes, beer is fine. I need a beer to combat this heat."

George looked for a waiter, and felt he was having a Deja vu. The discussion with Maggie reminded him of the morning when they were at Heathrow airport, on the day they left the UK for Brazil. The conversation was similar, and it was a strange feeling. The waiter noticed George and came over to take the order.

In the meantime, Antonio arrived to meet Felipe on the promenade across the road from the cafe.

"Where are the couple now?" Antonio asked.

Felipe pointed across the road.

"In the café opposite," he said.

Antonio looked across the road towards the café.

"Have they seen you at all?"

"No, I don't think they have, I've been careful."

"Right, I have a plan. I think it's about time we take them into custody to have a chat with them."

"Ok, boss," Felipe said.

"We'll drive up to the café in my car, and go inside together. Clear?"

"Yes, boss, very clear."

The road was a dual carriageway, so Antonio and Felipe drove to the next junction, performed a U-turn, and came back to park outside the café. They both got out of the car and entered the establishment.

George saw them coming through the door and, amazed, sat back in his chair.

"What the f…!" George said, "It's Antonio!"

Maggie looked around and saw the two men entering the cafe.

"What's happening now?" she asked.

Antonio approached the couple, while Felipe remained at the door to the café.

"Hello, Mr Peacock," Antonio said.

He then nodded towards Maggie and acknowledged her.

"Mrs Peacock."

George and Maggie remained silent; they were both surprised to see Antonio.

"I'd like you to come with me," Antonio said.

George became anxious, and his stomach began to churn. He went pale in the face, and the anxiousness immediately turned to fright.

"Where to?" George asked.

"To my office. You have some explaining to do, and I want to talk to you as well."

George looked at Maggie, then at Felipe, standing by the café door, looking grim-faced. George knew there was nothing he could do or say to avoid Antonio's request.

"Ok, Antonio, we will come with you, but where are you taking us?"

"Just back to my office, we need to talk."

Maggie remained silent; she was too scared to say anything and was shaking like a leaf. The couple stood up, and George glanced around at the people staring at them in the café. He felt utterly embarrassed and hung his head down in shame as they left the café. Antonio escorted George and Maggie to the car outside and drove them back to his office, the same one in downtown Rio where they met Antonio, the same office that had been ransacked.

The office was now tidy, compared to the last time George and Maggie were there, and they were requested to sit on the settee in the lounge area. Antonio and Felipe remained standing.
"Coffee?" Antonio asked.
George and Maggie remained silent but nodded their heads. They were nervous and unsure what was going to happen to them. Antonio looked over to Felipe.
"Can you make some coffee for us, please?" he asked.
He sensed George and Maggie were afraid, and tried to ease their nervousness.
"There is nothing to worry about," he said, "relax, and let me explain."
The couple looked at Antonio with anticipation of what he was about to say.

Antonio cleared his throat, looked down at the floor while scratching his head, and then looked up at George.
"Where shall I start?" he rhetorically asked.
He gave a wry smile and rubbed his chin with his hand.
"First of all, I think I should introduce myself properly. My name is Antonio Carlos Jobim. No, not the famous musician of the past. I am an MI6 agent working on an assignment for the Brazilian government..."
"You're what?" George asked.
"An MI6 agent," Antonio replied.
Maggie opened her eyes wide and raised her eyebrows.
"You mean a spy!" she said.
"Well, you could say so," Antonio replied, "I am Brazilian, and I live in London. I am currently on secondment to work for the Brazilian government."
George looked across at Felipe and moved his head from side to side.
"I don't believe my ears," he said.

Felipe nodded his head up and down.

"It's true," Antonio said, "believe it."

"What's this got to do with us?" George asked.

"Yes, why us?" Maggie asked.

"Everything," Antonio replied, "you see, you agreed to bring the Printed Circuit Board in exchange for money."

"Yes, that was the agreement," George said, "but what has it got to do with MI6?"

"Let me explain," Antonio said.

At that moment, Felipe brought over the coffee and placed the tray on the table in front of the couple. He then sat down nearby.

"Thank you, Felipe," Antonio said, and continued to talk to the couple, "as I was saying, let me explain about the PCB."

George and Maggie were unsure if Antonio was telling the truth or whether it was just another made-up story. The episode was all foreign to them, but they now felt a bit more relaxed, being with the supposedly 'good guys' rather than the 'bad guys.' Their eyes remained fixed on Antonio, and they waited to hear his explanation about the board.

"The PCB is a special circuitry board designed and developed in the UK," he said, "it is used in a drone, you know, one of those things that flies around, and operated by someone on the ground."

"Yes, we know what a drone is," George said.

"Very well," Antonio said, "this particular PCB can map and monitor the rain forest. It can identify different types of trees from high up, and even detect areas on the ground to mine."

George and Maggie remained perplexed, and both picked up their coffees to have a sip. Antonio took the opportunity to do the same.

"Why are we involved in this kind of thing?" Maggie asked.

"That's a good question," Antonio replied, "the PCB you brought over to Brazil was absolutely useless."

Antonio's comment stunned George and Maggie.

"Useless!" George said, "What do you mean by useless?"

"It is absolutely useless, it is a dud, and does not work at all."

"So why were we bringing it here to Brazil?" George asked.

Antonio looked over to Felipe for moral support. He knew he was about to say something that would infuriate the couple even more. He turned back to face George and Maggie.

"I know you are not going to like what I'm about to say, but here goes."

Antonio paused to collect his thoughts for a moment.

"Go on," Maggie said, "I'm intrigued."

"You were acting as decoys," Antonio said.

"DECOYS!" George and Maggie shouted together.

"What do you mean by decoys?" George asked.

"The genuine board was brought here by another MI6 operative, and you were the decoys."

"I don't believe my ears," George said.

"Damn right," Maggie added.

George and Maggie were now somewhat infuriated. Maggie leaned forward aggressively and threw her arms up in the air in anger.

"You used us as decoys?" she asked, "How dare you do that? Don't our lives mean anything to you? How could you put us in danger?"

Antonio then became embarrassed because of Maggie's reaction and bowed his head.

"Yes, I'm afraid so," he said.

George also became angry at Antonio.

"You put us in danger, you put our lives in danger, what the hell is going on?" he asked.

"It shouldn't have turned out this way," Antonio said, "There was not going to be any violence or danger. Things just got out of hand."

"I'll tell you what will get out of hand," Maggie said, "it's when we get back to the UK and make a complaint to the British government."

George and Maggie looked at each other in bewilderment, while Felipe tried to ease the situation by offering to make more coffee.

Antonio sat down opposite the couple, and all four reflected on the conversation.

After a few moments of silence, George felt guilty because Antonio divulged so much about himself, and decided to come clean about the Printed Circuit Board. He looked over to Antonio. "I've also got some news for you as well," he said.

"What's that?" Antonio asked.

"I don't have the PCB anymore, it's been sold."

"I guessed something changed," Antonio said, "you seemed reluctant to hand over the board to us. I detected you were making excuses when we last spoke, and I believe you also moved accommodation to avoid us."

"Yes, I'm really sorry about all the fuss," George said.

"No, don't be," Antonio said, "it was a dud anyway, and I'm sure you made more money than the amount we offered you. Am I right?"

George nodded his head.

"Who did you sell it to?" Antonio asked,

"It was a man dressed in black. He never gave us his name, so I don't know who the man was or who he represented. He was probably one of the gang members."

"Yes, possibly. It doesn't matter now, not for the moment anyway."

Maggie wanted to interject and raised her hand.

"What happens now?" she asked.

Antonio looked over to Felipe again.

"You tell them, Felipe, I've done enough talking for now."

Felipe was somewhat taken by surprise; he did not expect Antonio to ask him to speak. He thought Antonio would do all the talking.

"Er! What do you want me to say?" he asked.

"Tell them about the gang," Antonio said.

"Oh yes, the gang," Felipe said.

Felipe spent a few moments gathering his thoughts before speaking.

"Well, there is an international gang of criminals working out of the UK, with connections in Brazil. The organisation is large, and they have, how you say, fingers in many pies."

"What gang? What organisation?" George asked.

"They are called 'Money for All,' MFA for short. They got wind of the newly designed PCB, and wanted to get their hands on it..."

"You can see why," Antonio interrupted, "Imagine if they got their hands on such technology, they would be able to identify hardwood trees and mining areas, to log and mine illegally. It would be a disaster for the region."

Antonio looked back at Felipe for him to continue.

"The PCB design has not been formally released for use as yet. The British government wanted to get a sample board to the Brazilian government for trial purposes, without anyone knowing, but the MFA found out about it. We are not sure how; there must be a leak somewhere."

"Why did you not send it by normal 'spy' channels?" George asked.

As he spoke, George raised both hands to indicate quotations around the word 'spy.'

"As I said," Felipe continued, "the board has not been formally released for use as yet. So, we needed to think of a way to get the PCB across to Brazil, and at the same time, try to mislead the MFA gang."

"And that's the reason why you used us?" Maggie asked.

"Yes," Antonio replied, "It was fortunate for us that George was overheard in the pub in England, he stated you were coming to Brazil on holiday. It fitted into our plans quite nicely, and was the reason why we approached you."

George looked over to Maggie with raised eyebrows, and then back at Antonio.

So that's it," he said, "It's all over. I presume the real board has been delivered by now, and the dud board has been sold, so we can all go home now."

"No, not just yet," Antonio said.

He looked across at Felipe and nodded his head for him to continue.

George and Maggie also looked at Felipe, who smiled at the couple and then took a deep breath.

"Well, Mr and Mrs Peacock. Er, can I call you George and Maggie?"

George looked at Maggie and somehow thought they were about to be sweet-talked into doing something else.

"That's fine," George said, "What now?"

Felipe looked across at Antonio and then back at the couple.

"We would like your help," Felipe said.

"Our help!" George exclaimed, "What sort of help?"

"It could be dangerous for you, but you guys are best placed to help us."

"Dangerous? What do you mean? What sort of help?" George asked.

"We are planning a sting operation to flush out the MFA gang, and want you to help us."

Maggie sat back in the settee and folded her arms.

"Ha! You're joking, of course," she said.

"No, we're not," Felipe replied, "you have already made contact with the gang, and all we ask is for you to help us."

"Help you to do what?" Maggie asked.

Felipe bowed his head, feeling humbled. He knew he was going to ask the couple to do something outside their comfort zone.

"As part of the sting operation, we would like you to set up a meeting with the gang," he said.

"I think Maggie is right," George added, "you must be crazy, we're booked on a flight to the UK tomorrow."

"It won't take long," Felipe said.

"How long?" George asked.

Maggie looked across at George with disgust and wondered if he was really contemplating helping Antonio.

"Whoa there!" she scathingly said to George, "you can't be seriously thinking about this, after all we've been through?"

George was surprised by Maggie's interruption and her comment.

"I was just asking, that's all," he replied.

Felipe saw the opportunity to continue, and quickly interrupted the couple.

"A day or two, maybe three, no more," he said.

Maggie, still fuming at the suggestion, turned to George and gave him an objectionable look. George felt he should not upset Maggie anymore, and shrugged his shoulders towards Felipe.

"As I mentioned, we are booked on a flight out tomorrow," he said.

"We can take care of the flights, if that's all you are worried about," Antonio said.

"Stop, stop," Maggie shouted, "Where are we going with this? We shouldn't even be contemplating this."

"We can also compensate you for services to the government," Antonio added.

George looked at Antonio and raised his eyebrows. Even though it could be dangerous, he saw an opportunity to earn some extra money; it was always in George's nature to make a quick buck.

"What sort of compensation?" George asked.

"Well, first of all, we can change your return flight to first class, and of course, we can pay you cash for your services."

"Cash? What kind of cash? How much?" George asked.

"We would need to decide on the amount we can give you, and I would need to check if it's ok with my superiors."

"You'd have to make it really worthwhile for us, I'm not going to do this sort of thing for peanuts," George said.

Maggie was now very cross with George and stood up abruptly, interrupting the conversation.

"Can I have a word with my husband on our own, please?" she insisted.

All three men looked at Maggie and sensed her unhappiness with the suggestion.

"Ok," Antonio said, "let's have a break, Felipe and I will go into the next room, and leave you guys alone for a while."

Antonio and Felipe went into the adjacent office and closed the door behind them, leaving George and Maggie to talk on their own. Maggie shook her head from side to side and waved an index finger at George.

"You're crazy, you know," she said, "you are darn right crazy."

"I know it sounds dangerous, but think about it," George said, "all we have to do is possibly set up a meeting between MI6 and the MFA gang, and that's it."

"You make it sound so simple," Maggie said, "bringing the package here was supposed to be simple, and look what happened, it turned out to be a disaster."

"Just think of the extra money we would get, we could make thousands here, and think what we could do with it back home."
Tears began to form in Maggie's eyes, thinking about the consequences of endangering their lives.
"It's not the money," she said. "What about our lives? You were already shot once, doesn't that mean anything to you?"
"Yes, I agree being shot was serious, but we are here now, and we have an opportunity to make extra money."
"You're just greedy, George, that's your problem, you're just greedy."
Well, what do you say? Shall we do it?"
Maggie turned away from George and looked up at the ceiling. She remained silent for a minute while wiping the tears from her eyes.
"Well?" George asked, "They're waiting to hear from us. What are we going to do?"
Maggie turned around to face George.
"You are probably going to do what you want to do anyway," she said, "You always do, and I never have a say in it."
"It'll probably turn out all right. We will only be here for another day or so, and think we can travel back in first class."
George was now sweet-talking Maggie, and she knew it. She folded her arms and gave out a heavy sigh.
"I'm reluctant to do this," she said, "I'm frightened we could get hurt, but I will go along with it."
"Great!" George said, "Terrific!"
He walked across to Maggie and gave her a great big hug. She did not reciprocate the hug and kept her arms to her side. Maggie felt George had forced her into agreeing with him, and did not feel a hug was appropriate. George also felt uneasy; he pushed Maggie into the agreement and caressed her back to comfort her.
"You'll see," he said, "it will work out all right. Shall we call them back in?"

George opened the door to the adjacent office and popped his head through the doorway.
"Hi guys, we've decided to go ahead and help you with your plan," he said.

"Oh great," Antonio said. "Are you sure? Are you definitely sure?"

"Yes, we will help you."

Antonio looked at Maggie standing behind George in the doorway.

"Are you in agreement as well, Mrs Peacock? We have to be sure."

Maggie pushed past George and came through the doorway.

"Yes, reluctantly," she said, "but I have agreed to do it."

"You won't regret this," Antonio said.

He tried to ease the tense situation with an off-the-cuff remark.

"We might make spies out of you two yet," he said.

"One other thing," Felipe said, "while you were having your discussion, we spoke to our bosses, and agreed on the compensation for you."

"I hope it's good," Maggie said, "it better be worthwhile."

"What have you agreed?" George asked, "What can you give us?"

"We can pay you £5000 for your efforts," Antonio said, "we've taken into consideration the troubles you've had, and we feel £5000 will be sufficient for your inconveniences. What do you say?"

George looked across at Maggie and smiled at her, but she remained poker-faced. He felt excitement within because the adrenaline was flowing through his veins, and went over to shake Antonio and Felipe's hands.

"That sounds good," George said, "What do we do now?"

"Let's go and celebrate," Antonio said, "you guys must be starving. We interrupted your lunch, so I'm sure you're ready to eat something."

Antonio looked at his watch and continued.

"It's nearly 5 o'clock, and I could do with something to eat as well."

He then turned to his colleague.

"What about you, Felipe?" he asked.

"Yes, I am also starving, let's go to eat. Hopefully, we can continue the discussion there."

The foursome left the MI6 offices and headed to a nearby restaurant.

They ordered a meal and some wine, and then toasted the agreement made to catch the MFA gang. Antonio was very aware that others were seated nearby in the restaurant. He looked around to ensure no one was listening to them and spoke in a quiet voice.

"Listen," he said, "we must be careful our conversation is not overheard, so try to keep your voices down."

All of the other three nodded in agreement.

"You must have some contact details with which to get in touch with the gang. Mustn't you?" Antonio asked George.

"Yes, I had a telephone number."

"Have you still got it?"

"I'm not sure," George said.

George searched his pockets for the piece of paper the man in black gave him. He emptied all his pockets and eventually found the piece of paper with the number hidden among some Brazilian currency.

"Ah! Here it is, I've found it."

He handed the piece of paper to Antonio, who looked at the number.

"I'm not aware of the number," Antonio said.

He, in turn, handed the piece of paper to Felipe.

"Does the number mean anything to you?"

Felipe looked at the number and did not recognise it either. He searched on his mobile phone for the number, in case he had previously recorded it, but was unlucky with the search.

"No, I don't recognise it either," he said.

Felipe handed the piece of paper back to George.

"Ok, here is my plan," Antonio said, "I have given it some thought."

The other three listened intensely.

"You need to make contact with the gang again," Antonio said to George.

"That's cool, I can do that," George replied.

"You then tell them the printed circuit board you sold to them was a dud. Then you say that there were two boards, and you accidentally gave them the wrong board. Apologise to them, say you're deeply sorry, and make it sound real. Does that sound plausible to you?"

George looked at Maggie, then back at Antonio, and nodded in agreement.

"Now, before they say anything," Antonio continued, "you offer to meet with them again, to give them the correct board."

"What if they say something?" George asked in a raised voice.

"Shush," Antonio said.

He looked around the restaurant while George raised his hand in an apology, and covered his mouth in embarrassment.

"Sorry," he said, "I'm very sorry, I'll try to be careful."

"You'll have to play it by ear," Antonio said, "We will be listening in when you make the call, and can indicate what you need to say. Is that alright?"

"I suppose so," George replied.

All four remained silent for a few seconds, looked at each other, then Antonio continued.

"Any questions so far?" he asked.

George raised his hand to indicate he wanted to say something.

"Where shall I agree to meet them?" he asked.

"Well, I'll leave that up to you. Maybe somewhere convenient for you."

George looked over to Maggie for help, but she had a bewildered look on her face.

"What do you think?" he asked.

"I don't know what to think. This is really so strange, it's like being in a James Bond movie."

"What about the same restaurant where we met the man in black?" George asked Maggie.

"Hmm! Is that wise?" Maggie asked, "Maybe somewhere with a lot more people."

Antonio and Felipe were listening to the couple's conversation, and Antonio decided to add his thoughts.

"Yes, that's a good idea, somewhere busy," he said.

All four went silent again for a few seconds while thinking of an ideal place for the couple to meet the gang. George then had an idea and became enthusiastic.

"I know," he said, "what about the airport? We could arrange to catch our flight tomorrow, so maybe the airport would be the best place to meet. We could do our bit, and then catch our flight afterwards. We would be able to leave quickly and not get involved anymore."

"Sounds good to me," Antonio said.

He then looked over to Felipe.

"What do you think, Felipe?"

Felipe gave the suggestion a moment's thought and nodded his head in agreement.

"Yes, it could work," he replied, "I don't see any reason why not."

"Good, we'll have to arrange your flights soon," Antonio said.

"I'll take care of the flights," Felipe added.

"Right," Antonio said, "then all that remains is for George to make the call."

All three looked at George, and he became nervous at the thought of his part in the deal. His hands began to shake from the fear of making the call, and he felt he needed to say something to alleviate the tension.

"Ok, it's all down to me now," he said, "When shall I make the call?"

"After dinner," Antonio said, "let's enjoy our meal."

Dinner was served, and the foursome spent the next hour eating while reviewing the plan many times.

The time was now 6:30 pm, and after the meal, the group made their way back to the MI6 office. When they arrived, Paul was waiting for them. He was another MI6 operative, and turned out to be the man in the brown leather jacket George had seen before on many occasions. He was English and was introduced to George and Maggie.

"Paul is going to help us catch the gang," Antonio said.

George looked at Paul and thought he recognised him.

"Have we met before?" he asked Paul.

Paul shook his head from side to side.

"I don't think so," he said, "we've never met before."

"I could have sworn we crossed paths before," George said.

Paul was aware of George and Maggie and knew he may have been seen before by the couple. He was one of the men in the pub when contact was first made with George. He was seated in the café at London Heathrow Airport when the couple were having breakfast before leaving for Brazil. He was also on the plane to Rio, seated not far away from Karl and Helmut. And he brushed past George at Iguassu Falls, when the couple were escaping from the shooting. Paul tried to keep a straight face.

"No, I don't think we've met before," he said, "I'm sure I would remember."

"You've got me intrigued," George said, "I've got a good memory for faces. I'll think about it."

While George and Maggie were being introduced to Paul and having a subsequent conversation, Felipe contacted British Airways and rearranged the couple's flights back to the UK.

"All done," he said, "I booked you on a BA flight, first class, leaving at 1 pm tomorrow."

"Great," George said.

George then looked over to Maggie, all cock-a-hoot.

"A bit of style, eh!" he said.

"Yes, it certainly sounds good," Maggie replied.

"Ok, "Antonio said, "let's get down to business. Please sit down."

Antonio beckoned for George and Maggie to sit at one desk, and he sat at another.

"The plan is this," he said.

He paused for a moment, and the others listened intensely. Antonio then looked at George and spoke professionally.

"You're going to call the man in black and tell him there were two PCBs you were supposed to give them, and you only gave him one by mistake when you previously met. Then, arrange to meet him tomorrow at the International Café, in the departure lounge at the airport, to give him the other board. Tell him 12 noon, but in truth, we will be there by 11 o'clock. Does that sound plausible?"

George nodded his head in agreement and looked nervously at Maggie.

"I think so," he said, "but what if he asks me questions?"

"You'll just have to ad-lib; he probably won't ask you much, so you'll have to play it by ear."

"Ok, I'll try to be on the ball."

Paul looked over to Felipe, shrugged his shoulders, and opened his hands as if to ask, 'What is this all about?' He seemed perplexed that they were going to make contact with the gang again, and was intrigued by why the gang had been handed the wrong PCB. Paul had arrived at the office after the plans for the sting operation were formulated in the restaurant earlier, and missed out on the reason for arranging the meeting. It was a warm evening, and the ambient temperature in the office seemed to make Paul feel nauseous, so he made an excuse to leave to get some fresh air. He said he would be back in a short while.

Felipe attached a listening device to the phone George was going to use, and it enabled Antonio and him to listen in on the conversation.

"Are you ready for this?" Antonio asked George.

"Yes, as ready as can be," he replied.

George's hands began to shake nervously as he picked up the phone.

"Ok," Antonio said, "be calm, take a deep breath, and relax."

"Relax!" George exclaimed, "I've never done this kind of thing before, and I'm really terrified."

George took the piece of paper with the number on it from his pocket, unfolded it gently, and dialled the number on the paper. The phone rang for about a minute, and no one answered; George put the phone down. He felt tense, rubbed his forehead, and stood up to walk around the room to ease the tension. Felipe was sympathetic to George's unease; he offered to make some coffee, and soon disappeared into the kitchenette. A couple of minutes later, George sat back down and, still feeling nervous, rubbed his chin constantly. The others sat in silence, anticipating the upcoming telephone call. A few minutes later, and to everyone's relief, Felipe returned with the coffee.

"Try again," Antonio said.

George was still feeling nervous and dialled the number a second time. Maggie was seated next to him and rested her hand on his shoulder to give him moral support. This time, the number was engaged, and George slammed the phone down immediately. He waited a few minutes to calm himself and dialled again. This time, someone answered the phone.

213

"Hello," a voice said in Portuguese.

George tensed up again and was not able to speak.

"Hello, who is this?" the voice on the other end of the phone asked again.

Antonio beckoned with his hands for George to speak, but before speaking, George cleared his throat because it felt dry.

"Hello, this is George, the Englishman, the one with the printed circuit board."

"George! The Englishman!" the voice repeated in English.

"Yes, I met with a man dressed in black yesterday, and sold him a printed circuit board."

"A man in black?" the voice asked, "Ah, I know who you mean, I'll get him."

The man put the phone down, and George could hear footsteps walking away from the phone. There was silence for about a minute, then someone else picked up the phone.

"Hello, who is this?" the voice said.

"It's George. I met a man in black yesterday, and sold him a printed circuit board. Can I speak to him?"

"Yes, that would be me," the voice said, "How can I help you?"

George paused for a moment. He was about to tell some lies to the man on the other end of the phone, and was feeling very nervous. Maggie sensed this and massaged George's shoulders, which gave him the courage to continue.

"Er, Um, I only gave you one board yesterday."

"One board! What do you mean?"

"There were two boards, and I only gave you one by mistake."

"I see," the man in black said, "two boards."

There was silence on the phone for a few moments.

"How come there were two boards?" the man asked.

"I was given two boards, and meant to give them both to you, but I was nervous and forgot to bring the other one with me when we last met."

"So, what do you intend to do?" the man asked.

"That's the reason for calling, I'd like to meet you again to give you the other board."

The man remained silent, and George sensed he seemed perplexed. Antonio then beckoned for George to continue the conversation.

214

"Can we meet again?" George asked.

"Yes, I suppose so," the man said, "where do you suggest?"

"At the airport, tomorrow."

"What airport? And at what time?"

"Rio International, at 12 noon, in the departure area."

The man on the other end of the phone was silent for a while. George raised his eyebrows at Antonio, who subsequently raised his hand to George, telling him to be patient.

"Noon is fine," the man said, "tomorrow at noon."

"How shall I find you?" George asked.

"Don't worry, we will find you, we will meet you at the International Café."

There was a pause at the other end of the line, and George was a bit surprised that the man suggested the International Café.

"That's a coincidence," George said, "it was the same café I was going to suggest."

The man in black ignored George's remark and continued.

"And don't forget to bring the other board this time," he said.

George was now keen to end the call. He looked up to Antonio for guidance, who passed his hand across his throat, for George to end the call.

"Ok, goodbye," George said.

The phone went dead at the other end, and George put the phone down. He was relieved to finish the call and rubbed his forehead with his hand to alleviate the tension.

"Phew!" he said, looking at his hands, "I am shaking."

"Well done," Antonio said.

"Yes, well done," Maggie added.

Maggie then patted George on the shoulder to give him encouragement and moral support.

"Very good," Felipe said.

All three men shook hands across the desk and were pleased that the plans for the next day were coming to fruition.

Chapter 13 - The Double Cross

George was worried about something that concerned him, and before the couple departed for the hostel, he broached the subject with Antonio.

"One other thing," he said to Antonio.

"What's that?" Antonio asked.

He remained attentive to George and wanted to hear his concerns, not wanting to leave any loose ends.

"Something has been bothering me for a while," George said.

"What's that, my friend?"

Maggie was puzzled at George's comment and looked over to him, as if to ask, '*What are you going to say now?*'

"I've never been able to figure out how the gang knew about the package," George said.

Maggie had further thoughts, '*Oh no, here he goes again, what is he up to now?*'

"What do you mean, knew about the package?" Antonio asked.

Felipe and Maggie now became interested in what George had to say and listened attentively.

"Well, I was given the package in London to bring to Brazil," George said.

"Yes, that's right," Antonio replied.

"How did the gang come on to me straight away? I first noticed them at Heathrow airport, so don't you think it's a bit odd they were following us from that point onwards?"

Antonio nodded his head in agreement with George.

"Yes, I see what you mean."

Antonio then looked across at Felipe for moral support.

"Do you have any ideas?" he asked.

Felipe was none the wiser and shrugged his shoulders with open arms.

"No, boss," he replied, "beats me."

"And it was something the man in black also said on the phone a minute ago, which made me think that something doesn't seem right," George said.

"What did he say?" Antonio asked.

"Do you remember when I said I would meet him at noon tomorrow?"

"Yes."

"Well, he was the one who suggested meeting at the International Café. I did not mention the cafe to him before, so why did he choose it, and how did he know I was going to suggest it?"

"Yes, I remember now, he did say he would meet you there."

"That's right," Felipe added, "he did suggest the International Cafe."

George looked at Maggie, raised his eyebrows, and shrugged his shoulders, while Antonio looked across a bit puzzled at Felipe.

"The only people who knew the suggested meeting point were us, only us in this room," Antonio said, "we were the only ones who knew you were going to suggest the International Café."

"So why did he mention the café?" Maggie asked, "And how did he know?"

They all looked perplexed at each other, and the answer dawned on them in a Eureka moment.

"Paul," they all said at the same time.

"Where is Paul?" Antonio asked.

"He went outside to get some fresh air," Felipe replied.

"I don't believe it," Antonio said, "Paul wouldn't do such a thing, and he is so trustworthy. Having said that, we've suspected for some time that there was a mole in the organisation. Surely it can't be!"

The others remained silent, not yet understanding the consequences of Antonio's remark. Antonio then turned to Felipe.

"Go and find Paul, and bring him back. I need to talk to him."

"Yes, boss."

Felipe grabbed his mobile phone and exited the office immediately to find Paul.

Antonio looked at George and Maggie with open hands, indicating that he did not understand why Paul would do such a thing.

"Also," George said, "I thought it strange I kept noticing Paul over the last few days."

"How do you mean?" Antonio asked.

"Well, he wears a very distinctive brown leather jacket, and I noticed him on many occasions."

"Where was this?"

"Oh, different places. I first noticed him in England, in the pub. Then I saw him again at Heathrow Airport, and again on the plane. The last time was at Iguassu Falls, yes, that was the last time I saw him."

"But he only arrived in Rio two days ago," Antonio said.

George was taken aback and surprised at Antonio's comment.

"Couldn't have. I definitely saw him on the plane, and at Iguassu Falls. I'm sure it was him, and would bet my life on it."

George then turned to Maggie for moral support.

"Did you not see him as well?" he asked, "he was seated in the corner of the café at Heathrow Airport when we were having breakfast. Then we passed him as we walked along the aisle on the plane to stretch our legs. He was seated a few rows away from the Germans."

"No, I don't recall any of that," Maggie said, "but your memory is much better than mine."

George turned back to face Antonio.

"I'm telling you the truth, Antonio, I wouldn't make up something like this."

Antonio raised his hands and faced them towards George.

"Ok, hold on a moment," he said, "I believe you, let's see what Paul has to say for himself."

In the meantime, Felipe exited the building to look for Paul and found him smoking a cigarette on the pavement a few metres away from the office. He was also on his mobile phone. Felipe did not let on that they were suspicious of him.

"Hey, Paul," Felipe shouted, "The boss wants to see you."

Paul turned around and saw Felipe beckoning for him to come. Felipe noticed Paul had a guilty look on his face and ended the call immediately.

"What does he want?" Paul asked.

"I don't know, he just asked me to fetch you."

Paul took one more drag of the cigarette, threw it on the ground and stepped on it. He followed Felipe back into the building, and neither man spoke on the way.

Felipe and Paul entered the office, where the other three were still seated.

"You wanted to see me," Paul said to Antonio.

"Yes, come and sit here," Antonio replied, "I want to ask you a few things."

Paul sat down and looked across at George and Maggie. They stared back at him, and he sensed something was not quite right.

"You said you arrived in Rio from England two days ago." Antonio said, "Is that correct?"

Paul became nervous at the line of questioning, but kept a straight face.

"Yes, that's correct," he replied.

"And have you been in Rio all this time?"

"Yes."

Antonio looked over to Felipe, as if to ask the question, *'Is he telling the truth or not?'*

"Is there a problem?" Paul asked, "Why are you asking me all these questions?"

"We're trying to establish your whereabouts over the last few days," Antonio replied, "George said he saw you at Heathrow when they left England over a week ago, and again on the plane coming over."

"He must be mistaken. I only arrived in Rio two days ago."

George was furious at Paul's blatant lies and interrupted the conversation.

"That's not true," he shouted, "I did see you in the café at Heathrow Airport, and again on the plane. You were seated a few rows in front of the people we met at the airport. Furthermore, I saw you at other times, in the pub in England, and at Iguassu Falls."

Paul felt he needed to defend himself from George's accusations.

"I must have a twin then," he said.

George was not amused and felt Paul was trying to squirm out of the accusations. He became sarcastic towards Paul.

"Twin my ass," he said, "one who wears the same brown jacket? A double agent, most likely."

Paul stared at George in disgust, but remained silent.

"Hey, hold on there," Antonio said, "there is no need for that kind of talk, George."

"Well, he is calling me a liar, is he not?" George asked.

"It's your word against his," Antonio said, "but there is one way to prove this."

Everyone in the room looked at Antonio with anticipation, hoping he knew the answer to solve the dilemma. He turned to Paul.

"If you arrived two days ago, your passport would show the date you arrived in Rio," he said. "Can I see your passport?"

Paul needed time to think of an answer and thought for a moment.

"I don't have my passport with me; it's in my apartment."

Antonio was somewhat surprised at Paul's comment.

"You don't have your passport!" he said, "You should always have your passport. It is the rules of the organisation to carry our passports with us at all times. Is this a delaying tactic, Paul?"

"No, I don't have it with me, as I said, I left it in my apartment."

Antonio put out his hand towards Paul.

"Come on," he said, "come on, hand it over. I know you have it with you."

Paul remained silent and looked around at Felipe. He now knew they were on to him, and his passport would prove it. He needed to escape immediately and noticed there was no one between him and the office door. He stood up and dashed for the door. Felipe anticipated Paul's move and tried to stop him, but could not catch him in time. Paul exited the office and ran down the stairwell, closely followed by Felipe. He made it out of the building and onto the pavement, where he ran as fast as he could. Felipe soon reached the pavement, but could not catch up with Paul, and saw him disappearing into the crowds in the distance.

Meanwhile, back in the office, Antonio was very concerned about the new complication and spoke to George.

"It seems you were right all along. Paul may be the mole we suspected in the organisation."

"I told you I saw him, I was pretty sure," George said.

George felt smug and looked over to Maggie.

"See, I was right," he said.

Maggie nodded her head in agreement.

"Yes, George," she said, "you were right, you are always right, it's infuriating."

Antonio sensed a domestic argument might arise and needed to bring the two back on track.

"We must continue with tomorrow's plan," Antonio said, "we have to go ahead and complete the sting."

A few minutes later, Felipe returned to the office, breathing heavily.

"No luck," he said, while trying to take a deep breath, "Paul got away from me. He was much too fast for me."

"That's a shame," Antonio said, "He could jeopardise our plan, and spoil everything tomorrow. Which way did he head?"

Felipe was still puffing from the chase and took another deep breath.

"In the direction of his accommodation," he said.

"That's not good; he's probably going to collect his belongings and disappear from us. We must try to get to him before he collects his stuff."

"What are we going to do?" George asked.

"I don't know yet," Antonio said, "allow me a moment to think."

Antonio rubbed his forehead, while George looked up at Felipe and grimaced. Maggie sat nonchalantly and kept quiet, while Antonio thought for a bit longer.

"I know," he said, "it's our only chance. It might just work, but we will be taking a risk; otherwise, we may lose him."

"What do you have in mind, boss?" Felipe asked.

"Paul shares an apartment with another operative. I'll call John and ask him to restrain Paul until we get there; it's our only chance."

Antonio took out his mobile phone, searched for John's number, and dialled it.

The phone rang and John immediately answered it.

"Hi John, Antonio here."

John was about to speak, and was quickly cut short by Antonio.

"John, this is an urgent call. We need you to act swiftly to help us."

John sensed the urgency in Antonio's voice and that it was not a social call.

"What's up, Antonio?" he asked.

"We suspect Paul of being a mole."

"What? Our Paul?"

"Yes, our Paul."

"I don't believe it."

"Neither did I, but it seems it could be true."

"What do you want me to do?" John asked.

Antonio knew he was taking a chance with John and could not be sure if John was in cahoots with Paul, but he sensed he was on the level and willing to help. He had no alternative but to ask John for help.

"We were talking to Paul in the office a few minutes ago, and it seems he did not like the line of questioning. He suspiciously ran away and couldn't catch him. We believe he is heading back to the apartment to collect his belongings."

John now became concerned and was keen to help Antonio.

"So, what do you want me to do?" he asked again.

"Have a friendly chat with John when he gets back. Do not let on that we suspect him, and try to keep him in the apartment. We will be there soon."

"You want me to hold him here, is that it?" John asked.

Antonio realised he was asking John to detain one of their agents, one who may be unpredictable and dangerous.

"Yes, we don't want to lose him; otherwise, he will disappear, and we may never find him."

"Ok, I'll do my best."

"You've got to be careful, John," Antonio said, "if he thinks he's been found out, he may be dangerous; you've got to be on your guard."

"Ok, I'll take care of it, you can trust me."

"We're leaving now and will be with you in fifteen minutes."

"Ok, see you later."

The call ended, and they started their own course of action.

"Right, let's go," Antonio said, "it's now 7:30, and we've got lots to do."

Everyone in the office stood up in readiness. Antonio and Felipe both took out the pistols from inside their jackets and checked the ammunition. It was not the normal environment for George and Maggie, and they became nervous at the sight of guns. They felt unsure where they fitted in at this stage.

"Are we coming with you guys? George asked.

"If you want to," Antonio replied.

"But it could be dangerous," Maggie added.

"Yes, it could, so it's up to you if you come along," Antonio said, "you've been helpful so far, but if you come with us, you must follow my instructions."

George looked at Maggie, and they both felt a sense of adventure come over them. They nodded in agreement with each other.

"Ok, we'll tag along," George said.

All four headed down to the basement car park, where Antonio's car was located. The group bundled into the car and headed at speed to Paul's apartment.

In the meantime, John prepared himself for Paul's return to the apartment. He checked his gun and hid it in the top of his trousers under his shirt. He turned on the TV, slouched in the settee, and waited for Paul to return. John was anxious and did not pay much attention to the TV program being screened. It was not long before Paul arrived at the apartment and entered the lounge. He gave the impression of calmness and did not want to alarm John. Similarly, John also remained calm and acted as if he knew nothing of Paul's plight.

"Hi," Paul said.

"Hi mate, what's up?" John asked.

"Not much."

"How was your day?" John asked.

"Boring."

The conversation was very brief, and Paul went to his bedroom, leaving John alone in the lounge.

John was waiting for Antonio to arrive and wanted to check what Paul was doing in the bedroom. But first, he went to the front door of the apartment and unlocked it for Antonio to gain access. John then made his way to Paul's bedroom to find him packing his bags.

"What are you doing?" John asked, "Are you going somewhere?"

Paul was caught off guard by the question and needed to think of an answer quickly.

"Yes, I've decided to take a last-minute holiday, and booked it earlier today."

"Sounds good to me. Where are you going?"

Paul was caught once more with the question and needed to think of another answer.

"Er," he said, "down the coast."

Paul was anxious to pack his bags, and John needed to delay him. He felt he should strike up a conversation with Paul to try to keep him at the apartment. At least, until Antonio arrived, but was unsure when Antonio would get there.

"That's a sudden decision, isn't it?" John asked.

"Yes, these short breaks are normally a last-minute choice."

Paul packed two bags, picked them up, and brushed past John standing in the doorway to the bedroom. There was an urgency in Paul's action. He wanted to leave the apartment as soon as possible, and John felt he had to hinder Paul to stop him from leaving. He pulled out his gun and followed Paul into the lounge.

"Hold on a moment, Paul," John said.

John readied the gun and pointed it at Paul. Paul heard the click of the gun and immediately stopped in his tracks. He realised John must be aware of the situation.

"Put your bags down, Paul, you are not going anywhere."

Paul stood there with his back to John, but still held onto his bags.

"You don't mean that, do you, buddy? You are not going to shoot me, are you?"

"I will if I have to, now put down your bags, and sit down."

Paul had to think of a way out of the dilemma and needed to distract John. He dropped one bag to the floor, quickly spun around, and threw the other bag at John, who, in a reflex action,

224

tried to dodge the bag coming his way. But the bag collided with the arm holding the gun, and forced it upwards. John instinctively pulled the trigger, and the pistol discharged. There was a loud 'crack' and the bullet missed Paul by inches, lodging into the ceiling behind him. Paul took the opportunity to charge at John and managed to disengage the gun from his hand. The gun fell to the floor, and Paul quickly kicked it away. He tried to punch John in the face, but John ducked the punch and grabbed hold of Paul's body. Both men fell to the ground and wrestled for a minute or two, each throwing and receiving punches to the head and body. They were both trained MI6 agents, and their skills were almost equal, so they knew how to handle themselves. At one point, John shoved Paul away with his legs, and Paul crashed against the wall, falling onto the floor. He recovered quickly and noticed John's pistol on the floor a few inches away from him. John also noticed this and immediately tried to charge Paul, but was stopped in his tracks when Paul grabbed the pistol and aimed it at him. John stood still and raised his arms in surrender. Paul kept the gun pointed at John and stood up.

"Now the tables are turned, aren't they?" Paul asked.

"So, it seems," John replied, "It is true then, how could you do such a thing? How could you betray your own kind?"

"Needs must," Paul replied, "one has to look after oneself, and the opportunity came along, so I took it."

"What are you going to do now?" John asked.

Paul pointed the gun closer to John's head.

"Well, you are the only person who can stop me from escaping now."

John was now very anxious and hoped Antonio would arrive soon. He could see Paul's finger tightening on the trigger of the gun, and his stomach churned. He felt nauseous at the thought of the gun going off. Both men stared intensely into each other's eyes, and John wondered if this was the end for him.

Paul knew the sound of the previous gunshot would attract attention from the nearby residents, and he needed to act quickly. His back was to the door of the apartment, and he was about to pull the trigger when Antonio burst into the lounge behind him.

225

"Stop right there," Antonio shouted, "put the gun down."

Antonio arrived just in the nick of time to stop Paul from committing a heinous crime. It was nighttime, and because there was less traffic on the roads, Antonio was able to make his way to the address quickly. John's forethought of leaving the door ajar allowed Antonio to gain access to the apartment. Felipe and the couple followed closely behind. Paul was unsure whether to make a run for it, but hesitated. Felipe went around to the side of Paul and also held a gun on him. George and Maggie remained at the door, and the situation now became a stalemate.

"Put the gun down," Antonio repeated, "your last chance."

Paul thought for a moment and realised his exploits were hopeless. He eased off the trigger and put his arms in the air. Antonio grabbed the gun from him immediately, while Felipe still pointed his gun towards Paul. John felt utterly relieved and took a deep breath.

"Thank god," he said, "you came at the right moment, just in the nick of time."

Antonio turned Paul around so they faced each other. Paul looked dejected and glanced over Antonio's shoulder to see George and Maggie both smiling with delight.

"Well, my friend, it's all over," Antonio said, "for you anyway."

At that moment, two uniformed police officers pushed George and Maggie aside and burst into the room with guns ready.

"Everyone, stand still," one said in Portuguese.

"Put your guns down," the other said.

Antonio turned and looked at them.

"Internal Security," he said.

The two officers looked at Antonio strangely, and then at each other.

"I have ID, let me show you," Antonio said.

"Ok," one police officer said, "put the guns on the floor first, and let me see your ID."

Antonio lowered the two guns he held onto the floor and stood back from them. Felipe also did the same. Antonio and Felipe carefully took out their security badges from their jackets and showed them to the two police officers. They, in turn, scrutinised the badges and were satisfied that Antonio was telling the truth. "Ok," one officer said, "It seems you are really from Internal Security, and seem to have everything under control."

"Is there anything we can help you with?" the other officer asked.

"No, we're fine," Antonio said, "maybe you could deal with the crowd outside."

"Yes, certainly," one officer said, "we'll leave you to it."

The officers holstered their guns and departed. George and Maggie felt very tense and sat on the settee to relax. Felipe beckoned for Paul to sit in another chair, while Antonio had a quick word with John.

"Well done," he said, "good job."

He patted John on the shoulder and then turned to Paul.

"It seems you did this for nothing, Paul?" he said.

"What do you mean?" Paul asked.

"The PCB was a dud anyway, and you were wasting your time all along."

Paul looked perplexed at Antonio; he was unaware that the PCB brought to Brazil by the couple was not genuine.

"I thought it was real," he said, "The gang were expecting a genuine PCB."

"Well, you can't know everything," Antonio said, "another operative brought over the real board, and it is in safe hands now."

"But what about the meeting tomorrow?" Paul asked, "You arranged to hand over another PCB, what's that all about?"

"Only a decoy, my friend," Antonio said, "It's a sting to catch the gang."

Paul felt utterly embarrassed and held his head in his hands.

"Oh my god," he said, "What a fool I've been."

John thought it was time to make coffee and went to the kitchen, while Antonio made a few telephone calls to his colleagues for them to collect Paul. It was mid-evening before Paul was eventually taken away.

"Listen," Antonio said to the couple, "I have to arrange our end of the deal for tomorrow, so I need time to prepare."

"Ok, I understand," George said, "I think we need to get an early night anyway, maybe some fresh air as well."

"Yes, I could do with a walk," Maggie said, "I need to relax."

"I will pick you up from your hostel at 10 in the morning and take you to the airport," Antonio said.

"Great," George replied, "saves us getting a taxi."

All bid farewell, and the couple left the apartment. George and Maggie took a short walk to stretch their legs and to get some fresh air before returning to the hostel. The couple retired early that evening.

Chapter 14 – Final Day Sting

The following morning, a car arrived at the hostel at exactly 10 o'clock to collect the couple. George and Maggie made their way outside to the waiting car, to be greeted by a bright-eyed and restless Felipe.

"Good morning," he said, "I hope you are well today."

"Good morning, Felipe," Maggie said, "where is Antonio?"

"Hello," George added, "no Antonio?"

"He still has some preparations to do and will meet us at the airport," Felipe said. "I will take you there."

The couple put the luggage in the boot of the car and sat in the back. Felipe was eager to get going and sped off towards the airport. The traffic was heavy, as it was on most days in Rio, and the same problem in most cities worldwide.

"See the package on the back seat," Felipe said, "that's for you."

George and Maggie looked at the package, and George picked it up.

"What is it?" he asked.

George was hoping it was the payment of £5000 for them, and began to massage the package to find out.

"It's the Printed Circuit Board you have to give to the gang, you know, another dummy one."

"Ah, yes," George said, "the other dummy one."

George smirked at Maggie due to his sarcastic remark and put the package in his travel bag for safekeeping. He became anxious and began to bite his nails.

"How long will it take to get there?" George asked.

"Oh, not long," Felipe replied, "We'll be there in about 20 minutes."

All three remained silent for the rest of the journey and thought only of the events awaiting them. Felipe concentrated on the driving, while George and Maggie stared out of the window, taking in their final views of Rio de Janeiro.

The threesome arrived about 10:30 at the departure area of Rio's airport, the Galeão International Airport, and were met by Antonio. George assumed the gang members were already at the airport and cautiously glanced around the concourse.

Antonio noticed the couple were very nervous, shook their hands, and tried to ease the tense situation.

"Good day for travelling, eh?" Antonio said.

"Yes, not bad," George replied.

"And you, Mrs Peacock, how are you?"

Maggie sidled up next to George and held his hand.

"Nervous," she replied, "very nervous."

"Ok, just relax," Antonio said, "my men are in place and we're safe."

"Your men!" George exclaimed.

He looked around the concourse again to see if he could spot any of Antonio's men, but they were well hidden, and he could not identify any of them.

"Yes, I have a dozen men scattered around. You won't know who or where they are, and that's probably a good thing. However, they have been briefed, and they will protect you, I can assure you."

Antonio's comment made George and Maggie feel slightly more relaxed.

"We can't be seen together for obvious reasons," Antonio said, "we need to split up, but we'll meet up again afterwards."

George knew he and Maggie would be on their own for a while, so he squeezed her hand to comfort her.

"Ok," he said.

"Go and have some coffee, or breakfast," Felipe said, "it will help to pass the time."

"Not to worry," Antonio said, "everything is under control. The MFA gang said they will make contact with you, so relax and wait for them."

"I hope you're right," George said.

George then turned to Maggie and put on a brave face.

"Let's go, Maggie," he said, "let's get this done and dusted."

The couple grabbed their luggage and walked away from Antonio and Felipe without looking back.

"Don't worry," Antonio shouted at them, "we've done this kind of thing before."

The couple turned around, gave wry smiles to the two men, and continued walking. After a few moments, Antonio shouted at the couple again.

"Wait, wait. I've forgotten something."

He ran towards George and Maggie and put his hand into his inside jacket pocket.

"I've collected these for you; they are your tickets," Antonio said. He handed the tickets to George and ushered them along to get going.

"Now go and eat you two."

George and Maggie decided to check in their luggage early and headed for the British Airways desks. Several people were already waiting, and Maggie was anxious that they had to queue.

"Look at the number of people," she said, "we'll have to wait a long time."

"Not really," George said, "you remember, we are flying first class."

"Oh yes," Maggie said, "I forgot."

George and Maggie located the check-in desk for first-class passengers, and as they approached, they were met by a BA member of staff.

"First Class?" she asked them.

"Yes," George replied.

He handed the tickets to the lady, who quickly glanced at them. "This way," she said.

The staff member then ushered them to the first-class check-in desk, where there was no queue. This was a bonus for the couple; they were not accustomed to such quick service.

"Thank you," Maggie said, and smiled at the staff member.

George and Maggie checked in their luggage and waited for the boarding passes. The clerk behind the desk typed some details into the computer and printed the passes, which he handed to the couple.

"Have a pleasant trip," he said.

George and Maggie looked at each other with raised eyebrows, and George responded sarcastically.

"I wish," he said.

The clerk looked at George curiously as they walked away from the desk. The couple passed the queues of people for economy class who were staring at them with envy. George and Maggie felt embarrassed, and as they were not accustomed to first-class treatment, they quickly walked away from the crowd. The luggage was now taken care of, so the couple searched for the International Café to have breakfast, the café where they were to make contact with the MFA gang.

It was just after eleven o'clock when the couple sat down at a window seat in the cafe. They ordered breakfast and waited to be contacted by the MFA gang. Many people walked by the window, and almost every time, George and Maggie tried to determine if the person was a member of the gang. Some of the people could have been MI6 operatives, but it was hard to tell the difference. Time elapsed, and the couple became even more nervous; the meeting with the MFA gang at 12 o'clock loomed.

A waiter soon brought the food to the table.
"Breakfast," he said.
George and Maggie were startled at the interruption; their minds were occupied elsewhere as they watched the people outside the café. It seemed any noise or interruption made the couple jittery.
"Thank you," Maggie said.
"You're welcome," the waiter replied.
He walked away from the table, and the couple took one look at the breakfast in front of them and screwed up their faces. They did not feel hungry enough to eat breakfast.
"I'm not able to eat that," Maggie said.
"Me neither," George added.
They pushed the plates to one side and looked out across the concourse again. George spotted a man dressed in a suit with his back to them.
"Is that Antonio?" George asked.
"Looks like him," Maggie replied.
The man turned around to look up at the departure monitor, and it was not Antonio. George and Maggie began to think that everyone in a suit was either a member of the MFA gang or an MI6 agent. They were becoming paranoid. On one occasion, a man walked by the café and stared at the couple with a stern face.

"That's definitely a gang member," George said, "What do you think?"

"Not sure, could be," Maggie replied.

Both thought the man was one of the gang members, but his action was in response to the couple staring at him in the first place. Most of the people who passed by, however, were travellers, and some of them were business people. The couple picked at the breakfast, but were in no mood to eat. They constantly asked the waiter for coffee, in the hope it would ease their nervousness, but drinking coffee was something to do to pass the time. Both George and Maggie regularly looked at their watches, hoping the time would pass quickly, but in fact, it passed slowly for them.

"I really don't like waiting," Maggie said.

"Me neither," George added.

He tapped on the table constantly, a sign of nervousness which irritated Maggie, causing her to nag him many times.

"Stop doing that," she said, "it's annoying me."

And each time George gave the same reply.

"Sorry, nerves."

Twelve o'clock came, and to the couple's disappointment, nothing happened. No one made contact with them, so George began to tap on the table again, and a few more minutes passed by.

The couple, obsessed with looking out of the window, were interrupted by a man dressed in casual clothes standing behind them.

"Excuse me," he said, "are you the English couple? The English couple with the package."

George and Maggie turned around to see a man smiling at them. He was not the type of person they expected, and was dressed in casual clothes. They stared rudely at the man's attire for a while. Nevertheless, he must have been the contact they were awaiting.

"Yes, we're English," George said.

"Have you got the package?" the man asked.

"Yes, we've got the package," George replied.

"Ok, you'll have to come with me."

"Where to?" George asked.

The man looked at George nonchalantly and insisted.

"Just come with me," he said.

The man began to walk away from the table and beckoned for the couple to follow him.

"No wait," George shouted, "where are you taking us?"

"You will see, come with me."

George and Maggie looked at each other and realised there was no other option than to follow the man.

"I'll have to pay the bill," George said to the man, "we've just eaten breakfast."

"It's all been taken care of," the man said, "I took care of it. You come with me now."

The man walked on and beckoned again for the couple to go with him. George and Maggie quickly grabbed their hand luggage and followed the man out of the café.

"Where are you taking us?" Maggie asked.

The man ignored Maggie's question and kept on walking, closely followed by the couple. George and Maggie looked around the concourse to find Antonio, but could not see him. Hopefully, he was there watching them, but there was no alternative but to follow the man.

While this was happening, Antonio and his men remained hidden from the couple and saw what transpired. He uttered an instruction through his intercom to his colleagues.

"Right, they've made contact, they're on the move, let's follow them."

Antonio and Felipe began to follow the couple a few steps back, while the other MI6 operatives remained hidden. The man in casual clothes led the couple across the concourse until he came to a door with a sign 'Private Security.'

"We go in here," the man said.

"Where does this take us?" George asked.

"You'll see," the man said.

He opened the door using an electronic pass and went through it, closely followed by George and Maggie. The door led through to the baggage processing area, where a series of conveyor belts carried many pieces of luggage. The noise from the conveyor machinery was too loud to have a conversation.

"This way," the man shouted.

Antonio and Felipe saw the couple disappear through the security door and ran towards it. The door was locked, and they couldn't gain access. They tried their best to push the door open, with no luck.

"Quick," Antonio shouted, "let's find a security guard. They would be able to open the door."

Antonio and Felipe looked for a guard, but they could not see any in the vicinity.

"Where is a guard when you need one?" Felipe rhetorically asked.

Antonio then pointed in one direction along the concourse.

"You go that way," he shouted to Felipe, "and I'll go the other way."

"Ok, boss," Felipe replied.

Antonio continued to give Felipe some more instructions.

"Find a guard, and we'll let each other know by intercom when we've found one, and we'll meet back here. Go quickly."

Both men ran in opposite directions in search of a security guard, and about 30 seconds passed before Felipe found one. He identified himself to the guard and asked for his help in opening the door. Felipe immediately contacted his boss on the intercom.

"Antonio, I've found one, I've found a guard, meet you back at the door."

"Ok, see you there," Antonio replied.

Both men and the guard ran back to the security door through which the couple disappeared. Antonio also identified himself to the guard and had become anxious.

"Hurry, open the door, open up the door," he said.

In the commotion, the guard fumbled for his security pass, but eventually opened the door. Antonio and Felipe pushed past the guard and ran through the door leading to the luggage processing area. They looked for George and Maggie, but the couple could not be seen anywhere.

Antonio became really concerned. He lost sight of the couple and was unsure of their whereabouts.

"Damn," Antonio said, "we've lost them."

The baggage processing area was large, so Felipe and Antonio initially searched the immediate area, but could not find the couple. The entire area was fully automated with no staff present, so there was no one around to ask questions. They walked in one direction for a while, until they came to a dead end. They returned in the direction from which they came and spotted a man in the distance. He was smoking a cigarette and did not hear Antonio and Felipe approaching.

"You there?" Antonio shouted.

The man heard Antonio's call over the noise of the machinery and looked up. He saw Antonio and Felipe coming towards him, and immediately dropped the cigarette to the ground. The area was a non-smoking area, and the man knew he should not have been there. He stood on the cigarette butt to extinguish it and began to walk away from Antonio and Felipe.

"Hang on," Antonio shouted, "wait, I want to ask you something."

The man stopped and turned to face Antonio, who soon caught up with him. He seemed embarrassed because he knew he had been discovered smoking in a restricted area, and looked sheepishly at Antonio.

"What?" the man asked in Portuguese.

"Have you seen anyone in this area, in the last few minutes?"

For some reason, the man was reluctant to talk. Maybe he felt they might report him for smoking in a restricted area.

"Look, this is important," Felipe said.

He then took out his MI6 identity badge and showed it to the man.

"Look, mister," Antonio said, "I believe this is an unrestricted area, and a non-smoking area as well. It seems you shouldn't have been smoking here."

"Don't tell anyone." The man said, "I'll lose my job. I have a wife and children to look after."

"Look," Antonio said in a calm voice, "I'm not really interested in your smoking habits, even though you should not be smoking here, as it is dangerous. I want to know if you've seen anyone here in the last few minutes, two men and a woman."

The man paused for a moment.

"Yes, I have."

He pointed over his shoulder in the opposite direction from which Antonio came.

"They went that way, two men and a woman, going that way," the man continued.

"Are you sure?" Antonio asked, "Two men and a woman, the woman wore a blue dress."

"Yes, that's the one, the woman was in blue."

"Thanks," Antonio said, "let's go, Felipe."

The two men ran in the direction to which the man pointed. On the way and at all times, Antonio stayed in contact with the other MI6 operatives to update them on what was happening and their location.

In the meantime, George and Maggie were taken to the far side of the building, which opened out onto the airport tarmac. The man in black was waiting for them, accompanied by an older man in his late seventies. The older man was immaculately dressed in a grey suit, sported a grey goatee beard, and looked very distinguished. The man dressed in casual attire, who collected George and Maggie from the cafe, stood aside and remained in the background.

"Hello," the man in black said, "you've made it."

"Yes," George said, "hopefully for the last time."

The man in black looked at Maggie and acknowledged her with a nod of the head. He then turned to the man in the grey suit and introduced him to the couple.

"I'd like you to meet Senhor Mendoza," the man in black said, "He is intrigued with the whole episode about the package, and wanted to meet you."

George looked Senhor Mendoza straight in the eyes and shook his hand. For an older man, Senhor Mendoza still had a penetrating stare and a firm handshake. George felt he should be courteous to the older man.

"Pleased to meet you," he said.

George was reluctant to meet anyone else from the MFA gang and did not feel he belonged in this environment.

"Likewise," Senhor Mendoza said in a soft, dulcet tone, "I must say, you have given us quite a run around, haven't you?"

George felt embarrassed and was unsure how to answer the man, so he remained silent.

"Do you have the package?" the man in black asked.

"Er, yes, I do," George replied.

George opened the travelling bag and took out the package.

"Is this the correct one?" Senhor Mendoza asked.

George felt a rise of adrenaline in his body, for he knew he was about to give false information again. He plucked up the courage and cleared his throat.

"Yes, this is the correct one. I'm so sorry about the last one. I'm not sure why I gave you the wrong one."

The man in black held out his hand to receive the package, and George handed it partly over to him.

By now, Antonio and Felipe had crept up silently on the group meeting and were only a few meters away. They took out their handguns and readied them. Some of the other MI6 operatives, posing as airport workers, positioned themselves metres behind Antonio, while others were outside on the tarmac. At the moment the package was exchanged, Antonio and Felipe pointed the guns at the gang members.

"Stand still, everyone," Antonio shouted in Portuguese, "no silly moves."

The man in black and Senhor Mendoza were taken by surprise and looked up at Antonio. The casually dressed man who took the couple there tried to escape from the group, but was soon apprehended by two MI6 operatives. The man in black looked around quickly and saw other operatives closing in on them.

"You betrayed us," he said to George, "you bastard, you betrayed us."

He snatched the package fully from George and withdrew a pistol from his jacket. He then grabbed hold of Maggie by the arm, pulled her close to his body, and placed the gun to her neck. George became concerned at the situation and waved his hands frantically.

"No, don't," George shouted, "don't."

"Put your gun down," Felipe shouted.

Senhor Mendoza was confused at the sudden change of atmosphere and felt somewhat faint. For his age, he was long past this kind of activity, and he slumped to the ground.

"Stay back," the man in black shouted, "stay back or I'll shoot her."

He became very petrified, and now, surrounded by MI6 agents, was unsure what to do next.

"Put your weapon down," Antonio shouted.

Antonio approached the man slowly, not wanting him to act erratically.

"Stay back," the man in black shouted again.

He began to walk backwards and pulled Maggie in front of him for protection. No one wanted to fire their gun, in case they shot Maggie by mistake. The man in black moved out onto the open tarmac and held Maggie in front of him all the time. He was followed by Antonio, Felipe and George, who kept a safe distance away. All the MI6 operatives remained a safe distance from the man in case he decided to do something dreadful. He knew the situation was dire and decided to seize the opportunity. He fired a shot towards Antonio and, at the same time, pushed Maggie to the ground. The man in black began to run in the opposite direction from Antonio, who ran out onto the tarmac after him.

"Stop," Antonio shouted, "stop or I'll shoot."

The man kept on running, even though there were other MI6 operatives on the tarmac. Antonio stopped running, positioned himself firmly, aimed his pistol with both hands, and fired a shot at the man. The noise of the discharge echoed across the tarmac, as well as in the luggage processing area, and the bullet found its target.

"Aah!" the man in black shouted.

He was hit in the right shoulder by the bullet and tumbled to the ground, releasing his pistol when he fell.

"Oh shit!" he uttered.

The man held his shoulder while remaining seated on the tarmac. Blood was seeping through his jacket from the wound, and he was in obvious pain, as can be seen from the grimace on his face. Antonio approached the man slowly and continued to point his pistol towards him.

"Stay down," Antonio shouted.

He went over to the man's pistol lying nearby on the ground and kicked it away. A few seconds later, other agents crowded around the man, with guns at the ready. The man looked up dolefully at Antonio.

"I've been after you for a long time now," Antonio said, "we finally meet."

The man smirked at Antonio and remained silent. Another agent called for medics, who arrived a few minutes later to treat the man's wound. Later on, he was taken away in a police ambulance and escorted by protective guards.

In the meantime, Felipe remained with Senhor Mendoza, helped him up from the ground, and sat him down on a wooden box. Felipe was intrigued by the man's identity.

"Who are you?" he asked.

"My name is Senhor Mendoza, and that's all I'm saying."

Felipe was surprised by the comment, for the man was the leader of the MFA gang in Brazil and a huge catch for MI6.

"Ah, Senhor Mendoza," Felipe said, "We know about you, we've been after you for a long time."

Senhor Mendoza remained silent and felt there was no need to say anything else. Felipe looked out onto the tarmac to check what was happening, in case his help was required, but Antonio and the other operatives had the situation covered. After the man in black was taken away, Antonio returned to the luggage processing area, where Senhor Mendoza was seated.

"You'll never guess who we have here," Felipe said.

"Who?" Antonio asked.

"Senhor Mendoza."

Antonio seemed pleased at the capture of someone MI6 had been after for a long time.

"THE Senhor Mendoza," he stated.

Antonio looked triumphantly at the man.

"Well, well, well, what have we here?"

The man then looked up pitifully at Antonio.

"I want to see my lawyer," he said.

"You'll need more than a lawyer," Antonio said, "am I not right in thinking you are the main honcho of the MFA in Brazil?"

240

Senhor Mendoza remained silent; he did not want to let on either way.

"I didn't expect you to be here," Antonio said, "this is a bonus for us. What are you doing here anyway? An important man like you, collecting a feeble little package."

"He must have been bored," Felipe said jokingly.

"You have a lot to answer for, Senhor Mendoza," Antonio said. He then helped the Senhor up from the wooden box.

"Come with us."

Antonio took Senhor Mendoza over to the other MI6 agents, who were waiting to take charge of him.

"Look after the Senhor," Antonio said, "he is a big fish in the MFA, a big catch, and he's got a lot to answer for."

The operatives handcuffed the Senhor and took him away.

Meanwhile, George ran out onto the tarmac to help Maggie after she was pushed to the ground. He was anxious and knelt to comfort her.

"Are you alright, sweetheart?" he asked.

Maggie was shaking with terror, and tears filled her eyes.

"Yes," she said, "I bruised my knee when I fell."

"Let me have a look at it."

George looked at Maggie's knee and found a slight injury. It was a small cut to the skin with some bruising and a little blood seeping out.

"You'll survive," George said, "I've seen worse."

Maggie was somewhat taken aback and wanted a bit more sympathy from George, especially after the ordeal.

"Typical," she said, "typical of you. Is that all you can say?"

Having dealt with Senhor Mendoza, Antonio now approached the couple.

"Everyone alright?" he asked.

"Yes, we're fine," George said, "a bit shaken."

"A BIT!" Maggie exclaimed, "I was utterly terrified, you did not go through the experience I just did."

George and Antonio looked at each other with eyebrows raised.

"Let's get a medic to treat your knee," Antonio said.

He looked around and called a medic over, who set about to treat Maggie's knee.

Antonio then looked at his watch.

"Look, guys, you've got fifteen minutes to catch your flight, let's hurry," he said.

George and Maggie both looked at their watches.

"Oh Shit! Will we make it?" Maggie asked.

"We'll have to hurry," George said.

George helped Maggie to stand up, and Antonio grabbed their arms and led them away towards the departure lounge. He ushered the couple in front of him, and was closely followed by Felipe. They returned to the concourse through the luggage processing area, the same way they came in. George found a departure monitor and checked the departure times, only to see that the plane was now boarding.

"Hurry," Antonio said, "we don't want you to miss your flight."

They hurried along and soon arrived at the immigration desks.

"Well, I think you will be fine now," Antonio said, "you can go through the fast track, it will be quicker."

George and Maggie both looked at Antonio, feeling sad but excited at the same time; they were about to leave and return to England.

"Goodbye, Antonio Carlos Jobim," George said.

George shook Antonio's hand vigorously and smiled at him.

"Adeus," Antonio replied, "safe journey, my man."

They then gave each other a man hug.

Maggie approached Antonio, hugged him, and pecked him on the cheek.

"Goodbye, and thanks for everything," she said.

Antonio felt a bit of sadness as well and, with a croaky voice, replied.

"No, thanks to you, both of you, for everything."

George shook hands with Felipe, and Maggie kissed Felipe on the cheek.

"Go quickly," Antonio said as he waved goodbye.

"Wait," Felipe shouted, "the money."

"Oh yes," Antonio said, "wait, I have something for you."

He pulled an envelope from the inside pocket of his jacket and handed it over to George.

"Here, this is for you," he said, "It's the amount we agreed, £5000."

George took the envelope and shook it passionately.

"Thank you, thank you very much," he said, "this will come in very useful."

Antonio urged the couple to go quickly; he did not want them to miss their flight.

"Go, go now, hurry," he said.

He and Felipe watched as George and Maggie were processed through immigration. The MI6 men stayed for a while and watched as George and Maggie disappeared in the distance.

"You know what," Antonio said to Felipe.

"What's that, boss?"

"I really got to like those two, I really liked them."

"Me too, boss, me too."

"Such nice people. And you know what."

"What's that, boss?"

"I think George would make a good agent; he has the makings."

The End

Beecroft Publishing
Beecroft
Crittenden Road
Matfield, Kent
TN12 7EQ
United Kingdom

www.beecroftpublishing.co.uk

email: sales@beecroftpublishing.co.uk

EU Authorised Representative:
Easy Access System Europe
Mustamäe tee 50, 10621 Tallinn, Estonia

www.ingramcontent.com/pod-product-compliance
Lightning Source LLC
Chambersburg PA
CBHW071141170626
46809CB00002B/725